Praise for Maria Murnane

"Ms. Murnane is one of the funniest writers I have read in a long time..."
—*Joyfully Reviewed*

"Funny, fast-paced, adorable."
—*Publishers Weekly* (starred review), on *Chocolate for Two*

"[A] dynamic cast of characters ... and a plot well worth the read."
—*RT Book Reviews* (four-star review), on *Chocolate for Two*

"Meet the new Bridget Jones."
—*PopSugar Daily*, on *Perfect on Paper*

"[D]eftly written, thoroughly entertaining, and so painfully possible in this modern age of competing demands between what we want and what is demanded of us all."
—*Midwest Book Review*, on *Perfect on Paper*

Katwalk

Katwalk

Maria Murnane

Published by

LAKE UNION
PUBLISHING

Published by Lake Union Publishing, Seattle

www.apub.com

Amazon, the Amazon logo, and Lake Union Publishing are trademarks of Amazon.com, Inc., or its affiliates.

ISBN-13: 9781477849934
ISBN-10: 1477849939

Cover design by Debbie Berne

Library of Congress Control Number: 2013922588

Printed in the United States of America

To Jenny—I'm so glad I met you!

Chapter One

Katrina felt cool beads of sweat forming on her palms as she prepared to stand up. She placed her hands lightly on the desk and glanced around her tidy cubicle. As usual, there wasn't so much as a pen or a Post-it note—much less a paper clip—out of place. She quietly opened a drawer and removed her purse, turning her eyes to the calendar mounted on the wall as she reached inside for her makeup kit.

A small black circle was drawn around Wednesday, September 18.

Today.

It was finally here.

She ran a comb through her auburn hair, then checked her face in the mirror of her compact, applying a touch of powder to her fair skin and wishing, as always, that she didn't have quite so many freckles sprinkled across her cheeks and nose. She added a dab of rosy lip gloss, then rubbed hand sanitizer between her palms before putting her purse back in the drawer. She took a deep breath and closed her eyes, sitting silently, thinking about how many times she'd practiced this.

Opening greeting.

Main statement and supporting points.

Closing expression of gratitude.

You can do this, she told herself.

After a few moments, she opened her eyes and slowly stood up. She stepped away from her chair and carefully tucked it under the desk. Most of her coworkers were at lunch, so the office was quiet save for the chatter of a few account executives on the phone with clients. Every day around noon, especially when the weather was nice like today, the advertising agency emptied out in groups of two or three or four. Katrina usually brought her own sandwich, however. There was always so much work to do, and she had a hard time enjoying a lunch out knowing what was waiting for her when she got back to her desk. Besides, she wasn't exactly friends with her coworkers—not that she didn't want to be. She'd just never quite felt comfortable swapping stories about weekend exploits or gossiping about office politics with the same people who had to take her seriously as an accountant. And being shy certainly didn't help.

Everyone in the office knew Katrina Lynden could be counted on to finish her work on time and with a polite smile, but they didn't know how much she secretly wished someone would ask her to join them for drinks after work. Back when she first started, she had been invited out for happy hour a few times, but she always declined, citing work deadlines, and eventually the invitations stopped coming. It had been years since she'd received one, and she wondered if anyone knew how much she regretted having said no to those early efforts to include her.

She exited her cubicle and began walking down the long hallway. Conscious of her sweaty palms, she wiped them on her pants and forced herself to keep moving. Silently counting each step, she fought to ignore the voice in her head that told her to return to her desk, do what was expected of her, and get back to work.

Just like she'd been doing for years.

But she couldn't do that anymore.

It was too late.

She and Deb had made a pact.

She couldn't break her promise.

She walked gingerly across the hardwood floor leading toward the corner office, as though making less noise would make what was about to happen less real. She glanced at the placard on the open door that read JANICE HARRISON, CFO, then took a look inside at the plush interior, which was bigger than her entire living room. The older woman was alone, studying a sheet of paper, a thick folder of documents before her. Everyone knew Janice Harrison never went to lunch before one o'clock, if she took a break at all.

Katrina knocked gently and cleared her throat. "Janice?"

Janice lifted her head, her narrow face framed by a chic silver bob and expensive horn-rimmed reading glasses. "Katrina, hello." She looked a bit surprised, but not annoyed. "Do you need something?" Katrina rarely stopped by her office.

Katrina swallowed, then began her prepared remarks.

Opening greeting.

"May I speak with you for a moment?"

Janice removed her glasses and set them down. "Of course. Please, have a seat." She gestured to the black leather chair across from her sleek glass desk.

Katrina shut the door behind her, then walked over to the chair and sat down. She crossed her legs, careful to keep her ankles touching. Even though she reported directly to Janice, she'd been alone with her inside this office only a handful of times in her nearly eight years at the agency.

And never under these circumstances.

She reminded herself about the pact.

You can do this.

Now that it was finally happening, she was even more anxious than she'd thought she'd be.

"Are you okay, dear? You look a little pale." Janice gave her a concerned look. Janice was as professional as they came, but she often showed a warm, almost maternal side toward her team, something Katrina had always appreciated, given her own mother's lack of affection.

Katrina nodded and tried to control her nerves. "I'm fine. Thanks for asking." She tapped her foot lightly on the carpet.

Janice glanced at the stack of papers on her desk. "How can I help you?" The expression in her eyes was kind, but it was clear she was preoccupied. Things at the agency were always busy, and they had recently signed two new clients. It was about to become even more hectic for the entire finance department.

Katrina opened her mouth to speak but hesitated.

Her throat was dry.

Her foot was still tapping.

"Katrina?" Janice said. She picked up the top sheet of paper from the stack and skimmed it, already distracted.

Katrina took a breath.

Main statement.

Finally, she uttered the words she'd practiced in front of her bathroom mirror so many times. "I . . . I would like to give notice."

Janice looked up, her eyebrows raised.

"You're resigning?"

"Yes." Katrina felt her head nodding involuntarily in agreement. She couldn't believe she was going through with this.

"May I ask why?" Janice looked genuinely taken aback.

She had known her boss would be startled by the news. Why wouldn't she be? Anyone would. For years Katrina had carefully projected an image, however inaccurate, of professional satisfaction. She had a good job, an established career path, and the respect of her colleagues, if not exactly their friendship.

She forced herself to continue, just as she'd practiced.

Supporting points.

"I just . . . feel like it's time for me to move on, to begin a new chapter in my life." She spoke quietly and knew she didn't sound all that convinced of what she was saying.

"A new chapter? Why? You're doing so well here."

"Well . . ." She struggled to find an appropriate response to the question. She wondered what would happen if she told the truth.

I can't pretend I like my job anymore.

I never wanted to be an accountant.

I don't want to spend my life like this.

How had she let so many years slip by?

"Katrina?" Janice asked.

"It's, well, it's hard to explain," she said. Her foot was still tapping on the carpet.

Janice tilted her head to one side. "Do you have another job lined up?" The *Have you been interviewing on the side?* was implied. Talented accountants were hard to come by in the world of advertising agencies, especially so in tech-heavy Silicon Valley, where everyone wanted to work at a start-up in hopes of striking it rich.

Katrina shook her head. "Oh, no, it's nothing like that. Actually, I'm planning to take some time off." Saying it out loud made her decision feel suddenly real, as if she'd just jumped out of an airplane. Or off a building.

Janice didn't look convinced. "Are you sure you want to leave?" She knew how good Katrina was at her job. Janice's sincere appreciation for Katrina's ability with numbers was one of the things that made it so hard for Katrina to quit. Most people just thought she was boring. At least that's what she assumed they thought.

Katrina sat up straight and nodded with a confidence she wished were genuine. "Yes, I'm sure." She recited the line she'd practiced over and over. "I've given it quite a bit of thought, and I know this is the right thing for me to do right now."

She'd made her usual list of pros and cons about the decision, and to say it was lopsided would be an understatement. She hadn't wanted to face the reality of how unhappy she was, but once she'd seen it written in ink, it was hard to ignore.

Confident was hardly how she felt about the decision, however. At the moment *queasy* came closer to the truth.

"There's nothing I can do to change your mind?" Janice said.

Katrina squeezed the sides of the chair and glanced briefly at the ceiling, then willed herself to regain eye contact.

She shook her head. "Unfortunately, no." She knew Janice was referring to a salary increase, but she also knew that even a raise wouldn't help. This was more important than money. "I appreciate that you want me to stay, I really do. But I just . . . I need to try something new."

The look in Janice's eyes changed slightly. "Try something new?"

"Yes."

"You're getting out of accounting?"

"Temporarily, yes."

Katrina could tell Janice was waiting for her to elaborate, but when it became clear that she wasn't going to, Janice put her glasses back on and sighed. "Well, Katrina, I have to say I'm really sorry to see you go. You're an excellent accountant and a very nice person, and we've been lucky to have you here for this long."

Katrina smiled. Why couldn't her mother be more like that?

Closing expression of gratitude.

"Thank you, Janice. I've enjoyed working here. Oh, and just so you know, I've already finished my reports and e-mailed them to Erica." Erica was an admin who acted as a paperwork liaison between Janice and the accounting team.

Janice gave her a grateful look. "I'm not surprised, but thank you for doing that. I appreciate it and know the rest of the team will too." She picked up her phone. "I'll have Sheila from HR sort out the paperwork." Katrina knew that *giving notice* was just an expression. Due to the sensitive nature of the financial data she worked with, she would be leaving today—for good.

Katrina stood up. "Okay, well, thanks. I'll . . . get my things together." She turned to go as Janice dialed Sheila's extension.

She was nearly out the door when she heard Janice's voice.

"Katrina, dear?"

She turned around. "Yes?"

Janice covered the receiver with one hand and lowered her voice. "I hope you find what you're looking for."

Katrina smiled, trying to quell the rising panic at what she'd just done. "Thanks, Janice. I do too."

* * *

That evening Katrina sat at a high table at her favorite bar, Stephens Green on Castro Street, the main drag a few blocks from her apartment in downtown Mountain View. She nursed a Sprite and waited for Deb to arrive so they could swap stories.

She placed the round cardboard coasters in front of her in a tidy stack.

I can't believe I really quit my job.

She replayed the day's events, trying to wrap her head around the fact that she'd actually gone through with it. Her memory of the specifics of how it had all unfolded was somewhat blurred by nerves, but the end result was the same: she was no longer employed.

Katrina found changing brands of shampoo difficult. Quitting the only full-time job she'd ever had? Unfathomable. She knew her mother wasn't going to be happy when she heard the news, but she didn't want to think about that just yet.

Right now she just wanted to enjoy the moment.

She took a sip of her drink and tried to appreciate the emotions she was experiencing about what lay ahead. She was anxious, there was no denying that, but for the first time in a long time, maybe years, she also felt a stirring of something else.

Excitement.

She was *excited*, and the sensation, while pleasant, was striking in its unfamiliarity.

How had she become so . . . numb?

She continued to stack and restack the coasters as she examined her innermost thoughts.

She was apprehensive, for sure.

But she wasn't *terrified*, which she had expected to be, and for her, that in and of itself was a victory.

What she felt more than anything was . . . relief.

She had done it.

She was making a change.

It wasn't too late for her.

She and Deb had a few days to get ready. All she had to do was pack.

She sipped her drink and looked at her watch, then turned toward the entrance. Deb should have been here by now. Maybe her exit strategy hadn't gone as smoothly. While Katrina had chosen to resign at lunchtime, Deb had planned to break the news later in the afternoon, when she thought it would cause the least drama. Deb hated drama even more than she hated her boss.

Katrina pulled her phone out of her purse to see if there was a text or a missed call.

Nothing.

She's probably just caught in traffic. She'll be here soon.

"You need anything else to drink?" the waiter asked.

Katrina smiled. "I'm good for now. Just waiting for a friend."

As the waiter walked away, Katrina thought about the day, three weeks earlier, when she and Deb had made the joint decision to quit their jobs. Or, more accurately, the day Deb had convinced Katrina to quit her job. They had met up at their favorite sushi bar, Sushitomi, one evening after work.

Over a bowl of edamame, Deb complained about her unappreciative boss, and Katrina wondered out loud what would have happened if she'd had the nerve to stand up to her parents and pursue her love of art. As the waiter brought them a plate of California rolls and a sashimi platter, he smiled sympathetically and set down two steaming cups of sake.

"Sake's on the house. Sounds like you two need something stronger than sushi tonight," he said with a wink.

They both laughed and thanked him, but the moment he turned his back to walk away, Katrina pushed her cup toward Deb. As soon as she released her hand, Deb caught it and gave it a squeeze.

"He's right, you know."

Katrina nodded. "I'm not disagreeing with him. I just don't drink sake."

"I know, I know, you and your low alcohol tolerance. But I'm not talking about sake. I'm talking about us."

"What?"

"*Us.* We need to mix it up."

Katrina picked up a pod of edamame. "Mix up what?"

"Life. Our lives. We need to mix up our *lives.*"

"And how would we do that?"

"Let's quit."

"Quit what?"

"Our jobs."

Katrina gave her a look. "Quit our jobs? Are you crazy?"

Deb squeezed her hand again. "I'm serious, Katrina. Let's do it. What are we waiting for? Look at us. All we do is come here and complain about work, right?"

"Right."

"But we never do anything about it, right?"

"Right."

"Well, maybe it's time. Maybe we should quit."

"You're really serious?"

"Yes. I mean, why not? We're not married. We don't have kids. Neither one of us is even dating anyone right now. What are we waiting for? Let's quit and go do something adventurous before it's too late."

Katrina opened up another pod and thought about what her friend was proposing.

Quit and go do something adventurous before it's too late.

She wondered what her parents would think of that idea. As the only daughter of two overachievers who valued a person's work ethic above all else, the importance of getting a practical education had been ingrained in her since her days in a crib.

You need to be able to support yourself, Katrina.

Majoring in art history isn't going to pay the bills, Katrina.

You need to get your head out of the clouds, Katrina.

You can't expect a man to come along and rescue you, Katrina.

So getting a practical education was exactly what she'd done. She'd chosen a major that would lead to a steady job, a predictable career path, a growing nest egg, and, eventually, a mortgage. She'd done everything the right way.

The safe way.

The responsible way.

The *boring* way.

Until that moment.

She looked at Deb. "You really think we should do it?"

"I do."

"What would we do?"

Deb shrugged. "I don't know. We could go somewhere."

"Could you be more specific?"

Deb downed her sake. "I don't care. The beach. The mountains. The moon. Anywhere but Mountain View. I've had enough of Mountain View." She set down the cup and tapped her palms against the table. "Wait. I've got it! Let's go live in New York for a while."

"New York?"

"Yes. Why not? You know what they say, right? *Everyone should live in New York at least once.*"

"Who says that?"

"I don't know. People."

"For how long?"

Deb picked up Katrina's sake and downed it too, then set the cup on the table and tapped her chin with her finger. "I don't know . . . a month? Maybe two? Two months sounds good. Yes, let's do two."

Katrina's eyes got big. "Two months? Are you joking?"

"Do I look like I'm joking?"

"No."

"So there's your answer." She pointed to herself and shook her head. "Me. Not joking."

"Two months is a long time, Deb."

Deb waved a hand in front of her. "Please. It will fly by. If you want, you can sublet your place here to cover the rent." Deb never seemed to worry about money the way Katrina did. But then again, she didn't really need to. Her grandparents had made sure of that.

Katrina took a sip of water and considered the idea. Scary as it sounded, maybe Deb was right; maybe she *could* break out of her shell. Plus she hadn't had an extended vacation in ages. She'd started her job at the agency immediately after graduating from college, when most of her peers had gone traveling or at least taken the summer off to unwind after four years of books and exams. *Why wait to begin working?* her dad had said. *You've got to start supporting yourself,* her mother had agreed.

Katrina had listened to her parents, albeit reluctantly, and as a result, outside of one family trip to Washington, DC—which, frankly, had felt more like school than a vacation, given how structured it had been—she had never even left California. She'd gone to college just down the road from home, earned a degree in accounting—with honors—then had taken the job with the advertising agency and become a full-time number cruncher barely one week after graduation.

"Are you with me?" Deb extended her hand.

Katrina hesitated.

"Well?" Deb kept her hand out.

Katrina stared at the edamame bowl and thought about the pit she felt in her stomach whenever someone asked her what she did for a living. She'd been unhappy in her job for a long time, but for some reason it had never occurred to her to quit.

Not even once.

Quitting would be so . . . *unlike* her.

Deb was staring at her, her hand still extended. "You can do it, Katrina. I know you can. It would be good for you to take a chance for once, to try something outside of that safe little bubble you live in."

Katrina knew her friend was right, but she hesitated.

"Come on, you know I'm right," Deb said. "And I say that thing about your bubble with love, by the way."

"I know you do."

Deb raised one eyebrow. "So what do you think? Are you in?"

Katrina took a deep breath.

Maybe this is just what I need.

She sat up straight and shook her best friend's hand.

"Okay, I'm in."

* * *

"I'm so sorry, I'm so sorry, I'm so sorry." Deb finally came rushing up to the table nearly thirty minutes late. "Things got a little crazy at the office." She took off her jacket and sat down, then looked around for the waiter. "I'm dying for a stiff drink."

Katrina took a sip of Sprite and held up her guidebook. "No worries. I've been reading about all sorts of cool things we could do in New York. Did you know that in Central Park there's a—"

Deb put her hand on Katrina's shoulder. "I need to talk to you."

Katrina froze, then squeezed her eyes shut. "Oh no. Don't tell me."

Deb kept her hand on Katrina's shoulder. "I'm so sorry."

Katrina was silent for a few moments, then opened her eyes and looked at her friend with a sigh. "Okay, let's hear it."

Deb stood up. "Let me get that drink first." She hurried over to the bar.

Flush with panic, Katrina's mind began to race.

Is this really happening?

Is the rug really being pulled out from under me?

I just quit my job.

Her foot began to tap as one thought leaped in front of all the others.

What am I supposed to do now?

Deb returned, then pressed her palms against her temples for a moment before speaking. "Okay, here's what went down. When I told my boss I was quitting, he offered me a big raise, right then and there. He didn't even hesitate."

Katrina raised her eyebrows. "Really?"

"Yes, along with that promotion I've been wanting for like a year. He said he'd been planning to promote me at my next review anyway. Then he told me how he and all the other higher-ups expect me to be running my department one day."

"But I thought he didn't like you."

"I did too, which is why I was so surprised. I thought he had it in for me, but you should have heard him when I told him I was quitting. He went on and on about how good I am at my job, finally showing me the respect and appreciation I've wanted for so long. He sounded so sincere I couldn't help but believe him. He was close to *groveling*, Katrina."

"Why didn't he ever tell you any of that before?"

Deb lifted up her hands. "I know! Typical man. They never appreciate what they've got until they're about to lose it, just like most of my ex-boyfriends. Anyhow, after he said all that, I couldn't turn him down. I just couldn't. I'm so sorry." She made a pained face.

Just then the waiter appeared with Deb's drink, a vodka martini. She immediately took an enormous sip—or gulp. "So do you hate me? If I were you, I think I might hate me."

Katrina didn't reply. Instead, she straightened up the coaster stack, which didn't need straightening.

"Will you please say something? Even *I hate you* would be better than nothing right now."

"Of course I don't hate you. I could *never* hate you. I'm just disappointed that our big plan has sort of . . . imploded." The truth was, Katrina was devastated, but she didn't want Deb to know that. She didn't want her to know that she was paralyzed with fear. At least before, she'd had a plan. Now she had . . . nothing.

But what was done was done, and she didn't want her friend to feel any worse than she already did, so she maintained her polite exterior.

"I'm so sorry, Katrina. I truly thought they were never going to promote me. If I'd suspected there was even a baby chance they would counteroffer like that, I wouldn't have let you quit your job. I never imagined it would turn out like this."

"It's okay. I know how much you wanted that promotion." She also knew that despite Deb's occasional gripe about not being appreciated by her boss, she enjoyed her event-planning job and was generally happy with her career choice. Katrina, on the other hand, couldn't remember the last time she'd actually looked forward to going to work. Had she ever?

She certainly wouldn't be going to work tomorrow. She'd already cleaned out her cubicle and said good-bye to her coworkers—neither of which had taken very long—and turned in her security badge.

Plus she didn't want to go back anyway. On that she was clear.

The question was, what would she do now? She knew she could probably find another accounting job in no time if she put her mind to it, but she had already sublet her place to a friend of a friend of Deb's, a freelance writer from San Diego who was all set to move in on Monday. Plus she and Deb had already paid for the apartment they'd rented in Manhattan, beginning Tuesday, and it hadn't been cheap. Rearranging everything at the last minute was going to be not only complicated but expensive.

"Katrina? Are you there? What's going on inside that smart head of yours?" Deb snapped her fingers in the air between them.

Katrina blinked and realized she was tapping her foot again.

"I hope you're not thinking of ways to poison me," Deb said.

Katrina tried not to laugh as she took another sip of her Sprite. "I'm not exactly thrilled with you at the moment, but I'll get over it. I guess I'll just need to find a new job a little faster than I'd planned to. And a place to live until Thanksgiving."

"Why don't you go without me?"

"Go live in New York for two months *alone*?"

"Sure. Why not?"

"Are you crazy? Do you even know me?"

"Do I look like I'm crazy? People go traveling by themselves all the time. Why can't you?"

"Sure, *other people* go traveling by themselves. I can't even go to the movies by myself. You know that."

"Well, maybe it's time to shake things up a little bit. You're almost thirty years old. Time to spread those wings."

Katrina stirred the ice in her drink with the straw. "I've never gone anywhere alone for even a weekend. There's no way I could spend two months in New York City by myself."

"Yes, you could."

"I don't know anyone there."

"You'd meet people."

"Easy for you to say. You're not overcome with panic every time you walk into a roomful of strangers."

"You're not as shy as you think you are."

Katrina felt herself stiffen. "What's that supposed to mean?"

"It means that for whatever reason you *tell* yourself that you're shy, and then, unfortunately, you actually listen to yourself. You don't *have* to listen to that, you know."

"Again, easy for you to say. You're not me. And besides, going across the country by myself isn't quite what I had in mind when I signed up for this little adventure."

Deb picked up her drink. "I know going without me is light-years out of your comfort zone, but I'm just saying that you should think about it. You've already taken such a huge step by quitting your job. Wouldn't it be a shame to get another one right away instead of using this time off to do . . . *something*?"

Katrina shrugged. "Probably."

"Probably?"

She smiled weakly. "Okay, definitely."

"There you go. And it's not like you wanted to stay at your job anyway, right? I mean, would you want to go back there tomorrow if you could? Even if they offered you a promotion?"

Katrina answered without hesitation. "No."

"See? So this is for the best, no matter what happens next."

"I know, I know. All of this is just . . . scary."

"Life is scary. But that's what makes it so exciting, right? And for the record, I'm still paying for my half of the apartment, so if you decide to go, don't worry about that. I may be ditching you, but I'm not screwing you."

Katrina laughed. "You always have a way of making yourself come out of every situation smelling like a rose, did you know that?"

Deb bowed her head in thanks. "What can I say? It's from all those country-club lunches my grandparents used to drag me to. The ability to schmooze comes in handy in a pinch. So you'll think about it? And if you do it, I'll try to come visit you for a weekend."

"I'll think about it."

"Promise?"

"I promise."

"And you don't hate me?"

"I don't hate you."

"Promise?"

Katrina shook her head, then picked up a menu and whapped Deb lightly on the back of the head with it. "I promise. I could never hate you. But you're definitely buying me dinner tonight."

Chapter Two

After dinner, Katrina hugged Deb good-bye, then took her time walking home. Still trying to come to terms with the wrench that had been thrown into a meticulously constructed plan, she trudged up the stairs to the second floor.

Quit job, check.

Find place to live in New York, check.

Sublet apartment here, check.

Make airline reservations, check.

Figure out what to do now . . . ugh.

Once inside her apartment, she made herself a cup of hot chocolate, sat down cross-legged on the couch, and tried to picture herself in New York City.

Living in New York City.

Alone.

So alone.

Deb could never understand why Katrina had such trouble making new friends, especially because she worked at an advertising agency full of creative, sociable people. *Just chat them up,* she'd always say. *They're just people.* As if it were that easy. It had been ages since Katrina had felt comfortable making new friends. Thank God for Deb, who had been her best buddy since first grade.

Katrina hadn't always felt so awkward. Up through eighth grade, she'd been as outgoing as the next kid, with many friends in addition to Deb. But everything had changed when it came time to start high school. Her parents, consumed with preparing her for the future, had decided to enroll her in a private all-girls' school, and suddenly she had to start all over again. The student body was comprised mainly of outrageously wealthy girls who had been there since sixth grade, so from day one Katrina had felt like the only one lacking a tight-knit circle of friends. Without bubbly Deb by her side for the first time in her life, she was insecure. She wanted to make new friends, but she had never really learned how. She was always friendly when spoken to, but she couldn't quite shake the feeling that people thought of her as the shy girl who didn't quite fit in. It didn't help that her new classmates inhabited a world unlike anything she'd ever known.

Trust funds.

Luxury cars from Daddy on their sixteenth birthday.

Ski trips to Sun Valley or Jackson Hole, if not the French Alps.

Long weekends in Palm Springs.

Shopping trips along Rodeo Drive.

And with the bank accounts came a sense of entitlement and confidence that permeated the entire campus.

Deb could have held her own with these girls, but not Katrina.

Daunted by the cliques and inside jokes about vacation resorts she'd never visited and designer brands she couldn't afford, she didn't have the courage to sit down with anyone at lunchtime. Conspicuously alone one too many times, she began passing the hour in the library.

By herself.

Then one day she just stopped caring—or trying.

Instead, she put her head in her books and studied, spending most of her free time focusing on her homework. Almost before she knew it, freshman year turned into sophomore year, and so on and so on. When she graduated, she did so with a straight-A average but no truly meaningful friendships.

Her shyness abated somewhat in college, when she realized that no one knew—much less cared—what she had been like in high school. But it never disappeared entirely, because *she* knew.

She looked around her immaculate, minimalist living room. Would the subletter take good care of it? She hoped so. Deb had said he was neat, but she and Deb didn't exactly see eye to eye on the definition of *neat*.

She picked a tiny piece of fuzz off the couch, then closed her eyes.

Am I really too afraid to go to New York on my own?

Too scared to try something new?

Is this the person I want to be?

She thought of what Deb had said earlier: *You're not as shy as you think you are.*

For years Katrina had been telling herself she was misunderstood because of her shyness, but she wasn't sure about that anymore. While it was true that no one had made much of an effort to approach her back in school, how approachable had she made *herself* by hiding out in the library? Or, later, by declining social invitations at work? How much of her loneliness and isolation had she created, however inadvertently, over the years?

Maybe it was time to stop making excuses.

She glanced at her laptop on the kitchen table.

If she stayed in Mountain View, she'd soon be sitting in front of that computer screen, probably down the road in her childhood bedroom at her parents' house, where she'd be forced to live until her subletter's term was up. She'd be meticulously updating her résumé and then embarking on a job search that—when completed—would bring her right back where she'd started.

She glanced at the laptop again.

If I don't do this, will I regret it for the rest of my life?

* * *

Before going to bed, Katrina headed to the bathroom to perform her nightly routine.

Remove eye makeup with cotton ball.

Wash face with gentle foaming cleanser.

Apply night cream.

Floss and brush teeth.

She carefully returned her toothbrush to the cup on the sink, looked at herself in the mirror, then turned and walked into the living room to get her phone. If she didn't call Deb tonight, she knew she'd lose her nerve. She had to say it out loud to make herself accountable, to make her decision real.

Deb answered on the first ring. "Please tell me you're still going."

Katrina closed her eyes as she replied. "I'm still going."

Deb's surprise came leaping through the phone. "You are?"

"Yes. I just need to get on the plane before I change my mind. Will you go shopping with me tomorrow to help me pick out some new clothes? Maybe a good coat? I need to be prepared for the New York weather."

"Definitely. I'll call you right before I leave work. And I'm proud of you. I knew you could do it."

"You really think I can do this?"

"I know you can. And trust me, you're going to have the most memorable time of your life."

Katrina sighed. "I hope you're right. But I've got to move fast before I change my mind."

* * *

The following Monday evening, a few minutes after six o'clock, Katrina turned her apartment keys over to the subletter. Then she drove her silver Audi to nearby Los Altos Hills. She was spending her last night in town at her parents' house.

The sky was clear and bright as she merged northbound onto Highway 280. She looked at the dashboard to check the time. Her parents were expecting her for dinner, and her mother got upset if she was even five minutes late. Given their less than enthusiastic reaction to her recent news, she didn't want to upset them further by not showing up on time. She was already dreading the inevitable conversation about her decision to quit her job, and the one to spend eight weeks—alone—in New York even more so.

The sun was just beginning to set as she took the Page Mill exit and made her way up the winding roads to her parents' secluded ranch-style house. She pulled into the spotless garage, careful to park equidistant from her dad's shiny black Range Rover and her mom's pristine silver Lexus sedan, stopping precisely when the tennis ball attached to an overhead string gently touched her windshield to indicate she'd pulled in far enough—but not too far. When she stepped out of her car, she glanced at the gleaming tools hanging on the opposite wall, then removed her suitcase from the trunk and rolled it across the cement floor.

At the entrance, she kicked off her shoes and lifted the bag to avoid tracking anything onto the white carpet, then carried it into one of the guest bedrooms. She took out a fold-out luggage stand from the closet and set the bag down on it, then stopped in the bathroom to wash her hands and check her hair. After one last look in the mirror, she took a deep breath and walked through the large house to the kitchen. As she approached, she could hear her parents' voices and the classical music they always had playing.

Her dad was stirring something in a tall pot, her mom chopping celery on a sleek wooden cutting board. They were both standing in front of the island that divided the kitchen from the expansive entertainment room behind them.

Her dad smiled. "Well, hello there, sunshine. Always nice to hear the sound of your footsteps in the house."

Katrina pointed to her stocking feet. "You know I'm not wearing shoes, Dad." No one ever did, except for guests.

"Did you shut the garage door?" her mom asked.

Katrina walked over to peer into the pot. "Park the car, check. Shut the door, check. Something smells really good. What are you making?"

"Roast beef, homemade vegetable soup, and a fresh tomato-and-mozzarella salad. You better have brought an appetite, young lady," her dad said.

"Henry, please don't encourage her to overeat," her mom said. "Once she turns thirty, it isn't going to be so easy for her to maintain her figure without exercising."

Katrina plopped down on one of the bar stools bordering the island. "Bring an appetite, check. Don't overeat after I turn thirty, check. It's been a while since I had a real home-cooked meal. Are Eric and Emily coming over?" Her older brother and his wife lived up in San Francisco.

Her dad tossed a cup of chopped celery into the soup pot. "He canceled, unfortunately. Said he had to work late."

"Again? He's always working late." Eric was an investment banker at a big firm in the city.

"At least someone is," her mom said.

Katrina sighed. "Mom, it's been less than a week since I quit. Can you please not start?"

Her mother set down her knife and put her hands on her hips. "Your father and I just think it would have been smarter to line something up before traipsing off to New York like this. It's not like you to be so . . . *reckless*."

Katrina felt her whole body stiffen. "You think I'm being reckless?" She looked at her dad for support.

He gave her a sympathetic frown. "It *is* a bit impetuous."

Katrina balled her hands into fists in her lap. She had worked at the same job for *eight years*, and her parents thought she was rash?

She took another deep breath, then calmly stood up and walked across the kitchen toward the cabinets. "What time do you think we should leave for the airport?" She pulled down a large glass.

"Remember, you promised us you'd look for a job from there," her mother said. "You can't go back on that promise."

Katrina opened the refrigerator to retrieve a pitcher of water. "I won't." Even though looking for a job was just about the last thing she felt like doing, she'd never broken a promise to her parents and didn't intend to now.

Her mother picked up the knife and started chopping again. "It's important to keep up with your networks, however limited they may be. If you let them idle for too long, you may be in trouble when you get back, especially in this economy."

"I know, I know," Katrina said. "You told me that yesterday, remember?"

"Well, it's worth repeating. You know networking isn't your strong suit."

"Yep, got it." Her back to both of them, Katrina set the pitcher on the counter and closed her eyes. *Please stop.*

She heard her dad's voice behind her. "Not that you're not a top-notch accountant, sunshine. We know how smart and capable you are with numbers."

"Got it," she said without turning around.

He cleared his throat. "We just know you have a little trouble . . . on the social side of things . . . you know, putting yourself out there."

"Uh-huh." She squeezed the handle of the pitcher.

"Now, if it were your *brother* going, we wouldn't be so concerned. He's so charismatic he'd be able to land a job from anywhere," her mom said.

Katrina slowly poured herself a glass of water, then turned around and forced a smile. "Of course. Now, what time do you think we should leave for the airport?"

Chapter Three

The following evening—after battling a last-minute bout of cold feet wrapped in self-doubt—Katrina landed in New York.

It was the last week of September, and as she stepped outside baggage claim, the evening wind swirled up and around her with an intensity she'd never felt in the Bay Area. Her hair flew into her face, blocking her vision. She dug around in her purse to find a ponytail holder, then pulled her hair out of her eyes and into a haphazard bun.

Now she could see.

She soon found the taxi station, and despite what she'd read on the Internet about monstrous waits at JFK, there were only a dozen or so people in line. A few minutes later, she found herself in the back of one of New York City's famous yellow cabs.

"Where to, ma'am?" the driver asked.

"Oh, here you go." She leaned forward to hand him the address, then exhaled and sank back into the leather seat.

"Long flight?"

"Sort of. From San Francisco."

"Never been, but I hear that's quite a pretty city."

She gazed out of the window. "Yes, it is."

"First time in New York?"

"Yes." She was surprised at how chatty he was. Weren't New York cabdrivers famous for their sullen demeanor? Her mother had certainly warned her enough times about getting ripped off by anyone and everyone.

You know how naïve you can be, Katrina.

They'll eat you alive if you let your guard down, Katrina.

"Well then, welcome to town. I'm Enrique."

"I'm Katrina. It's nice to meet you."

She closed her eyes, and Enrique let her rest as they merged onto the expressway.

In a few minutes—and for the next two months—she would officially be one of New York City's eight million inhabitants.

Eight million inhabitants, of whom she knew a grand total of one.

If she counted Enrique.

Actually, that wasn't exactly true. Thanks to social media, she knew that a tiny handful of people from college lived here, and she'd already made plans to meet up with one of them tomorrow night. She was planning to contact the others as soon as she got settled. Granted it had been almost a decade since they'd graduated, but at this point, seeing any familiar face would be a good thing.

Forty minutes later, the cab slowed to a stop in front of her temporary home in Manhattan, a modest brownstone on East Twenty-Second Street between Second and Third Avenues. Enrique unloaded her suitcase and handed her a card. "Enjoy your time in New York. I'm starting my own car service next week, so let me know if you ever need a ride anywhere," he said with a smile.

"Thanks. I will." She hated that she was suspicious of him just for being friendly, hated that her mother had succeeded in instilling doubt about her ability to navigate the city on her own.

After paying Enrique the standard flat airport rate—no, of course he hadn't tried to gouge her—plus a tip, she stood at the bottom of the steps looking out at her surroundings.

Both sides of the street were filled with parked cars, but there were only a couple of people strolling by, so it was relatively quiet. The entire block was lined with brownstones, most of them similar in size and color and most of them in need of a power wash. The street was pretty enough, but she couldn't help but think it looked like a slightly neglected version of *Sesame Street*. Deb had found the place through a rental agency and had assured Katrina that the neighborhood was safe, centrally located, and the best they could do in their price range.

As the cab pulled away, she turned around to face the four-story building. She looked up at the windows, wondering which one belonged to her new apartment.

Despite her nerves, she felt a small shiver of excitement.

I can't believe I'm really here.

She lugged her suitcase up the front steps, then set it down and hunted around in her purse for the set of keys the rental agency had mailed her. As she struggled with the lock to the front door, two women opened it from the inside. The first, a blonde who looked to be in her midtwenties, was dressed in workout gear. The second, a tiny Asian closer to Katrina's age, was wearing a sleeveless purple dress and carrying a cardboard box the size of a small microwave oven.

"Looks like you could use some help." The blonde took a step backward and held open the heavy wood door. On the other side of it was a small vestibule with mailboxes along one wall. Beyond that was another door, this one glass, leading to a steep staircase covered in dark-green carpet.

Katrina smiled as she wheeled her suitcase into the building. "Thanks. I think I packed too much."

"Are you moving in or just visiting?" The short woman pointed to the suitcase.

"Subletting, actually. For a couple of months."

"Which apartment?"

Katrina looked at the key in her hand. "Three A."

The blonde smiled. "Cool. That's Ben's place. I remember he said he was leaving the country on some research project. I'm Shana, by the way. I'm in Two B."

"I'm Grace." The second woman saluted. "Commander of apartment Four A. Welcome to the building. God knows we could use some fresh blood around here since the murder, no pun intended."

Katrina's eyes got big. "Murder?"

Grace waved a tiny hand in front of her. "Just kidding. What's your name?"

"I'm Katrina. It's nice to meet you both."

Shana tucked a loose strand of blonde hair behind her ear. "Where are you from?"

"California. Silicon Valley, actually."

Grace pumped her fist. "Cali—*nice!* I grew up here but went to law school at UCLA and loved it. You've never seen an Asian girl so tan."

"I've never been to California, but it's on my list," Shana said. "I'm from Ohio. Haven't made it to the West Coast yet." She pressed her hands against her milky-white cheeks. "And I'm *never* tan. Are you here for work?"

Katrina shook her head. "I just quit my job, actually. I'm here . . . I guess, just to relax and have fun for a couple of months."

This was the first time she'd said those words aloud, and she could only imagine the look on her mother's face if she'd heard them.

Shana smiled. "Groovy. Well, listen, I'm off to teach a yoga class right now, but my boyfriend and I are grabbing a drink a few blocks away later. Want to join us?" She turned to Grace. "You're coming too, right, Gracie?"

Grace tapped the top of the box with her free hand. "I may be a little late, depending on how this goes, but I'll try to stop by if I'm not too wiped."

Shana looked back at Katrina. "What do you think? Want to come along?"

Katrina looked at her watch. It was eight fifteen.

"What time?" she asked.

"Probably around ten."

Katrina stifled a cough. *Ten o'clock on a Tuesday night? The streets in Mountain View would be deserted by eight.*

She was about to politely decline out of sheer habit, but something stopped her. Instead, she found herself nodding with a small smile.

"Okay, sure. Why not?"

Shana smiled and turned to go. "Coolio. I'll knock on your door on my way out. See you soon."

"Okay, thanks. I guess I'll see you later."

"Catch ya on the flip side," Grace said with a nod.

Katrina watched them walk down the block until they turned a corner and disappeared. Then she picked up her suitcase and hauled it up the stairs.

Drinks at ten o'clock on a Tuesday night.

Wow.

Welcome to New York.

The small two-bedroom unit was fully furnished, and while it was very clean, it was clearly a single man's apartment. Black leather couch. Big flat-screen TV. Black halogen lamp. The three staples of every bachelor pad Katrina had ever seen. Not that she'd seen many. She'd gone on dates from time to time for as long as she could remember, but her dance card had never been exactly full. And she'd never been in a serious relationship, which was a greater and greater source of embarrassment to her the closer she got to thirty.

In the first bedroom she stepped into, she was greeted by a shiny black bedspread and multiple posters of Metallica and various other heavy-metal bands, so she immediately turned on her heel.

The second bedroom was a bit smaller, but its white walls were bare save for a modest print of a flowerpot above an old wooden desk. The queen-size bed was covered with a thin white quilt embroidered with small green flowers, plus two large white pillows with green trim and matching shams, an ensemble that, while pretty, looked decidedly out of place in a single man's apartment. Katrina figured the entire bedding set had to have been a gift from Ben's mother, if not his grandmother. This was definitely the guest room, but she found it much more appealing, so this was where she would stay.

She pulled her bathrobe and slippers from her suitcase and decided to rinse off before unpacking the rest of her things. After dropping her clothes into a hamper in the corner of the bedroom, she took a towel from the hall closet and headed to the bathroom, wary of how clean it would be. She was pleasantly surprised to discover that it was spotless—or at least as spotless as the old fixtures and floor tiles would allow. She performed a quick inspection.

Tub, check.

Toilet, check.

Sink, check.

Floor, check.

Medicine chest, check.

All clean.

Ben had certainly fulfilled his end of the rental agreement. Even Katrina's mother couldn't have disapproved of the state of things.

She turned on the showerhead and held her hand under the water until it got hot, then took off her robe and stepped inside the tub. As the soothing water ran over her neck and shoulders, she closed her eyes and tried to forget the seeds of concern her parents had planted in her mind during dinner the night before.

It wasn't easy.

It's foolish to quit a job without a new one lined up, Katrina.

Being an adult means having responsibilities, Katrina.

Life isn't just about having fun, Katrina.

New York is dangerous, especially for someone who has never traveled anywhere on her own, Katrina.

To blot out the negative thoughts, she focused on her plans for that night. In her tidy new apartment, with a date for drinks with friendly neighbors, so far New York wasn't anywhere near as daunting as she'd expected.

She changed into jeans and a tank top, then methodically began to unpack her things.

T-shirts, jeans, and undergarments in the bureau.

Skirts, blouses, sweaters, and dresses in the closet.

Toiletries in the medicine chest.

The rental agency had assured her the place had an iron *and* an ironing board, which she found in the hall closet. She ironed everything in her suitcase that needed it, then carefully rehung the items in the closet.

When she was done, she looked around and smiled.

All set.

After she'd stored her empty suitcase in the hall closet, she picked up her phone to call Deb, excited to give her an update on her first hours in the big city. Disappointed but not surprised to reach her voice mail, she left a brief message:

"Hey, it's me. Made it safe and sound! I'm nervous, but excited too. Thanks for making me do this. Love you lots."

She hung up the phone, then plugged her laptop into the outlet next to the desk and booted it up. As the screen flickered to life, she studied the orderly room, trying to picture the last person who had lived here, wondering what Ben was like, what his life in New York was like.

Wondering what *her* life in New York was going to be like.

She turned her attention to her LinkedIn profile and debated whether to change her status of employment at the advertising agency from current to previous. She stared at the screen and pursed her lips. She was tempted to switch it, but somehow that seemed so . . . *permanent.*

She decided to keep it as it was. No need to announce to the world what she'd done—at least not yet.

She thought about doing a cursory search for accounting jobs, then changed her mind. She switched off the computer and decided to check out the flat-screen TV in the living room instead.

* * *

Before Katrina knew it, it was nearly ten o'clock. She was applying a dab of blush at the bathroom mirror when she heard knocking. She ran into the bedroom to grab her purse, then opened the front door.

"Hey, neighbor, you ready for your first night out in New York?" Shana stood there smiling.

Katrina still couldn't believe she was going out at ten o'clock—what would her mother think?—but she forced herself to smile back and nod. "Let's do it." Should she tell Shana she never did anything like this? Or would that make her sound boring?

She decided to keep that information to herself.

"Did you get unpacked okay?" Shana asked as she opened the front door of the building. "Ben left the place in good shape for you, I hope."

"I did, thanks. And the place is *extremely* clean. I was pleasantly surprised, actually."

"I'm not. Ben's sort of a neat freak," she said before skipping down the steps. Katrina couldn't tell if Shana thought that was a good thing or a bad thing, so she didn't share the fact that she was a neat freak too.

"You teach yoga?" Katrina asked.

"Yep. There's a studio not too far from here. Are you a yogi?"

"There's a yoga studio near my place at home, but I've never tried it," Katrina said. The truth was, she'd been *afraid* to try it, afraid to look foolish.

"You should come to one of my classes sometime. Yoga's great for the soul."

They walked several blocks to a small pub on Avenue A called The HorseBox. As they strolled through the front door—always an awkward moment for Katrina, no matter who she was with—Shana scanned the room.

The place was dark and smelled of beer, with the brick walls and wood paneling typical of a dive bar, but it looked perfectly clean. To the left of the entrance was a dartboard, to the right a Big Buck Hunter machine. Beyond that, Katrina spotted an old-school cash register, complete with push buttons, perched atop the scratched wooden bar. A half-dozen or so TV screens showed various sporting events, most of which appeared to be the Yankees game, and a hand-ful of large oak barrels to one side provided a convenient place for standing patrons to set down their drinks. The place was a little more than half full, with a mixed crowd that appeared to range broadly in age from early twenties to mid or even late sixties, mostly male.

Shana smiled and pointed to the back of the room. "There's Josh."

Katrina's eyes followed. Seated at a high round table was a short barrel-chested man with a dark full beard and glasses. In front of him rested a glistening pitcher of beer. When he noticed Shana approaching, he immediately stood up, although it didn't add much to his stature. Katrina couldn't help but think that he looked a lot like a peanut M&M.

"Hey, handsome." Shana gave him a quick kiss, then turned to Katrina. "This is my boyfriend, Josh. Josh, meet my new neighbor, Kat, who just moved here today from California." She looked at Katrina as she climbed onto a bar stool. "Is it okay if I call you Kat?"

Katrina paused. No one had ever called her anything but Katrina, not even when she was little. Although Katie might have seemed like a reasonable nickname for a child, her mother had specifically instructed her elementary-school teachers not to call her that. *Katie is too pedestrian*, her mother had always said, long before Katrina even knew what the word *pedestrian* meant.

So it had always been Katrina. Not Katie. But *Kat* had never even crossed her radar.

She liked the sound of it.

She looked at Shana and shrugged, trying to look nonchalant but secretly thrilled. *I'm Kat here!* "Sure. Why not?"

"Well, hello there, *Kat*." Josh held out a hand and gave her an exaggerated nod. "It's nice to meet you, and may I be among the first to welcome you to our humble city?"

Katrina shook his hand. "Thanks, Josh. I'm excited to be here. A little nervous, but excited."

"And may I also be the first to pour you a beer in said humble city?" He gestured to the waitress to bring another glass.

"That sounds great. Thanks." Katrina wondered where New Yorkers had gotten their reputation for being so unfriendly. They couldn't all be this nice, could they? She figured it was only a matter of time before someone in a hurry pushed her into a gutter.

Once Shana and Katrina each had a full beer in hand, Josh took off his round horn-rimmed glasses and cleaned them with the tail of his light-blue button-down shirt. "So, Kat, what brings you to New York? Work? Love? Mafia ties? I'm always curious how people end up here."

Katrina thought about how to respond—there was no simple answer, was there?—but before she could say anything, Shana jumped in.

"Adventure," she said with bright eyes. "She just quit her job. She's going to live here for a couple of months and just have fun. Isn't that magnificent?"

Josh raised his eyebrows. "Is that so? Here to get into some trouble, are you?"

Katrina laughed. "Not really. I was actually supposed to come with my best friend, but she had to cancel at the last minute because of work, so I decided to come anyway."

"Really?" Shana asked. "That's too bad."

"Impressive that you're on your own," Josh said. "That takes guts."

"Totally," Shana said. "I don't know if I could do it."

They were clearly impressed, but Katrina still felt the familiar discomfort that arose anytime she had to talk about herself. She noticed her foot had begun to tap. "Thanks. So, Josh, what do you do? Shana told me she teaches yoga."

Shana pointed to herself, then to Josh. "I also go to auditions that never turn into any real work. *Josh*, however, is a highly paid tax attorney and is thus buying our drinks tonight." She playfully tousled his thick hair.

Josh caught her hand and kissed it. "With pleasure."

Katrina looked at Josh. Tax attorney was about the last thing she'd have guessed. He looked more like a history professor. Or a lumberjack dressed in a nice shirt. Or a peanut M&M model.

"What kind of auditions?" she asked Shana.

Shana pushed her long blonde hair behind her shoulders. "Acting. I can't sing, that's for sure."

"You sing great," Josh said. He turned to Katrina. "You should see her rock it at karaoke."

Shana put a hand on his chest. "Such a sweet man, yet so delusional."

"How long have you lived here?" Katrina asked Josh.

This time Josh pointed to himself and then turned to Shana. "Me, six years. You're five, right, hot bug?"

"Almost." Shana sipped her beer. "Time goes by so quickly here. You'll see, Kat."

"How long have you two been dating?"

Shana held up two fingers. "Two years, this time around. We went on a couple dates when I first moved here, but then he ditched me like I had the plague. We ran into each other a few years later, and by then he'd come to his senses. Lucky for me."

Josh coughed. "As I recall, you had a boyfriend back home on the farm. A tall, dashing sort. Remember him?"

She giggled. "Okay, maybe you're right. But regardless of how it went down, it worked out in my favor."

Katrina studied the unlikely couple. Shana looked like a head cheerleader. She was perky and pretty and a good two inches taller than rotund, bespectacled Josh, who hardly seemed the type to engage in any sort of aerobic activity, much less yoga. But despite the physical mismatch, there was no questioning their sincere affection for each other. Katrina found it very sweet.

"Do you live around here too?" she asked Josh.

He pointed his thumb over his left shoulder. "I'm on the Upper East Side. I'm not hip enough to live in this neighborhood. I don't even own a fedora."

"You're hip enough for me," Shana said.

"Well then, I'm not young enough."

"How old are you?" Katrina asked.

"Twenty-nine."

Shana pointed at herself. "Twenty-six."

Katrina followed their lead. "Twenty-nine." Then she pointed toward the exit. "Our building is in Gramercy, right?" she asked Shana. "That's what the rental agency said."

Shana nodded. "Technically, yes, but I tend to say I live in the East Village, because I like to be associated with the East Village. I just can't afford to live there."

"Where's that?" Katrina asked.

Josh pointed west. "A couple blocks that way. I'm *definitely* not young enough *or* hip enough to live there."

"Technically we're in Alphabet City right now," Shana said. "But it's all walking distance from Gramercy. You'll see."

Katrina sipped her beer. "I'm going to need a geography lesson. I feel like I have quite a steep learning curve ahead of me."

Josh shook his head. "Don't worry. You'll get it down fast. We all did."

Shana held up her phone. "Plus, if you're directionally challenged like I am, there's always this little guy to help in a pinch."

"Well, hello there, beautiful people in a scary dive bar." The sound of a woman's voice made them all turn their heads.

Josh stood up, and Katrina was again impressed by his manners. "Hey, tiny one," he said to Grace. "Good to see you."

"Hi, Gracie." Shana kissed her on the cheek and gestured to an empty bar stool. "Have a seat."

"Hi, Katrina," Grace said. "I'm glad you came out for a drink."

"We've decided to call her Kat," Shana said.

Grace raised an eyebrow as she climbed up on the stool. "Is that so?"

Shana nodded. "I think it suits her. Don't you?"

Grace looked at Katrina. "She's known you for what, two hours, and now you're a pet?"

Katrina smiled. "I sort of like it, actually. No one's ever called me that before."

"I like it too," Shana said. "Goes well with the adventure-in–New York theme, like this is just one of your nine lives." She made cat claws with her fingers.

Grace tapped her palms on the table. "Then Kat it is. Meow. Uncle Josh, will you procure me a beverage, please?"

Katrina crinkled her nose. "Uncle Josh?"

Grace gestured to him. "Look at that face. Does he look twenty-nine to you? Hell no. I'd put my money on forty-five."

"I've had a full beard since I was about fifteen," Josh said with a shrug. "I was buying beer as a junior in high school—without an ID."

Grace wiggled her fingers at him, then pointed to the bar. "Yo. Uncle Josh. Focus. Beverage."

"Okay, okay." Josh signaled to the waiter to bring them a fresh pitcher of beer, plus another glass for Grace. "God forbid I upset Queen Gracie."

"How did the meeting go?" Shana turned to face Grace. "Tell us everything."

Grace stiffened a tiny bit—not much, but just enough to be noticed. "Outcome uncertain. I think she liked the line, but she's going to get back to me next week. So that probably means like a month. You know how flaky these buyers are. It's ridiculous."

Katrina wondered what kind of meeting she'd had at such a late hour, but before she could ask, Shana put a hand on her arm. "Grace makes the most beautiful jewelry."

Katrina looked at Grace. "Jewelry? What kind?"

Grace shrugged. "Mostly necklaces and earrings, all silver, some with various stones."

"Show her, Gracie," Shana said.

Grace pulled out two boxes from her purse and set them carefully on the table, then opened them one after the other. Inside one lay a long, delicate chain holding a thin silver triangle about an inch long on each side. The pendant on the second necklace consisted of two interlocking silver circles, one the size of a silver dollar, the other half as big.

"Wow, they *are* beautiful," Katrina said. It was just the type of jewelry she'd always wanted to wear . . . but never had.

"Aren't they stunning?" Shana said.

"Yes." Katrina realized she was whispering. She found both pieces striking for their bold simplicity.

Grace handed one of the necklaces to Katrina. "This is sort of the general style of all my stuff. I'm into class, not trash."

"I adore them," Shana said.

Grace smiled at her. "Thanks, babe." Then she looked at Katrina. "I'm trying to get some retail shops to carry them, which is turning out to be way harder than I ever thought it would be. It's really starting to piss me off, actually."

Josh laughed. "Everything pisses you off."

"You piss me off," she said to him.

The waitress set down a pitcher, and Josh began to pour everyone a fresh drink, starting with Grace. When it was Katrina's turn, she covered her still half-full glass with her hand.

"I'm good. Thanks, though," she said. Then she said to Grace, "How long have you been making jewelry?"

"Since I was two."

Katrina felt her eyes get big. "Since you were *two*?"

"Kidding. Not that long. Full-time for about a year now."

"Oh," Katrina said.

"It takes a while to get used to her," Josh said to Katrina.

"But it's well worth it. You'll see," Shana added.

Grace narrowed her eyes at Josh. "Did you hear that, old man? I'm well worth it."

"We're the same age," Josh said.

"What were you doing before this?" Katrina asked.

Grace took a sip of her beer, then set down her glass on the table. "I was a tax attorney. But I dabbled in jewelry in my spare time for a couple years before finally taking the plunge."

Grace is a tax attorney too? Katrina turned to Josh, who smiled at her and nodded. "We used to work together."

"You mean you used to work for me," Grace said, pointing at him.

He held up his palms. "What is with all the revisionist history tonight? We used to work *together*. We were the shortest attorneys in the firm."

Grace pointed at him again. "We were the shortest *people* in the firm, not limited to attorneys. Unless it was bring your kid to work day, of course."

"They used to call us the munchkins," Josh said.

Katrina laughed. "So why did you leave?" she asked Grace.

"I had to get out of there. I was totally getting office butt. Everyone was."

"Hey now, I still work there," Josh said.

"Have you *seen* your butt?" Grace sliced the air in a flat line with her hand.

"I love his office butt," Shana said.

Josh cleared his throat. "I think it's time to change the subject. What about you, Kat? What did you do out in California?"

Katrina swallowed. "Oh, I . . . I used to work at an advertising agency."

"Ah, so you're a creative type too," Grace said with a nod. "My kind of person."

Katrina shook her head. "Actually, no. I worked in the finance department."

Shana looked surprised. "Really? You don't strike me as that . . . personality type."

"Definitely not," Grace said.

Katrina hoped that was a compliment. No one but Deb had ever questioned how her chosen profession matched up with her personality—aside from herself, of course.

"Do you have friends who live here?" Grace asked as she took another sip of her beer. "New York City can be a bitch to navigate solo."

Katrina gave Shana and Josh a hopeful look. "Do you two count?"

Shana smiled. "Of course we do."

"Then I have three friends, counting the cabdriver I met tonight. Or four, if I can count you too?"

Grace shook her head. "Thanks for the offer, but I don't think so."

Shana laughed and put a hand on her shoulder. "Be nice, Gracie."

Grace held up her glass to Katrina. "Totally kidding, dude. Count away."

Katrina smiled. "Then I guess I have four friends here."

"That's more than enough to get you started in this town," Shana said. "You'll see."

* * *

When she got back to the apartment later, Katrina changed into her pajamas and promptly headed to the bathroom to perform her nightly routine.

Remove eye makeup with cotton ball.

Wash face with gentle foaming cleanser.

Apply night cream.

Floss and brush teeth.

She climbed into bed and gazed at the pretty flowers on the quilt as she listened to the sounds of the street outside and reflected on her first night in New York. She'd been in town only a few hours and she already had friends, a more lively social life than at home, and a new name.

It certainly hadn't begun the way she'd planned, but maybe everything was going to turn out okay after all.

Chapter Four

The next morning, Katrina laced up the brand-new sneakers she'd bought for the trip and went for a stroll around the neighborhood.

The surrounding blocks were a blend of brownstones, row houses, and bland apartment buildings, some better maintained than others. The myriad trees dotting the sidewalks were still leafy and green, and she was surprised at how many there were smack in the middle of Manhattan, which she'd so often heard described as a "concrete jungle."

She walked along Twenty-First Street toward the East River. After crossing First Avenue, she found herself approaching a development whose signage identified it as Peter Cooper Village. Enclosed by a fence and connected by a series of crisscrossing cement pathways, the handful of brick high-rises inside formed a small campus that reminded Katrina of college dorms. She wondered if the residents had a similar feeling about the enclosure—if by living there, they enjoyed a sense of a small community inside such an enormous city. Maybe that was the secret to New York—carving out your own niche within the vast metropolis.

She crossed the busy six-lane FDR Drive, then walked a few blocks south along the narrow esplanade hugging the riverbank below. Several cyclists passed by in either direction, as did a couple of ferries full of tourists cruising along the East River, on the other side of which lay the skyline of what Katrina suspected was Queens. Or was it Brooklyn? She made a mental note to look it up on a map when she got home. In the meantime, her already tired legs were reminding her how out of shape she was. At least she'd bought comfortable sneakers. Maybe she could use her time here to finally get into an exercise routine.

For no reason in particular, she veered west on Sixteenth Street, and eventually found herself at a park enclosed by a wrought-iron fence with open gates on two sides. A placard near the east entrance said STUYVESANT SQUARE. She wandered in and took a seat on one of the many benches dotting the colorful garden. Although it hadn't been mentioned in any of her travel guides, she found it tranquil and quite pretty.

After Katrina had been sitting there for a few minutes, a young couple approached her, and the woman held out her phone. "Excuse me. Would you mind taking a picture of us?"

"Sure. No problem." As the couple positioned themselves in front of the fountain in the center of the park, Katrina noticed the tower of Saint George's Episcopal Church in the background and adjusted her angle to include it in the photo.

She waved good-bye to the couple and gazed back up at the historic church, admiring the nineteenth-century architecture nestled between the more modern neighboring buildings, all a stone's throw from this beautiful public garden. The juxtaposition was surprising, yet somehow welcoming, as if it were somehow stating that this was a city with room for everything.

With room for every*one*.

Suddenly, Katrina had an urge to paint. It had been years since she'd touched a canvas, but there was something in the peaceful coexistence of such dissimilar entities that called out to her. Why not give it a go right now? She pulled out her phone to look up the closest art store, then rushed off to buy some supplies.

* * *

Nearly three hours later, Katrina put the finishing touches on her painting of the church and gardens. Though she was clearly a bit rusty, it wasn't bad. The painting captured the essence of how this place made *her* feel, which was all she really cared about. It wasn't like anyone else was ever going to see it. She'd stopped showing her work to anyone long ago.

After carefully packing up her easel, paints, and brushes, she picked up the canvas, preparing to go home. As she exited the park, she turned her head to look back up at the church tower one last time.

A centuries-old church, an oasis of serenity in the middle of a modern city.

She smiled.

On the way home her stomach began to rumble, so she wandered around until she spotted a small coffeehouse. At least it appeared to be a coffeehouse. A steaming mug painted on what looked like a homemade sign was the only outward indication of what type of business it was.

She pushed open the heavy glass door and the delicate ringing of chimes announced her entrance. She was slightly embarrassed by the attention it drew to her arrival, but no one else seemed to notice. She looked around the small shop, admiring the way the dark hardwood floor highlighted the pale-blue walls. The interior was bigger than she'd expected but still not very large, with just a handful of wooden tables occupying the open space in front of the counter. Classical music played in the background, much like at her parents' house. In contrast to the sterile chill she always felt there, however, the vibe here was warm and inviting. Though she had yet to speak to a soul, she already felt at home.

She studied the large chalkboard mounted above the cash register. A list of menu options was displayed in bright purple. It didn't matter what the choices were, however. She already knew what she would order, assuming they had it.

"Hi, there. What can I get you?"

She blinked and saw the man standing behind the counter smiling at her. His face was a bit unshaven but not sloppily so, his eyes green and friendly. He wore a plaid flannel button-down over a white T-shirt, both untucked, and jeans. She guessed he was probably in his mid to late thirties. She cast her eyes downward, suddenly aware of the number of details she'd ingested so quickly.

"Do you have blueberry scones?" she asked.

"Sure do."

"I'd like one, please, and a skim latte." She kept her eyes fixed on the hardwood floor.

"To stay or to take away?"

"Oh, to stay, please." She'd never heard either term but figured they were the equivalent of *for here* and *to go*. Her answer surprised her, as she hadn't planned on eating here, but there was something about the place that she found so appealing that she didn't want to leave just yet.

"You okay there?"

She forced herself to look up at him. "Excuse me?"

He put both palms on the counter and smiled again. "You look a little rattled. It's just espresso in the latte, I promise. We run a clean operation here."

Katrina swallowed. "Oh, I'm okay, thanks." She realized she was almost whispering. He was clearly trying to be friendly. Why couldn't she at least laugh at his joke? She never knew when an attack of shyness would hit, but for some reason, she felt struck with timidity by this man's friendly overtures.

"I take it you're not from here?"

"Is it that obvious?" She offered a weak smile and wished she weren't so awkward around strangers, especially such amiable ones. Or handsome ones.

"Just a little. Were you just painting?" He nodded at her folded-up easel.

She felt her cheeks turning pink. "It's not very good."

He smiled. "I doubt that. If you'd like to have a seat, I'll bring over that latte when it's ready. Here's your scone." He gestured toward the tables and passed her a plate, and when he lifted his left hand she immediately saw the ring on his third finger. She averted her eyes again, mortified that she'd even noticed.

"Are you sure you're okay?" he asked.

She knew she should regain eye contact, that any normal human being would simply look him in the eye, but she couldn't make herself do it. Despite being flustered, she wanted to say something friendly in return, at least *thank you*, but all she could bring herself to do was nod politely. She turned around and silently cursed herself as she scanned the room for a place to sit.

Most of the tables were empty, so she headed toward one near the front windows and spread out the *New York Times* she'd bought earlier. She'd always enjoyed reading it at home, but doing so in Manhattan felt so much more right. Plus she wanted to get her mind off the awkwardness of that encounter. She was all too familiar with her reaction and hated the way she came across when she got shy, but hating it didn't make it any easier to change.

She put her head down and began to read.

"Here's your skim latte, ma'am." The sound of a male voice startled her out of the article she'd been reading about a new community center in the Bronx. She'd regained control of her nerves, and this time she was determined to be pleasant, approachable, *normal*. She looked up with a semiforced smile, but the face wasn't the same one as the friendly man behind the counter. This one belonged to a scraggly youth who looked painfully bored.

"Oh, thank you," she said as he set down the steaming cup in front of her.

"No problem."

As he sauntered away, she casually glanced over her shoulder at the counter.

Flannel Shirt Barista was gone.

* * *

Katrina ran into Grace on her way back into her building, carrying the same box she'd had with her the night before.

"Hey, Kat. How's your first day here going?"

"Honestly? I think I need a nap. And maybe a massage."

Grace held up her free hand for a high five. "Way to overdo it right out of the gate. I like it. What's up with the art supplies?"

Katrina high-fived her back. "Oh, just a little painting I did. Nothing fancy."

Grace raised her eyebrows. "You paint?"

"I *try* to paint. I don't know if I actually *paint*. What are you up to?"

Grace patted the box. "Another meeting with a potential buyer. More getting my hopes up, more dreams dashed, the usual. I swear to God this is worse than online dating."

"Is it really that hard to get someone to carry your jewelry?"

"Actually, it's even harder than that."

"I'm sorry, Grace. For what it's worth, I think the necklaces you showed me last night are beautiful. I've never seen anything like them."

"Do you want one?" Grace set down the box and opened it. "I have an overstock situation going on here." She pulled out one with the interlocking circles.

"I'd love one! How much are they?" Katrina asked. She didn't have much cash in her wallet.

"Shut up," Grace said. "Consider it a welcome-to–New York gift."

Katrina put a hand over her mouth. "Really?"

"Of course. Here you go." Grace handed her a small plastic pouch, then bent down and picked up the box. "I've gotta skedaddle. Wish me luck."

Katrina pressed the pouch against her chest. "Good luck. And thanks so much for this. I really appreciate it."

Grace nodded at Katrina's easel. "No problem. Maybe in return you can paint me in the buff sometime."

Katrina's jaw dropped.

"Kidding, just kidding," Grace said. "See ya."

* * *

That evening, wearing her brand-new necklace with a simple green sheath and black flats, Katrina went to have a drink with a woman who'd been an RA in her dorm during her freshman year of college. Her name was Brittany, and she worked at an investment firm on Wall Street. She'd suggested they meet in Tribeca at a trendy Mexican restaurant called Super Linda that was a few blocks from her place. Given Brittany's busy work schedule—and Katrina's lack thereof—Katrina didn't mind hiking across town to see her.

Katrina arrived a few minutes early and took a seat at the far end of the downstairs bar. Quietly nursing a soda water with lemon, she watched the scene unfolding around her. It was only Wednesday, but the place was quickly becoming as full as any bar in Mountain View on a Friday or Saturday night. She had her purse sitting on the bar stool next to her and hoped Brittany wouldn't be late. Otherwise, she knew she wouldn't have the nerve to hold the seat much longer.

"You okay there?" The bartender pointed to her drink.

Katrina nodded as she straightened the small stack of cardboard coasters she'd created on the bar. "I'm fine for now, thank you." She felt a little silly ordering soda water at a place like this, but she wasn't comfortable ordering an alcoholic drink by herself. Sitting at a bar alone was awkward enough. She'd never been much of a bar person, and here she was, out for the second night in a row—and midweek to boot! Deb would be so proud of her.

"Katrina Lynden, is that really you?"

Katrina turned at the sound of the raspy voice behind her. She stood up and smoothed her dress as a tall blonde wearing what appeared to be a black cape approached and gave her a hug.

As Katrina hugged Brittany back, she was surprised to realize how happy she was to see a familiar face, even though it had been more than ten years since she'd laid eyes on it.

"Brittany, hi. It's so nice to see you."

As a freshman in the dorms, Katrina had always thought of Brittany as an adult figure, though in reality she was only three years ahead of her in school. Impressions made as a teenager were hard to break, so even now, in Katrina's eyes, she still seemed much more grown-up. It might have been her chic black outfit, or the way she had her blonde locks swept up in a classic twist, but Katrina felt like a girl of eighteen around her. She wondered whether Brittany still thought of Katrina as a kid just out of high school. She ran her fingers over the silver pendant and tried to stand up straight, hoping to make a good impression.

Her hands still on Katrina's shoulders, Brittany took a step backward and smiled at her. "Wow. It has been *ages*, hasn't it? I can't believe you're all grown-up and here in New York City. You look great. I *love* that necklace. It looks gorgeous with your fair skin." She glanced at Katrina's glass. "What are you drinking? I'll get you a refill."

Katrina's eyes followed. "Oh, I was actually just drinking some soda water."

Brittany gave her a strange look. "Soda water . . . as in *only* soda water?"

Katrina offered a sheepish smile. "I'm not much of a drinker."

"You don't drink? Oh, wait, I'm sorry. Are you . . ." Her voice trailed off into an awkward pause.

Katrina knew what Brittany was thinking and quickly shook her head. "Oh, no, I *do* drink, just—just not all that often." Hardly ever, actually.

Brittany waved a hand in front of her. "Well, we must put a stop to that immediately. This is *New York*, after all, where drinking is the city pastime. Do you take your margaritas with salt?" She leaned over the bar and flagged down the bartender, who was a good ten feet away, then snapped her fingers. "Hey there, hon. Two top-shelf margaritas, please."

The man nodded back in acknowledgment, and Brittany asked Katrina again, "Salt okay?"

"Okay, sure. Thanks." She was too embarrassed to tell the truth, which was that she had no idea.

Brittany turned back to the bartender, who was approaching them. "Both with salt, and make them strong, thank you very much, you handsome thing." She pulled her credit card out of her wallet and handed it to him.

"That's all you have to say to me?" he asked.

Brittany winked at him and nodded toward Katrina. "I'm busy catching up with an old friend. We'll chat later."

"Does your friend have a name?" The bartended turned to Katrina and smiled. "I'm Kevin."

"I'm Katrina . . . er . . . Kat . . . either is fine," Katrina said. "It's nice to meet you, Kevin."

Brittany looked at her. "You go by Kat now?"

"In New York I think maybe I do." She managed a nervous smile. "I'm still trying it on."

Brittany nodded. "I like the sound of it. Has a bit of that What-happens-in-Vegas-stays-in-Vegas vibe to it, you know what I mean?"

"I'll leave you two ladies to get reacquainted." As Kevin walked away to prepare the drinks, Katrina wondered how well they knew each other. Or did Brittany call everyone *handsome*?

Brittany took off her cape and plopped down on the bar stool. "I'm so glad today is over, can I just tell you that? I'm exhausted."

"Bad day at the office?"

"Nothing out of the ordinary, just exhausting. It's always exhausting. But let's not talk about me right now. I want to talk about *you*. How are you doing? You really do look amazing, by the way. Your hair is gorgeous. I don't remember it being this long." She reached over and petted Katrina's wavy auburn locks.

Katrina felt her cheeks flush at the attention. "Thanks. I'm doing well." Even though they were both sitting down, she felt even smaller in Brittany's imposing presence than she remembered feeling in college. Her foot began tapping against the bar stool and she forced herself to stop.

"I'm so happy you got in touch. What brings you to New York?" Brittany asked.

Katrina swallowed. "Well, my best friend, Deb, thought it would be fun for us to quit our jobs and move here for a couple months. It's not normally the sort of thing I would do, but—"

"I love it! I like how this Deb thinks."

"It took some convincing on her part, but she finally got me to take the plunge."

"She sounds like someone I want to meet. Where is she tonight?"

"Oh, well, unfortunately her side of the bargain fell through at the last minute, so she didn't come."

Kevin set two margaritas in front of them along with Brittany's credit card. "Ladies, on the house."

"Thanks, handsome." Brittany touched his arm, then raised an eyebrow at Katrina. "You came here by yourself?"

"Yep."

"Do you know anyone here? I mean, besides me?"

"Not really. There's a handful of people from school I'll probably meet up with at some point, but they're not exactly buddies." Although *two* could hardly be called a handful, she didn't feel like admitting just how few people she knew here in New York. They also hadn't e-mailed her back, another depressing factoid she didn't feel like sharing.

"Wow. Good for you for flying solo. I wouldn't ever have expected you to make such a bold move, but I guess everyone grows up eventually. You were such a shy little thing back in the dorms. Quieter than a baby hamster."

Katrina realized how accurate—if not exactly flattering—the description was. But she didn't take offense. It was clear Brittany hadn't meant it as an insult, and that she didn't see Katrina as a wallflower anymore . . . even though Katrina knew all too well that she was just as much of a "shy little thing" as ever. She glanced at the sliding stack of coasters and quickly moved to straighten them.

Brittany held up her glass for a toast. "Cheers to you for having a pair, and welcome to New York. It's a damn fun place to be, I'll tell you that much."

Katrina clinked her margarita against Brittany's and took a small sip, trying her best not to visibly flinch at the strong kick of tequila. The crowd around them was getting louder, so she raised her voice a few decibels. "How long have you been living here?"

Brittany closed her eyes and tapped her forehead with her index finger. "How long have I been living here? Oh Jesus, let's see. . . . I came here straight out of business school . . ."

Katrina watched her do the math in her head.

"So that puts it at eight years now." Brittany opened her eyes. "Damn! Scary how fast time goes."

"So I've heard," Katrina said. "You work in investment banking, right?"

"Yes, ma'am. I'm in mergers and acquisitions at Goldman Sachs."

Katrina took another sip of her drink. "Do you like it?" Despite her own mundane experience in accounting, Katrina had always thought investment banking sounded like the more glamorous side of the number-crunching world—and with much better perks.

Brittany raised her eyebrow again. "Do I like it? Now *that* is a loaded question."

"What do you mean?"

She stirred her margarita. "Well . . . I love the money, I hate the hours. I love the challenge, I hate the politics. I love the intellectual stimulation, I hate being on the road so much. I love the lifestyle, I hate the lifestyle. Need I go on?"

Katrina smiled. "I think I get the picture. Are there a lot of women in your field? I think you're the only investment banker I know, male or female. Actually, that's not quite true. I went on a few dates with a banker once, but then he stopped calling." Katrina stiffened and wondered why she was being so candid with that information. Was the tequila already affecting her? Or was it just the fact that she was in a new environment? Regardless, it felt nice to share, and Brittany didn't seem to find the comment odd at all.

"Yes, there are women, just not even close to as many as there should be. But you could say that about most high-paying jobs in this country, couldn't you?" She took a big sip of her margarita and glanced around the room, then put her hand on Katrina's arm. "So tell me, what have you been up to since college? I don't think I've seen you since you were a freshman. Just a baby, you were."

Katrina hesitated, embarrassed at the dearth of interesting stories she had to share about her life since then. She squeezed the stem of her glass. "Not much, really. I've been living in Mountain View since I graduated."

"Mountain View? Why on earth would any recent college graduate want to live in Mountain View?" Brittany looked sincerely perplexed. "Nearly everyone I knew in school moved to San Francisco."

Katrina shifted on her bar stool. "I, um, I got offered a job at an advertising agency there a few weeks before the end of my senior year, so I took it. I started the week after graduation, and before I knew it, I'd been there for eight years." Saying it out loud made her even more self-conscious. *How did that happen?*

Brittany's eyes brightened. "Advertising? Sounds fun. What sort of campaigns have you worked on? Anything I might have seen?"

Katrina cleared her throat. "Oh, well, actually I worked in the finance department, so I wasn't involved in the campaigns. I was an accounting major."

"Oh." The brightness in Brittany's eyes disappeared. Despite her genuine interest in Katrina, she was clearly—however understandably—underwhelmed by this information.

Katrina slouched a little on her stool, wishing she hadn't led such a boring life. No wonder she avoided social situations. She never had anything interesting to add to the conversation. "What did *you* major in?" she asked, hoping to deflect the focus from herself.

Brittany shrugged and glanced around the bar. "Econ. Pretty standard in my industry. Where are you staying while you're in town?"

Katrina perked up a little bit at the reminder that she was no longer working at the agency and, at least for the moment, no longer living in Mountain View. For once, she *did* have something interesting to say. "I've sublet an apartment in Gramercy. Although my neighbor told me I should say the East Village because she thinks it sounds cooler."

Brittany smiled. "Your neighbor sounds funny. And young. Is she young?"

"I think she said she's twenty-six."

Brittany pointed at her. "Bingo. Everyone in their twenties wants to live in the East Village and go dancing like a rock star every night. Then one day they turn thirty, and soon they start wearing earplugs to sleep and bitching about the piles of trash they have to navigate on the way to work. And then, eventually, they realize it's time to find a new neighborhood."

Katrina winced. She'd been wearing earplugs to bed since her freshman year in college.

"Did you leave anyone back home?" Brittany asked.

"You mean a boyfriend?"

"You think I was talking about a cat?"

Katrina laughed awkwardly. "No, no boyfriend." She said the words quickly. *Too* quickly, she thought, as if she'd replied *Of course I don't have a boyfriend! Why would I have a boyfriend?* Was it really that odd a question?

Brittany polished off her drink. "Well, that's a good thing, because there are plenty of men here. Not many are worth bringing home to Mom and Dad for the holidays, but believe me, if you're looking for a good time, men are *everywhere* in New York." She pointed at the bartender and lowered her voice. "That one, for example."

Katrina's eyes followed Brittany's index finger. Kevin was at the other end of the bar, chatting with two women who were both smiling a bit too eagerly at him.

"You dated him?"

"*Dated*? No."

Unsure how to respond to that, Katrina just said "Oh."

Brittany shrugged. "He's cute enough, but the sex wasn't anything special, so that was the end of that. He makes yummy margaritas though, doesn't he? Do you want another?"

Katrina looked down at her glass. It was still more than half full. "Oh, no, thanks. I'm okay."

"You sure? You've been nursing that one for quite a while."

"I'm sure. Thanks though."

Brittany caught Kevin's attention and ordered another drink, then turned to face Katrina and lowered her voice. "I think he's still a little bitter that I blew him off, but whatever. I'll tip him well if he actually lets me buy a round."

Again, Katrina didn't know how to respond, so she didn't. Instead, she asked "What about now? Are you seeing anyone?"

Brittany waved a hand in front of her face. "Hon, I'm *always* seeing someone. It's just a different someone every few weeks."

"Really?" Katrina usually went months between *first* dates. Second dates were even fewer and farther between. Third dates almost never happened.

"Yes, really. I work too much and travel way too much to get serious with any one person."

"Your life sounds so glamorous."

Brittany shrugged. "Sometimes. Other times it's just draining. But whatever it is, it suits me. I'm not one to settle down for the long haul. Never have been, really."

"Didn't you have a serious boyfriend when you were my RA? A guy with glasses?"

"Good memory. His name was Scott. We dated for like three years, but he wanted to get married and have lots of babies, and I didn't, so we broke up."

"That's too bad." Katrina couldn't even fathom what it would feel like to date someone for three years.

Brittany yawned and stretched her arms over her head. "Oh gosh, don't feel sorry for me for even a minute. It was for the best, believe me. I'm definitely not the marrying type, and certainly not the having-babies type. Plus no one should get married before the age of thirty anyway. That's insanity, in my opinion."

"Do you still talk to him?"

She shook her head. "Not in ages. It's ancient history now."

"And you still don't want to get married?"

Brittany pulled a lipstick out of her purse and discreetly applied it. "I don't think so. I'm too much of a free spirit for that. Maybe one day, when I'm much, much older, but for now I'm just not interested in coming home to the same man every night and fighting over who takes out the trash every morning."

"But what if you fell in love again?" *Doesn't everyone want to fall in love?* Katrina thought. She certainly did.

Brittany smirked. "I doubt that's going to happen, and love ends up turning to dust most of the time anyway. So I just prefer to have fun and focus on myself. Life is much easier that way. Plus sometimes sex is more fun when you know you're never going to see the guy again. You should try that sometime, if you haven't already."

Katrina had never heard a woman speak so nonchalantly about sex and relationships—especially a woman in her thirties. Most of the women she knew back home were either married, well on their way there, or actively looking for Mr. Right—or at least hoping to run into him. *She* certainly was—however passively—and had always assumed everyone else was too. Could she be wrong?

She glanced at the small stack of coasters—it was still intact—and searched for something interesting to say in response to Brittany's comments. She wanted to be livelier, bolder, cooler—to come up with something witty, if only to mask how surprised she was at the brazen remarks.

Before she could say anything, Brittany said, "Hold on a second. That's my phone buzzing." She dug her phone out of her purse, then smiled at the text message and put a hand on Katrina's arm without looking up. "I'm so sorry to be rude, but given what we were just talking about, I need a quick second to reply to this."

Katrina welcomed the break in conversation and took the opportunity to stand up. "No worries. I'll just run to the ladies' room. Be right back."

Brittany nodded, still not looking up from her phone.

Katrina navigated her way through the crowd to the restrooms in the back. While in line, she glanced around and noticed several couples sitting on oversized lounge chairs on the left. While most of them were cuddled up, some of them looked obviously uncomfortable, and she wondered if they were on first dates. Would that be her soon? She hadn't been on a first date—any date—in months, but she'd always felt awkward on them. She hated feeling like she was on some kind of audition, and often buckled under the pressure of trying to impress someone new.

But maybe it would be different here?

Maybe *she* would be different here?

Perhaps it was because of all the movies she'd watched over the years, but the idea of going on a date in New York seemed so . . . *romantic*. And despite what Brittany had just said, Katrina still hoped that love might, someday, somehow, find her.

Maybe New York was where it would finally happen?

Where she'd finally meet a man who understood her?

One who saw her for who she really was . . . and loved her for it?

When she got back, Brittany was chatting with Kevin. It looked like she was flirting. Maybe she'd changed her mind about him?

"That was quick," Brittany said as Katrina took a stool. "I thought you'd be gone for ages."

Kevin pointed to Katrina's drink. "Can I get you another one?"

"Oh no, I'm fine. Thanks." Katrina covered the glass with her palm.

"Okay, just let me know. Britt, give a shout if you need anything." He smiled at both of them and headed back to the women at the other end of the bar.

"He's trying way too hard," Brittany said under her breath when he was well out of earshot.

Just then a hand appeared on Brittany's shoulder. She swiveled around, then jumped up to hug the man standing behind her. He had dark brown, perfectly coiffed hair and equally dark almond-shaped eyes that suggested intelligence—in addition to notable good looks.

"Damn, that was fast. I want you to meet my friend from college." Brittany turned to Katrina. "Katrina, I mean *Kat*, Lynden, this is Reid Hanson. Reid, Kat just moved here from Silicon Valley."

Katrina extended her hand. "It's nice to meet you, Reid."

"The pleasure's all mine, Kat." He smiled and shook her hand before pointing to the bar. "Do you ladies need another round?"

Katrina noticed a wedding ring on his left hand and shook her head. "I'm still working on my first, thanks."

"Enough nursing," Brittany said. "Yes, Reid, she needs another one. I'll take one too."

There were no more available stools, so after Reid ordered the drinks he stood behind Katrina and Brittany, forming a little half circle between them and the bar that succeeded in slightly insulating them from the noise.

"That was Reid who texted me before," Brittany said. "He was asking what I was up to, so I told him to come join us for a drink."

Katrina glanced at her watch. "Did you just come from work?" It was close to nine o'clock.

He nodded. "Yes, but let's not talk about that. Work is the last thing I want to be thinking about right now. So Brittany says you and she met in college?" He narrowed his eyes and looked back and forth between them. "Let me guess. Same sorority?"

Brittany shook her head. "I wasn't in a sorority."

"Were you represented by the same modeling agency?"

Brittany rolled her eyes. "Spare us, please."

He snapped his fingers. "I got it. Cheerleaders for the football team?"

"Stop it. I was Katrina's RA."

He looked confused. "What's an RA?"

Brittany gave him an are-you-serious look. "Resident adviser? In the dorms?"

Reid nodded. "Ah, got it. Sorry, it's been a long time since I lived in the dorms."

Brittany took a sip of her margarita. "My senior year I got free room and board for keeping the freshmen out of trouble." She leaned over and squeezed Katrina's knee. "Not that this one ever got into trouble. She was as pure as the driven snow."

Katrina felt her cheeks flush again, but neither Reid nor Brittany seemed to notice her embarrassment. How could they know how little she had changed since then? Her history of getting into trouble read more like a greeting card than a novel.

As Reid made eye contact with Katrina, she felt a shiver of anxiety course through her. "So, Snow White, is it? What brings you to New York?" he asked with a polite smile.

She swallowed and tried frantically to think how to respond, desperate to sound more fabulous than she felt. "I guess you could say . . . adventure."

His smile grew into a grin. "Oh really?"

"She quit her job and came here *by herself* to have fun for a couple months," Brittany said. "Pretty badass, if you ask me."

"That *is* pretty badass," Reid said. "You sound like my kind of woman, Snow White."

Brittany playfully batted him on the arm. "You should be so lucky. So how's life at Morgan Stanley treating you?" She looked at Katrina. "Reid's in banking too. We used to work together."

"I'm hanging in there. The European market sure took it on the chin today. That's why I was at the office so late."

"Ugh, let's not talk about the European market." Brittany stuck out her tongue. "I've been hearing about that disaster all day."

Kevin brought over the drinks, and as he set a second margarita in front of her, Katrina quickly picked up her first one and took a sip, hoping it wasn't too obvious how full it still was. As she took another big gulp, she tried once more to ignore the burning in her throat. She also tried not to notice the fact that she'd just knocked over her coasters.

Brittany was holding up her margarita for another toast. "Here's to old friends and new friends."

"And future friends," Reid said.

"Hear, hear," Brittany said. "Can't forget future friends."

Katrina clinked her glass against theirs, then forced herself to take another big gulp. Then another, and another. Each one set her throat on fire, but she finally finished the first margarita. Her eyes watering, she set down the empty glass and picked up the full one. Brittany and Reid didn't appear to notice; they were staring across the room at someone they thought used to work with them.

"I don't think that's her. She's not that tall, right?" Reid said.

"I think it is," Brittany said. "I always hated her."

Reid turned back to face the bar, then pointed at the full glass in Katrina's hand and smiled. "Hey, look at that—Snow White's finally on her second drink."

Katrina, her throat still stinging, managed a smile in return. "Surprise." She averted her eyes and tried to straighten the coasters with her free hand, although it suddenly wasn't as easy to arrange the little stack as before. She stared at the slightly lopsided pile for a moment, then looked back at Reid. "Do you live in Tribeca too? Brittany said she lives just a few blocks from here." She was determined to participate in the conversation and not just observe it, which was what she would normally do in this situation. Not that she'd ever found herself in a situation quite like this before.

Brittany turned around. "I said what?"

"You said you live just a few blocks from here, right?" Katrina said. The words came out a bit thick, and much more deliberately than she'd intended. She also hadn't meant to repeat herself verbatim, but she couldn't help it. She wondered if Brittany and Reid could tell how much one margarita had affected her. She hoped not.

Brittany nodded. "I did say that."

"So, um, do you live in Tribeca too?" Katrina asked Reid again.

"I'm in the West Village."

"Where's that?"

"A little farther north than Brittany's loft, but still not too far from here. I could walk home, but I'm too lazy, so I'll cab it."

"Who has the energy?" Brittany said with a shrug. "I take cabs everywhere."

Katrina wondered if either of them ever took the subway. She doubted it. "What does Tribeca stand for?" she asked.

"Triangle below Canal Street," Brittany and Reid said in unison.

Katrina shifted on her stool. "Got it. From what little I've seen, this part of town seems less rowdy than the East Village—a bit cleaner, more grown-up. I like it." What she really meant was that it looked more expensive, but she wasn't sure how couth pointing that out would be.

Reid took a gulp of his drink and set it on the bar. "Is that where you're staying? The East Village?"

Katrina smiled at him, finally beginning to relax. "Actually, I've already learned that the appropriate answer to that question depends on the demographic asking it. So since that demographic is you, I'll say Gramercy."

"Say what?" He looked confused.

Brittany elbowed him gently. "Her prepubescent neighbor thinks living in the East Village is cool, but I've already explained the migration pattern to her."

"Ah, the East Village migration pattern. So true, so true. That hood is for postcollege kids looking to dance on bars. Me no do that anymore."

"Unless your wife's out of town, of course," Brittany said.

Katrina looked at her and wondered if she was kidding.

Reid tossed back the rest of his drink and held his thumb and pinkie up to his ear and mouth to indicate a phone. "Speaking of the wife, will you ladies excuse me for a minute? I need to make a quick call."

"Of course," Brittany said. "Go do what you gotta do."

He set his empty glass on the bar. "Be back in a flash. Will you order me another?"

"Consider it done," Brittany said.

"Thanks. You're a peach." He turned and rapidly disappeared into the crowd.

As soon as he was gone, Brittany shook her head. "Poor guy is miserable."

Katrina gave her a confused look. "He is?" He'd certainly seemed happy to her.

"Miserable."

"Why?"

"He's married to a bitch."

Katrina felt her eyes get big. "Really?"

"Major bitch. Super frosty."

"You've met her?"

"Once, but that was enough. I steer clear now. It's not worth engaging."

"If she's so awful, why did he marry her?"

Brittany shrugged. "Because that's what men here do."

"What do you mean?"

"I mean, they marry bitches, or at least the pretty ones who come from money."

"They do?"

"Yep."

"All of them?"

"A lot of them."

"Oh." Katrina exhaled. "That's a bummer." She was too insecure to even imagine being a bitch.

"I see it a lot with bankers in particular. Once they turn thirty, they all feel the need to find some trophy wife, usually from a wealthy family, and almost always with a mean streak. It's like they need to prove something to the world."

"What are they proving?"

"What else? That they're *men*."

"Oh." Despite her momentary surge in confidence, Katrina felt her naïveté bubbling to the surface again. She had no idea how marrying an ice queen could prove someone's manliness.

"Sometimes it works out, but from what I've seen, usually it's downhill after the fancy wedding, because how can you top that whole princess-for-a-day thing? It's hardly my problem though, so I don't let it bother me."

Reid returned with a grin and poked his head back into the conversation. "You don't let *what* bother you?"

Brittany waved a hand in front of her. "All the unwanted attention I get from men who don't interest me sexually, present company included."

"Ouch." Reid pretended to stab himself in the heart.

Katrina blushed. Brittany was too much.

Reid stood up straight and smoothed his hands down the front of his shirt. "Okay, I'm recovered from the heart stabbing. You ladies ready for another round?"

"I'd love a glass of water, actually," Katrina said. She was only about two sips into her second margarita but already knew she wouldn't be able to drink it without getting a little tipsy. Actually, who was she kidding? She was already a little tipsy, and if she drank another margarita, she would be full-on *drunk*. She didn't want Brittany and Reid to see what a lightweight she was, even if she *was* new in town.

Brittany stood up and reached for her purse. "I'm going to visit the little girls' room. I don't need another drink, but Reid, would you be a love and watch my seat?" She pointed to her stool before disappearing into the crowd.

"Don't mind if I do." Reid ordered a glass of water for Katrina and another margarita for himself, then took a seat on the empty stool. Katrina detected the lingering odor of cigarette smoke, as well as a slight five o'clock shadow on his face.

"When did you roll into town?" His chocolate eyes were warm and curious, and Katrina's nerves began to jump again.

The bartender set down their drinks, and Katrina picked up her water right away and took a sip, grateful for an excuse to avert her eyes. "Yesterday," she said into the glass.

"Just yesterday? For real? Then that calls for a welcome shot." He flagged down the bartender again. Kevin was clearly less than thrilled at the addition of a man to the equation, but he maintained a professional demeanor and came back to take Reid's order.

Katrina hoped Reid couldn't see the fear in her eyes. "Did you just say *shot*?"

Reid smiled. "Of course. It's not every day you move to New York, especially for the sole purpose of having an adventure. It's time to celebrate!"

Before Katrina could object, he ordered three tequila shots from Kevin, who nodded politely but didn't smile as he poured the drinks.

Katrina tensed and looked around the room, hoping Brittany would return soon. As she inspected the crowd, she wished she didn't feel so uncomfortable. So Reid wanted to buy her a celebratory shot. What was the big deal? She knew this was just his way of being friendly—and she wanted to preserve the budding rapport she had with the few people she knew in the city. But she blanched at the prospect of more tequila going down her throat.

The truth was, she'd never done a shot before.

Ever.

Even in college.

Though she'd graduated with a stellar academic record and an impressive résumé dotted with awards, she hadn't experienced many of the rites of passage typically associated with being a college student—at least the social ones.

She'd never dared try anything just for the sake of . . . fun.

Or adventure.

Or excitement.

"So why now?" Reid asked.

Katrina blinked. "What?"

"Why New York?"

Kevin set a saltshaker and a small plate holding three slices of lime next to the three small glasses, then promptly disappeared. "My friend Deb convinced me that I needed a change, and New York is about as different from Mountain View as it gets."

He smiled. "Change is good. I could use some of that myself, to be honest."

She wasn't sure what to say to that, but it didn't matter, because the sound of Brittany's voice made them both turn their heads. "Reid Hanson, is that your calling card I see sitting on the bar?" She pointed at the shot glasses.

Reid grinned at her. "You know me so well. We're doing a welcome round for Kat. And you're joining us, of course."

Brittany joined her hands in a prayer position and slowly shook her head. "I would love to, but alas, I must leave you two crazy kids to carry on this party without me. I have a six o'clock flight in the morning, and I haven't even packed yet."

Katrina checked her watch. It was almost ten o'clock. She wished she had Brittany's boundless stamina.

Brittany gestured to Kevin to tell him she was leaving and to pay whatever pittance she owed, but Reid waved her away. "I got it."

"You sure? You always pay."

"And I always will."

"Such a gentleman." She smiled at him, then gave Katrina a warm hug. "It was so nice catching up with you. My travel schedule is nuts the next few weeks, but I really hope we can get together again before you leave town."

"I hope so too," Katrina said. "It was great to see you."

Brittany turned to Reid. "You'll make sure she gets home safe?"

"Are you really asking me that?"

She kissed him on the cheek. "Don't do anything I wouldn't do." Without saying good-bye to Kevin, she disappeared into the crowd.

As soon as she was gone, Reid turned to face Katrina. "And then there were two."

"Looks like it." She knew it was awkward to stay there with him, but she couldn't just get up and leave after he'd ordered the shots, could she?

Should she?

She was tempted to bid him a polite good-bye and take a cab home. If she were in Mountain View right now, without question she'd be at home alone, on the couch, watching TV, or maybe reading a book. That is, if she were even *awake*. She was usually fast asleep by ten thirty.

The thought startled her.

Wow. Can a person possibly get any more boring?

Yes, she could bid him a polite good-bye and head home to the brownstone.

But what kind of adventure would that be?

Was that why she'd come to New York? To sit on the couch and channel surf? She could've stayed home if she was going to do that, right?

She could almost hear Deb's voice in her head, telling her to calm down and stay put.

Relax, Katrina.

There's nothing to be afraid of.

Take a chance.

One shot isn't going to kill you.

Loosen up for once.

Have some fun.

Reid didn't appear to notice her distraction. Instead, he handed her a shot glass and smiled. "Okay, Snow White. Are you with me?"

Deb's voice was right. The old Katrina *would* go home and watch TV. Wasn't it time for the new Katrina—for *Kat*—to chart a new path?

Her foot tapping against the stool again, she cleared her throat and forced a smile. "And then there were two."

* * *

Katrina and Reid ended up chatting at the bar for another hour. She was amazed at how well they got along, despite how different their lives were. Then again, it might have been the drinks that got her to open up. At first they'd bantered back and forth about favorite foods and movies, but at some point she found herself candidly explaining how her parents' expectations that she find a stable job had pushed her into a major—and eventually a career—that had left her feeling unfulfilled.

And discouraged.

And lost.

"So your boss had no idea you were going to quit when you walked into her office?" Reid asked.

"Not a clue. It was pretty out of character for me, to say the least. I tend to walk in a straight line, if you haven't noticed."

"You must have been really unhappy," he said. It wasn't a question.

Katrina nodded and took a sip of her margarita. "I guess you could say I'm having an early midlife crisis." She let out a small hiccup. She wasn't sure where all this forthrightness had come from, but Reid appeared to be really listening to what she had to say.

"And then you moved here for a couple months, with no plan for what to do after that?"

She hiccupped again. "Looks like it. To be honest, I still can't believe I did it. It's really not like me at all. I'm usually very . . . organized." She glanced at the stack of tilted coasters on the bar.

"That took a lot of courage." He looked genuinely impressed.

"My parents certainly don't look at it that way." She offered a weak laugh. "They told me I was being reckless."

"Reckless is good sometimes."

"You think so?"

"I know so. I bet you got straight A's in high school. Am I right?"

Katrina nodded.

"More of the same in college?"

She nodded again.

"I think a lot people do that, especially straight-A high-school students."

"Do what?"

"Put their heads down, study to get a degree, get a degree to get a job, get a job to get a paycheck, get a paycheck to buy a house.

Everything's focused on the next step, and before they know it, they've spent all their best years always aiming for the future and never really enjoying the present."

Katrina squinted at him. "How do you know so much about life? You seem so, I don't know . . . so *wise*."

He smiled and put a hand on her head. "And you're like a baby deer, all doe-eyed and innocent."

She hiccupped again. "And a little boring. I wish I were more like my brother."

"Trust me, you're far from boring. You're reserved, but's that's hardly a crime. I do get the feeling you take yourself a bit too seriously though."

Katrina frowned. "I know."

"I'm not saying that to be mean. It's just an observation."

"It's okay. I know I can be a little . . . stiff . . . but I'm working on that." She was surprised at her newfound frankness.

"Well, you've already taken a huge step in that direction by coming here, right?"

"Thanks." She smiled and felt—for the first time in a long time—a little . . . proud.

"In my humble opinion, I think you're definitely ready for an adventure."

"I hope you're right about that."

He held up his drink. "And the more reckless the adventure, the better."

After chatting for a while longer, they finally stood up to leave. Katrina steadied herself against the bar, hoping it wasn't obvious how buzzed she felt. Reid was clearly a more seasoned drinker and appeared to still be stone-cold sober.

They walked up the narrow back staircase and out onto the sidewalk, not speaking, the silence comfortable yet also a bit awkward. Reid stopped and looked as if he were going to say something, but then appeared to change his mind. Instead, he turned toward the street to hail Katrina a cab. When he opened the door for her, he looked at her and grinned.

"Well, Kat from California, this was a rather unexpected pleasure."

She smiled back. "I would have to agree."

He reached into his pocket and pulled out his phone. "What's your number? I'll give you a shout if there's a party or something that can't be missed."

After giving him her number, she ducked into the cab and waved out of the window as the driver pulled away into a sea of uptown-bound cars, taxis, and buses, then leaned back against the seat and exhaled. The relentless energy of Manhattan was unlike anything she'd ever experienced, and after just twenty-four hours here she was already exhausted.

But thrilled.

First drinks with her new neighbors and now this unanticipated encounter with Reid barely twenty-four hours later. It was completely out of character for her to chatter away so openly with virtual strangers, but she'd done it, twice. And tonight it hadn't been just small talk. She'd opened up to Reid in a way she normally did only with Deb—and survived. And she'd had *fun*. And the amazing thing was, Reid had seemed to enjoy her company. He could have left at any time, but he hadn't. He'd stayed to talk to her. He'd asked her questions. He wanted to *know* about her.

She'd even made him laugh a couple of times. She hardly ever made anyone laugh, not even Deb.

Katrina smiled to herself.

It was just one evening with a man she'd probably never see again, but it felt like a major step forward.

* * *

Once back at the apartment, Katrina changed into her pajamas, then headed to the bathroom to perform her nightly routine. When she was done, she sat down in front of her laptop to check her e-mail. Her mother had forwarded the names of two acquaintances she wanted Katrina to contact as part of her job search, along with a suggestion to "act quickly so they know you're serious and not just gallivanting around New York."

She thought about sending the e-mails right away, then stopped herself and logged off.

She'd do it tomorrow.

Just as she was climbing into bed, she heard her phone chime from the kitchen, where she'd plugged it in to charge overnight. She plodded into the kitchen to pick it up. It was a text from a number she didn't recognize.

It was really nice to meet you tonight.

Chapter Five

"Hey, Katrina, how's life in the big city?"

"Actually, so far—"

"Before you answer that," Deb said, "I'm about to head in to our Friday-morning staff meeting, so you have about five minutes to fill me in. If it were anyone but you, I wouldn't have picked up."

"Okay, I'll try to talk fast. So far . . . I must say . . . it's been really fun."

"For real?"

"For real!" Katrina smiled into the phone.

"So no meltdown?"

"No meltdown. I'm taking a walk in Central Park right now. *Central Park.* How cool is that?"

"Oh man, I'm so jealous. Right now I'm in a *cube.*"

"It's so beautiful here, Deb. The air is crisp and clear, just like in the movies. It's like this morning fall decided to show up, grab a microphone, and announce to the whole city that it was taking over."

"Ah, fall in New York City. I can only imagine how pretty that must be."

"It's breathtaking, Deb. I can't wait for the leaves to start turning."

"You should see *me* turning right now—as in green with envy. How's the apartment?"

"It's perfect. My parents wouldn't approve of the dusty exterior, but the building's a classic brownstone, and in a pretty good location. It's like any minute I expect the camera crew to show up and start filming."

"I'm a darker shade of green now."

"And, perhaps best of all, the apartment itself is extremely clean."

Deb laughed. "Hallelujah! You'd freak if it were anything less than spotless. Is it tiny? I've heard New York apartments are like matchboxes."

"It's not Buckingham Palace, but it's plenty big just for me. I hate seeing what should be *your bedroom* sitting there across the hall empty though. It makes me sad."

"Ugh, don't remind me. I know I got what I wanted by staying here, but that doesn't mean I don't totally wish I were there with you right now."

"Are you still going to come visit?"

"Prognosis undetermined. It all depends on these new accounts I've been chasing. If they come through, my workload is going to be off the charts."

"So for you to come out here, I have to hope you *don't* get the accounts?"

"Exactly."

Katrina kicked a pebble and frowned. "That doesn't make me feel like a very good friend."

"Please. You're a great friend. So what have you been doing? Have you already been to the Empire State Building? Touristy as it may be, I'm dying to go there."

"Not yet. Except for walking through Central Park, I haven't done anything really touristy yet. I've sort of been getting my feet wet, just exploring the neighborhood. Believe me, compared to Mountain View, even the ordinary city streets here are plenty exciting. Yesterday

I saw a man walking down the street with a parrot perched right on his shoulder. A *parrot*."

"I'm sure you'll get to the touristy stuff soon enough. I know you must have a huge list of things to see and do. In fact, I bet you have it with you right now."

Katrina tapped her palm against her pocket. "Oh yes, of course. I've got my list, but to be honest, I think I could spend entire days just wandering around aimlessly, not even looking at it."

"Really? That's so unlike you."

"I know, isn't it? But it's been great exploring the nooks and crannies. There are indie boutiques, tiny bodegas, and hip coffee bars on pretty much every block, and don't even get me started on all the art galleries. And then, of course, there are the *people*, who are out on the streets all the time and are from every corner of the world, constantly chattering away in a million languages. Just sitting on a park bench and watching them could keep me occupied for weeks. That reminds me—I even painted something a couple of days ago."

"You *painted*?"

"Yes. Nothing much, just a park, but it felt good."

"That's awesome, Katrina. It's been forever since you painted anything, hasn't it?"

"Yes. Years, actually. I can't remember why I stopped, although I imagine it had something to do with my parents telling me to."

Deb laughed. "Well, it's great that you finally started again, and I'm thrilled that you're enjoying yourself out there. Have you met anybody yet?"

"Yes, my neighbors: Shana and Grace."

"I thought nobody knew their neighbors in New York."

"Me too, but we thought wrong, because I literally met them the moment I arrived from the airport. They're really nice."

"Is one of them like eighty? In the movies, the heroine always seems to have an eighty-year-old neighbor. Meddling, yet wise. Cranky, but with a heart of gold."

"Hardly. They're our age. And they're super friendly. They even invited me to join them for drinks that night."

"Did you go?"

"Yes."

"*You* went out for drinks on a weeknight?"

"I had one beer. Don't get too excited."

"I'm excited. You can't stop me."

"They call me Kat."

"*Kat*? I bet that weirded you out."

"It did a little, at first, but I think it's sort of fun. You know, new city, new name, new me?"

Deb's excitement bubbled through the phone. "Oh my God, I'm loving this! Painting? A nickname? Not immediately plowing through your to-do list? Going out for drinks in the middle of the week? You have no idea how much I'm loving this."

Katrina leaned down and picked up a leaf. "I also met Shana's boyfriend, Josh. He's very friendly too, even paid for all our drinks."

"Ooh, boyfriend Josh. I like the potential in that. Does boyfriend Josh have any single friends for Kat to meet?"

"I didn't ask him, given that I'd only been *Kat* for like . . . five minutes."

"Touché. Kat can ask him next time. You should also have her ask her new friends for fun things to do that don't show up in any of *Katrina*'s guidebooks. I bet that could keep you both busy for quite a while."

"Kat will make a mental note to do that."

"Good. So what else do you have to tell me? You have like a minute left, by the way."

Katrina held up the leaf and admired it in the sunlight. "Wednesday night I had drinks in Tribeca with my RA from college."

"Drinks again? As in two nights in a row? I think I may need to lie down."

Katrina laughed. "Going out for drinks after work seems to be the MO around here." She didn't mention meeting Reid, unsure how to bring him up or even what she should say. It wasn't like anything inappropriate had happened between them, but she felt a bit weird about the text message he'd sent her. She hadn't replied because she couldn't for the life of her think what to say. Part of her thought it was a tad out of line for him to contact her, but maybe she was reading too much into it. He had noted that she took herself too seriously. Maybe this was one of those times?

"Well then, who are you to buck tradition? In my opinion, the world is a happier place when people go out for drinks after work. Did Kat go for the trifecta last night? Please tell me she did."

Katrina folded the leaf in her hand and felt it crackle into little bits. "I wish I could say she did, but last night I stayed in and worked on my résumé."

"Did you just say you worked on your *résumé*?"

"Maybe."

"I'm hanging up now. Katrina's back."

"Don't start, okay?"

"Fine. You're down to thirty seconds. What's on the agenda for Kat after her leisurely stroll through the park? Glad to hear she's putting those new sneakers to good use, by the way."

"I'm not sure yet. I guess she'll have to tell you the next time you two talk."

"Deal. Please tell her to keep having enough fun for both of us. Or all three of us, if you count Katrina."

"I will. I'm sure she'll try her best."

"I'm proud of her. I'm proud of you too. But no more working on your résumé, promise?"

Katrina laughed. "*Thanks, Mom*—though we both know my mom would never say that."

When Katrina hung up the phone, she saw a new text message had come in during the call.

It was from her mother, reminding her to update her LinkedIn profile.

She tossed the leaf bits into the air and kept walking.

* * *

Katrina spent nearly an hour strolling through Central Park, covering more ground than she'd meant to, but she was so mesmerized by the charm and beauty surrounding her that she didn't realize how far she'd gone until her legs began to ache. While exploring the seemingly endless walkways, recreational fields, and grassy knolls, she stumbled across the zoo, the Boathouse, and the reservoir, plus multiple ice-cream carts, whose distinctive bells triggered vivid childhood memories of hot summer days. She also encountered countless wide-eyed tourists who appeared to be similarly awed by the bright autumn light and tree-lined paths.

She felt aimless and carefree.

And wonderful.

When she finally made it back to her neighborhood, Katrina wandered into the coffeehouse near her apartment, the third day in a row she'd done so. Today it was more crowded, and she wondered if she'd be able to find a seat to read her newspaper. As she waited in line to order, she pulled out her phone and began typing a reply to her mother's text. She could postpone getting back to her mother, but she couldn't outright ignore her.

"Well, hello again."

She looked up in surprise. The green-eyed barista who had taken her order the first day was standing behind the counter. She hadn't seen him when she walked in, and she hadn't seen him yesterday either. He was dressed much as he'd been the other day: a plaid shirt over a white T-shirt, both still untucked, with jeans. His face had the same five o'clock shadow.

"Hi," she said, suddenly tense. *Why am I nervous? Why am I noticing his outfit?*

He smiled. "What can I get you today?"

"I'll have a skim latte and a blueberry scone, please."

"Isn't that what you ordered the other day?"

She nodded.

"I bet you order that every day. Am I right?" He pointed to her newspaper. "You strike me as a creature of habit."

She gave him a shy smile. "Maybe. I'm trying to become more adventurous though."

"Adventure is always good. And so are our blueberry scones. Some even say they're the best in town—although when I say *some,* I really mean *me.*"

"They are pretty good." She looked around the room and saw an unoccupied table in the corner, the only one in the place.

Reading her mind, he gestured to it. "Grab it," he said. "Real estate in here can be a bit tricky this time of day, so you've got to pounce when you can. I'll bring you the latte when it's ready." He placed a scone on a plate and handed it to her.

"Thanks." She hurried to the table, sat down, opened the *Times,* and spread it out in front of her. After the long walk in the park, she was looking forward to relaxing as she immersed herself in the news.

She was in the middle of an article about the latest round of Israeli-Palestinian peace talks when the barista appeared with her latte. "Anything exciting happening?" He set down the cup on the table and rubbed his hands together.

She looked up from the paper. "I guess so. I mean, not really, but sort of." She realized how ambivalent her answer was and cringed slightly. She followed current events and took pride in knowing what was going on in the world, but for some reason she felt like going into detail about the Middle East might make her come across as too serious—or boring. She reached for the latte and hoped the awkward moment would pass.

"Got it: not really, but sort of." He half-laughed and turned to go. "Enjoy your scone."

She felt her cheeks flush. Had she offended him? She hoped not.

* * *

Katrina spent the next half hour engrossed in the newspaper. When she finally looked up, the coffeehouse had nearly emptied out. She noticed the classical music in the background again, which she'd managed to shut out as she read. It was soothing and just the right volume. She recognized it as Beethoven's *Moonlight Sonata*, one of her dad's favorites.

Whoever chooses the music here has good taste, she thought.

She picked up her mug, deciding to get a refill.

The barista with the green eyes was behind the counter, his back to her. She cleared her throat to get his attention. "Excuse me, could I get another skim latte, please?"

He turned around and took the empty mug. "Sure thing. How's that newspaper treating you? You seemed pretty focused over there."

She felt embarrassed that he had noticed. "Not quite finished."

"You read it every day?"

She nodded. "I try to."

"It's nice to see someone reading a real newspaper. Most people these days just seem to scan the headlines on their phones, if that. They're all too busy texting or updating their Facebook status."

She smiled. "I think you may be right about that. Personally, I get a headache if I read too much on a tiny screen. Too much squinting." She tapped her palm against her temple.

He laughed. "I do too! I bet half the kids who come in here are going to need reading glasses by the time they're thirty. We might have to keep a pair on the counter to help them make out the menu."

She smiled again as she paid for the latte, hoping she'd smoothed over whatever slight she'd inadvertently committed. She took a step away from the counter, then hesitated before returning to her table.

He'd be a good person to ask, she thought.

She looked back at him, poised to speak.

"Did you want to order something else?" he asked. "Another scone?"

Suddenly she felt uncomfortable. "No, I'm fine. Thanks for the latte." She visibly stiffened, disappointed in herself, in her inability to control her nerves.

He gave her a strange look, clearly picking up on her swift change in demeanor. "Gotcha."

She began walking toward her table. Why hadn't she asked him? It was a simple request. Why was she so timid?

Halfway there she stopped.

It's just a question, Katrina.

You can do it.

Stop being so afraid of normal human interaction.

This is your chance to change things.

She forced herself to return to the counter.

"Excuse me?" She cleared her throat again.

He looked up, an amused expression on his face. "Yep. Still here."

"Can I ask you something?"

"Sure thing."

She swallowed. "Well, I'm in town for just a couple of months, and I've made a long list of things I want to see . . . or do . . . while I'm here. But I'm learning that some of the best things about New York don't necessarily appear in guidebooks, so, um, I was just wondering if you could offer any suggestions of other things I should see . . . or do." She cringed at how awkward she sounded. By now he had to have noticed how socially inept she was.

He smiled. "What's your name?"

She hesitated before responding, which made him chuckle.

"It's not a trick question," he said.

She took a quick breath. "Katrina . . . er . . . Kat . . . I mean . . . either is fine, I guess."

He chuckled again. "You sure about that?"

She nodded weakly.

"Okay then, we'll go with Kat. Kat from . . . ?"

"California. Silicon Valley, to be precise."

He raised his eyebrows. "Really? I'd have pegged you as a Midwestern girl."

She understood why he thought so. Silicon Valley was hardly known as a hotbed of reserved personalities. She shrugged and held up her palms. "Sorry."

"Well, Kat from Silicon Valley, it's nice to meet you. I'm Justin from Long Island."

"It's nice to meet you too." She flinched at her faux pas. Why hadn't she asked him his name back? She hoped she hadn't offended him . . . again.

If she had, he didn't let on. He placed his hands on the counter. "So, sightseeing . . . I assume you've already got the basics on your list."

She nodded. "I think so. The Statue of Liberty, the Empire State Building, Times Square, the 9/11 Memorial, a Broadway show. I'll be sure to do all that stuff."

"So you're looking for cool things that aren't on the first page of every guidebook? A little off the beaten path?"

She nodded. "I guess you could say that. I'm trying to be adventurous, but I'm thinking more along the lines of *a hidden gem of a museum* than *a secret underground rave*. I'm not much of a partier, if you couldn't already tell." She managed a weak smile.

"You? Never." He picked up a wet rag and began wiping down the wooden counter. "Hmm. Just going off the top of my head here, I'd say some good ones up north are the Bronx Zoo and the Cloisters, but those are probably already on your list. And renting a bike in Central Park might sound a little touristy, but it's definitely worth doing. Off the beaten path in Brooklyn, I'd suggest checking out Bedford Avenue over in Williamsburg, a stroll through the Fulton Mall downtown, and of course the Brooklyn Flea, a weekend market in Dumbo filled with all sorts of homemade everything. And while you're over there, you've got to eat at Grimaldi's Pizzeria—and check out the Brooklyn Botanic Gardens, too. Oh, and since it's right in this neighborhood, I highly recommend an afternoon of people-watching in Tompkins Square Park." He pointed in the direction of the East Village. "And you *must* check out the—"

Katrina held up a finger to interrupt him, then glanced over at her table. "I'm so sorry, but would you mind repeating all that for me when I have a pen and paper in hand? It's a fantastic list, but I'll never remember it all."

He smiled. "No problem, Kat. I'm happy to help."

"Thanks, Justin." She found herself smiling slightly as she went to retrieve her purse. *That wasn't so hard*, she thought. She pulled out a notebook and was digging around for a pen when she heard her phone chime with a new text message. She took it out and looked at the screen.

It was from Reid.

How goes the adventuring? Any interest in grabbing a drink later?

She read the message again.

Today was Friday.

He wants to have a drink with me on a Friday night?

He couldn't be suggesting a *date* because he was married, so maybe he was just being friendly. They had clearly enjoyed talking with each other the other night. They could be friends even though he was married, couldn't they?

Glancing at the counter, Katrina saw that Justin was busy serving a new customer. She took a seat and considered the invitation, which seemed harmless enough.

Would it be okay to go?

Is it appropriate?

Things are different in New York, right?

She tried to think of the best way to reply to the message. She began typing a response several times but deleted each one and started again. Nothing she wrote seemed to convey the attitude she wanted to project, probably because she wasn't even sure what that was.

She sat there for a few moments, staring at her phone, then finally typed a brief note saying sure, it'd be fun. It was just a drink, right? That was allowed. He didn't need to know she found him attractive. They could have a friendly chat about how she was settling into New York, and maybe he'd give her some good tips on things to see while she was in town.

As soon as she pressed *send* she noticed someone approaching her table. She looked up and saw the skinny young barista standing over her.

"Justin asked me to give this to you." He handed her a folded piece of paper.

"Oh, thanks." She opened the note and read it as he walked away.

It was a list of insider things to do in New York.

She looked over at the counter, but Justin was gone.

* * *

Katrina spent an hour or so exploring the East Village, which was sprinkled with dozens of boutiques, antique stores, thrift shops, and sidewalk vendors, each of which somehow managed to be unique and trendy in its own highly distinctive way. Every few steps she spotted something she'd never see in Mountain View. A girly pink purse covered in peace symbols hanging next to a black tank top painted with an angry skull and crossbones. An array of coffee mugs featuring vulgar yet humorous slogans that made her blush. A vintage lace dress on a headless mannequin. A small mountain of well-worn political and religious books piled atop a sagging card table.

The gritty streets were a veritable bastion of the hip and cool, with just enough touristy knickknacks on display to make more mainstream visitors like Katrina feel comfortable. At first she felt like a fish out of water as she popped in and out of bohemian stores and browsed the myriad sidewalk displays of funky jewelry, clothing, artwork, and albums, but there were so many other people there from all walks of life that she soon relaxed and began to enjoy the energy pulsating around her. By the end of her jaunt, she felt almost like a veteran. In one postage-stamp-sized shop she even bought a pink neck scarf, a knitted blue hat, and a pair of dangly silver earrings, all three of which breached the boundaries of her normal conservative style—but which she found absolutely adorable. Whether or not she would ever feel comfortable wearing any of these things was another story, but she was proud of herself for having purchased something other than yet another pair of black pants.

She bought a ham-and-cheese sandwich at a deli on East Seventh Street and stopped by her apartment to pick up a fresh canvas before heading out to Tompkins Square Park, the place Justin had said was good for people watching. Once there, she sat on a bench and set up her easel, then unwrapped the sandwich and took in the scene as she ate.

Justin hadn't been kidding. It was a crisp weekday afternoon in October, but she could just as easily believe it was a warm summer Saturday, given how much was going on around her. To her left, a group of older men were intently watching two of their peers battle it out in a game of chess. To her right, a young couple lay side by side on a blanket, fingers interlaced, each holding an e-reader in the air with their free hands. Nearby, a young man with a long ponytail played guitar and sang folk songs, the large case propped open at his feet to collect tips. A boisterous pickup game of street hockey was being waged on the basketball court behind him. And in the midst of it all, a constant stream of foot traffic—young and old, hipster and business casual, every skin color—was crisscrossing the cement pathways that cut through the grass in all directions. Katrina estimated that 25 percent of the people were carrying Starbucks cups and 40 percent were wearing headphones.

After watching the world go by for a few minutes, she neatly folded the empty paper sandwich wrapper in half before tossing it into a nearby trash bin. Then she began to paint. For her subject she'd chosen the bench where she'd been sitting, which was now empty and framed by a background buzzing with passersby.

Calm, surrounded by chaos.

Another unusual juxtaposition, yet it was exactly how she felt at that moment.

When she was done painting an hour or so later, she picked up the canvas and folded up her easel, then stretched her arms over her head, satisfied with what she'd accomplished. She dropped two dollars into the ponytailed guitarist's case and decided it was time to head back to the apartment.

She ran into Shana on her way into the building.

"Hey, Kat. How's your first week in New York going?"

"So far, so good. There's just so much to do here, I almost don't even know where to begin. I'll never be able to fit it all into just two months. I seriously think I could spend several days just watching people in Tompkins Square Park. It's a whole world unto itself."

"Tell me about it. I think I could live here for five more years without even scratching the surface. But that's why New York's so fun, right? It's nothing like where I grew up. Going to the mall is a big deal in rural Ohio." She pointed at the canvas. "Were you just painting?"

Katrina felt her cheeks flush and nodded.

"Can I see?"

"I'm not very good. I'm pretty rusty, actually."

"I draw stick people, so let me be the judge of it." Shana reached for the canvas and turned it around, then let out a little gasp. "Oh, wow, Kat, it's beautiful."

"You think so?"

"I love it. What are you going to do with it?"

Katrina shrugged. "I have no idea. I hadn't thought that far ahead. Before this week I hadn't painted in years."

"I'd love to hang it in my living room."

"Really?"

"You bet. I don't have money to pay you for it though. I'm sorry."

"Oh gosh, don't worry about that. I can't believe you think it's worth hanging."

"I do. Not that I know a lick about art, but I love it."

"Well, consider it yours." Katrina began to hand it to her, then pulled it back as she eyed Shana's workout clothes. "Are you off to teach?" I can hold on to it for you."

"Yep. Friday evenings I teach at six and again at seven thirty. You should come to a class sometime."

Katrina stiffened. "I don't know. I'm not very athletic. I can barely keep my balance on the stationary bike."

Shana put a hand on Katrina's arm. "That's okay, a lot of people who come to my classes aren't athletic. That's why they do yoga, or at least the kind of yoga I teach. Come on, give it a try. I can get you in for free. I know it's not much compared to that painting, but at least it's something."

Katrina hesitated. She wanted to go, but she had agreed to meet Reid for a drink in the Meatpacking District.

"How long is the class?"

"Just an hour." She squeezed Katrina's arm, her eyes bright. "Come on, it'll be fun! I promise."

"Do I have to wear special clothes?"

"Anything you'd wear to the gym is fine, as long as it's not too loose. And I have an extra yoga mat you can borrow. But I've got to leave *now*, so if you're going to come with me, we've got to get a move on."

Katrina thought about it for another few seconds, then made a decision. "Okay, I'll do it. Can you give me five minutes to change?"

"Make it three. And hurry."

"Got it." She turned and rushed upstairs with a hint of a smile on her face. With each step she climbed, she realized that she was acting less like *Katrina* and more like *Kat*, and it felt . . . *good*.

* * *

Shana set Katrina up with a mat near the side wall of the yoga studio, close enough but not completely front and center. The room wasn't too crowded, which helped assuage her self-consciousness about being a complete beginner.

"I hope I don't make a fool of myself," Katrina whispered as she rolled out the mat. "I'm not very coordinated."

"You'll be fine," Shana whispered back before tiptoeing across the wooden floor. "Just copy the person next to you if you get lost."

Katrina took a seat on her mat, interlacing her hands in her lap and waiting for the session to begin.

Shana turned down the lights, and soft music began to play. She lit a candle and sat cross-legged in front of the group, then opened a notebook. It looked like she was about to begin reading but she suddenly closed it. Katrina noticed that all the other students had their eyes closed, so she followed suit.

She heard Shana inhale deeply, then begin to speak. "I recently met a woman who has truly inspired me, who has made me remember how important it is to take chances in life. She came to New York alone, without a job, without knowing a soul."

Katrina opened her eyes and looked up at Shana. *Are you talking about me?*

Shana smiled at Katrina and gestured for her to close her eyes again, then continued.

"This woman didn't *plan* to come to New York by herself, but when her travel companion had to bow out unexpectedly, instead of canceling the trip, she came *on her own*. She didn't know a soul here, but she didn't let that stop her. She might not even realize it yet, but I think on some level she came here *by herself* to learn *about herself*. And meeting her has inspired *me* to keep learning about *myself*. We all need to keep learning. If we never take chances in life, if we never venture out of our comfort zones, we'll never grow. And we all need to keep growing. The day we stop growing is the day life stops mattering."

Katrina kept her eyes closed even after Shana finished speaking, stunned by her new friend's perception of her. Was she really that person? A person who took chances? A person who wasn't afraid to step out of her comfort zone? A person who inspired others?

I want to be, she thought.

* * *

Katrina loved the class. As Shana had predicted, she did get lost several times at the beginning, and nearly fell over more than once trying to balance on one leg, but no one seemed to care. The basic sequence of positions repeated itself much like the chorus of a song, so when she got the hang of it, she was able to relax and enjoy the experience. Shana's description of yoga had been accurate; the postures were geared more toward strengthening and elongating the muscles than providing an intense cardiovascular workout, and they did their job. Though she wondered how sore she'd be the next day, Katrina felt like she'd just gotten a massage, and her mind was calm.

"You did great, Kat." Shana came over and handed her a bottle of water. "How do you feel? Did you enjoy it?" Though she kept her voice low, it was brimming with positive energy.

Katrina took the water and opened it. "It was just what I needed. Thank you so much for getting me to come. I wasn't expecting that part at the beginning though. You surprised me."

Shana smiled. "What can I say? I was hit with a bolt of inspiration, so I went with it. I hope you don't mind."

"Oh gosh, not at all." If Shana only knew how rare it was for Katrina to inspire anyone.

"Were the poses too challenging for you?"

"A little, but not terribly. At first I felt really self-conscious, but by the end of the class I was able to relax and get into it."

"I'm so glad to hear that."

Katrina nodded before taking a sip of water. "I was impressed by how well you speak, but also by the way you ran the class. You have a really gentle way about you. Very soothing."

Shana smiled. "Thanks. Maybe if there's ever a role as a yoga teacher on Broadway, I'll get the part."

"You'd be great at it."

Shana squeezed her shoulder. "It was fun having you here. You should come to another class sometime."

"I'd love to come back—assuming I can walk tomorrow, that is. I'm not sure how my hamstrings are going to respond to holding all those poses." She pretended to grimace. Or half-pretended. Getting out of bed in the morning was going to be no joke, especially after all the ground she'd covered earlier in the day.

Shana laughed and headed toward a broom closet at the back of the room. "You're sweet. Now scat so I can get this place ready for the next class. I don't want to get yelled at by Blair."

"Who's Blair?"

"The studio owner. She's teaching next, and she gets upset when my classes run over even a little. She's very particular and likes time to prepare before the students show up." Shana lowered her voice. "And she's a little scary, if you ask me."

"Got it."

Out on the street, Katrina passed a tall, thin woman with ivory skin and black hair slicked back into a severe bun. She looked to be in her late thirties or early forties. Katrina smiled weakly at her, immediately intimidated. The woman nodded back but didn't smile.

As she walked down the sidewalk, Katrina turned back and watched the woman enter the studio.

She hoped Shana had finished sweeping the floor.

Chapter Six

When she got back to her apartment, Katrina quickly showered and got dressed. After much thought, she'd made the decision that she would meet Reid for one drink and then leave. Regardless of whatever New York social etiquette was, she didn't feel comfortable spending time alone with a married man she barely knew, no matter how nice he was.

Or maybe because of it.

She remembered what Brittany had said about his unhappy relationship.

She shook her head and told herself to stop thinking that way.

He was married, *period*.

She fixed her hair and makeup and studied herself in the mirror, once again wishing her freckles would magically disappear, that one morning she'd wake up with her mother's flawless complexion. After agonizing over what to wear, she'd finally settled on a sleeveless black sheath cut two inches above the knee. She wanted to look nice but not like she was trying *too* hard. Unfortunately, she had zero idea what that meant in New York.

Does this look okay for a drink?

Black goes with everything, right?

One drink. Where's the harm in that?
She switched off the bathroom light and went to grab her purse.
She was halfway out the door when she remembered. She turned on her heel and hurried back into the bedroom, her eyes scanning until they landed on the shopping bag in the corner. She pulled out the pink silk scarf and silver earrings, put on the earrings and tied the scarf around her neck, then took a quick peek in the mirror above the dresser.
She smiled.
She wasn't looking at *Katrina*.
Katrina would never dress like this.
She was looking at *Kat*—and she liked what she saw.
I'm going out for a drink in New York!
She turned out the lights and skipped downstairs to find a cab.

* * *

A few minutes after eight o'clock, Katrina entered the lobby of Soho House, a private social club in the heart of the übertrendy Meatpacking District. After giving her name to the glamorous young woman at the front desk, she rode the elevator to the sixth floor. As she ascended silently, wondering why the walls were padded in green leather, she suddenly feared that the pink scarf looked silly. How quickly her newfound confidence had waned.
The doors opened onto what appeared to be a foyer or reception area, which led to an expansive room divided into two distinct sections. To the right was a saloon-style bar, complete with high red leather stools and dark hardwood floors. A sea of sparkling liquor bottles framed an enormous mirror mounted on the wall. A handful of plush velvet couches and love seats separated the bar from a dining area; a roaring fire in the large marble fireplace set against the back wall emitted a cozy glow. To the left was a large, beautifully appointed lounge filled with clusters of friends and couples chatting away over drinks. A few people even sat alone, quietly reading books with glasses of wine in one hand. Crisply attired waiters in white

shirts and black bow ties and vests moved silently among the guests, gracefully refilling glasses and whisking away empty ones.

Katrina immediately loved everything about Soho House.

She soon spotted Reid. He was chatting at the bar with two men, one taller than he, one shorter. All three of them were wearing sport coats and ties. She lifted her hand to yank off the scarf and tuck it into her purse, then willed herself to stop.

No.

You're in New York now.

You look fine.

She took a deep breath, smoothed her hand over her dress, and walked toward the bar. She was about ten feet away when Reid looked over and saw her. He grinned and set down his drink.

"Well, hello there, Snow White." He gave her a quick kiss on the cheek. "Thanks for coming. It's great to see you."

She smiled. "Thanks for inviting me. It's nice to see you too."

Reid gestured toward the two men. "Kat Lynden, meet Ryder Schaffer and Colby Sinclair. Kat's new in town, from California."

They each held up their glasses and nodded in salutation, then Colby gestured to the bar. "Welcome to New York. What can we get you to drink? We're doing scotch and soda."

Katrina looked up at him and guessed he had to be six foot three, maybe even taller.

She lightly touched one of her new earrings and tried to conceal her nerves. "A glass of wine would be lovely. Thank you."

"Could you be more specific?" He looked amused.

"Oh, yes, of course. Sorry. Red would be fine. Thanks."

He laughed. "Still need more direction."

"How about a pinot?" Reid put a hand on her arm. "They have an excellent Kosta Browne."

Ryder nodded. "The oh-nine Sonoma Coast. Good call. Stellar year for that blend." He glanced at Katrina's chest as he spoke.

"Sound good to you?" Colby asked her.

She had no idea what that was, but she smiled and nodded. "Sure, that sounds nice."

"One glass of the oh-nine Sonoma Coast, coming right up." As Colby turned to the bar to order, Katrina noticed he was wearing a wedding ring. So was Ryder. It was Friday night. Where were their wives? Where was Reid's wife? Was this really how things worked here?

"Did you find this place okay?" Reid asked her.

She nodded. "I love the cobblestone streets in this neighborhood. It sort of makes me feel like I'm in a movie set in old New York."

"How long have you been in town?" Ryder asked. The way he looked at her made her slightly uncomfortable, and she found herself taking a tiny step backward.

"Just a few days. This is the first time I've been to the Meatpacking District."

He sipped his drink. "What part of California are you from?"

"The Bay Area."

"Is that so? Where exactly?"

"Mountain View."

He nodded very slowly. "Niiiiiice. I went to business school at Stanford. Dammit, I love the weather out there."

She noticed he was slurring his words a bit and wondered how many drinks he'd had.

"It's pretty nice, no arguing that. I'm excited for fall here, but I'm not sure how well I'll be able to handle New York if it starts snowing," she said.

"Why did you move here?"

She swallowed. "I didn't actually *move* here. I'm just staying for a couple months."

"For work?"

"No, just . . . for fun."

Reid grinned. "She's being adventurous."

Ryder nodded. "I dig it. New York is the place to be if you want adventure."

Katrina looked at Reid and then at the others. "Do you all work together?"

Reid shook his head. "Same industry, different firms. It's a big city but a small community."

"How do you know our man Reid here?" Ryder asked.

"She went to college with a friend of mine," Reid said. "You know the tall blonde, Brittany?" He held his palm up to about his eye level.

Ryder nodded. "Ah, yes. That woman isn't someone a man can easily forget."

Colby turned around and handed Katrina a glass of wine. "Who's that now?"

"Brittany Levin," Reid said. "We used to work together. I don't think you've met her."

"Believe me, you want to meet her," Ryder said. "Killer rack."

Katrina let the comment pass. Ryder was clearly not her type of person, but she willed herself to be friendly. She took a sip of her wine and forced a smile. "Do you both live in Manhattan?"

Colby shook his head. "I'm in Westchester."

"Westchester?" Her eyes were blank.

"The northern suburbs that begin right after Manhattan ends," Reid said. "Moving there is sort of par for the course here once people get married and start having kids. Either that or Long Island. Or New Jersey."

"Oh, do you have kids?" she asked Colby.

He smiled. "One in the oven."

"Wow, congratulations." She turned to Ryder. "What about you?"

"I'm in Montclair, which is in New Jersey." He pointed in the direction of the fireplace, which she assumed meant west. "And downtown." He motioned behind the bartenders.

Reid saw the confusion on Katrina's face and explained. "That's par for the course around here too. A lot of guys in the banking industry who are married have houses in the burbs but keep apartments in the city because of the long hours."

Katrina nodded and took another sip of wine. "Got it." She wondered where Ryder would be sleeping tonight. This lifestyle was so foreign to her.

"What about you?" Colby asked. "Where are you staying while you're in town?"

"I'm subletting a place in Gramercy."

"Cool. And how are you liking New York so far?"

She smiled. "So far I've had a lovely time, although I've barely skimmed the surface. There's so much to do here that I can't seem to get anything done."

Reid held up his glass. "That's why they call this city Disneyland for adults. *Everything* here is worth doing."

Katrina looked at him. "Disneyland for adults? I hadn't heard that, but I like it." She turned back to Colby and Ryder. "What about you two?"

"What about us *what*?" Ryder said, his eyes a little glassy.

"What do you like to do when you're not working? Any recommendations for things I should add to my adventure list?"

Ryder took a gulp of his drink and gave her a suggestive look. "I like to get into trouble. You interested in joining me?"

Reid shook his head. "Don't be an ass, man. I'm sorry, Kat. We've been here for a few hours. Just ignore him."

"Can't blame a guy for trying," Ryder said with a shrug as he polished off his drink.

Katrina didn't want to think too much about what kind of trouble he was referring to. Whatever it was, she wanted no part of it, or him.

Reid squeezed Ryder's shoulder. "Don't you have dinner plans?"

Colby set down his drink and looked at his watch. "I think my hall pass is up too. Lisa's got dinner waiting for me."

"Okay, okay." Ryder held up his hands in surrender. "I can take a hint." He gestured clumsily to the bartender for the check. "Sure you and Kat can't join us?" he said to Reid. "We're going out hard tonight."

"Maybe next time," Reid said.

Katrina wondered who Ryder meant by *we*, but she also didn't really want to know.

* * *

After Ryder and Colby left, Reid and Katrina moved to the far corner of the bar, which was closer to the fireplace and much less crowded. She was able to relax a little, now that it was just the two of them.

"Alone at last," he said. "Sorry about Ryder."

"I thought he seemed . . . nice enough." She gave him a polite smile, figuring it was best to keep her misgivings to herself. "Colby too."

He chuckled. "You're so gracious. It's very charming. Ryder's not all bad, but he can be kind of a prick when he drinks. Amelia can't stand him."

"Who's Amelia?"

"My wife."

She hesitated. "Oh." He hadn't mentioned his wife by name before, but Katrina still felt a little silly for having asked. Her foot had begun to tap, and she forced herself to stop it. "Where is Amelia tonight?"

"She's out with friends." There was noticeable tension in his voice. "Can I get you another drink?"

She shook her head. "Thanks, but I'm still working on this one."

He gestured to the bartender, and Katrina gazed into the fireplace as he ordered. "Don't the men in New York ever go out with their wives?" she mumbled under her breath.

"What was that?" Reid asked.

She blushed. "Oh, nothing."

"Come on now, you said *something*. Out with it, Snow White," he said, wiggling his fingers in a come-here gesture.

"I . . . was just wondering if any men here go out *with* their wives. Do they?"

He half-smiled, then shrugged. "Depends on whose wife you're talking about."

She had no idea what he meant by that remark or how to respond to it, so she just took another look around the room. "Is Soho House only for bankers? It's beautiful here."

He shook his head. "Not at all. In fact, Colby and I may be the only members who work in finance. This club is more for artsy types—a lot of writers, musicians, theater people, that sort of crowd."

"Ryder's not a member?"

"No way. He hates this place. Too lowbrow for him. He's a member of the Union League Club. That's much more up his alley."

"How so?"

"Let's just say it's the type of place where you might run into a Rockefeller or a Roosevelt. Or maybe even a Morgan."

"Got it." She studied the dozen or so people lining the bar. Despite the swank surroundings, most of the women were dressed in jeans and cute tops. Unlike Reid, most of the men weren't wearing ties.

"If there aren't any bankers at this club, why did you decide to join it?" she asked.

He gave her an amused look. "You don't know many bankers, do you?"

She shook her head.

"Clearly not, because if you did, you wouldn't ask that question."

"Not your favorite personality type?"

He leaned toward her and lowered his voice. "Completely stereotyping here, but you might say that where Colby is the exception, Ryder is the norm."

"The norm?" She didn't really want to know what he meant. Snobbish? Rude? Lecherous? All of the above?

He tapped a finger on her nose. "Let's just leave it at that. So are you hungry? They have great appetizers here." He nodded to the bartender, who set two menus in front of them.

She gave him a grateful smile, glad to be changing the subject. "Actually, *yes*. I'm starving."

* * *

"Want to see the roof-deck?"

Katrina looked up from a plate of calamari. "There's a roof-deck here?"

He nodded. "It's packed in the summertime. Kind of a scene, actually."

"I'd love to see it."

After they'd finished eating, Reid asked the bartender to bring him the check. When Katrina tried to offer her credit card, he waved her hand away. "Please. You're my guest."

"Are you sure?"

"Of course I'm sure. Unlike Ryder, I'm a gentleman, remember?"

"Okay, well, thank you then. I appreciate it." She slipped the card back into her purse and stood up. "Will you direct me to the powder room, please?"

He pointed toward the elevators, then gestured back toward the bar. "You want another glass of wine?"

"No, thanks. I'm good." She turned on her heel and strolled across the room, adjusting her scarf as she walked. She felt a little silly for having been so anxious about meeting him. Given his opinion of Ryder, she'd clearly erred in perceiving his overtures as anything more than friendly. She exhaled and was surprised when she felt a bit relieved. It was nice to know she'd made a new friend. Over their appetizers, he'd surprised her with how many ideas he had for things for her to do in town, as well as suggestions for galleries she should check out.

When she returned a few minutes later, Reid was signing his credit-card receipt. He put his wallet in his pocket and stood up, then pointed to two fresh drinks on the bar. One was a scotch and soda, the other a goblet of pinot noir.

He grinned at her. "I overruled you and got us both roadies. You ready to check out the deck?"

Though she didn't want another glass of wine, she didn't want to appear rude. "Show me the way."

He pointed to her scarf. "I'm liking that look, by the way. It's very Audrey Hepburn."

"Oh, thank you." Her hand flew up to her neck and touched the pink silk. She smiled awkwardly, unaccustomed to being complimented on her appearance.

They walked across the bar and entered the crowded lounge area, which had filled up since she'd first arrived, then climbed the stairwell one floor to the roof-deck. Reid held open the door for her, and when she walked outside Katrina caught her breath. Although they were only on the seventh floor, two entire sides of the roof deck were enclosed by glass walls, offering a stunning view of the neighborhood—building after building illuminated in sparkling lights—as well as the night sky above.

"It's gorgeous up here, Reid."

"Told you so."

She turned to admire the pool. It was deserted, the water still.

"It looks like glass," she said softly.

"They'll cover it soon for the winter. I've always thought it would be cool if they just let it freeze though."

"It would freeze?"

"Not all the way through. The top layer would."

She sipped her wine, taking in her surroundings. A row of crisp lounge chairs was perfectly aligned around the rectangular pool, the outer perimeter dotted by closed sunshade umbrellas and strings of white lights that reminded her of Christmas. A tented section near the stairwell housed a bar, this one with a marble counter, as well as a handful of round marble tables, all gleaming in the soft moonlight.

They strolled to the far end of the pool to take in the view. "I can see why people would want to spend time up here in the summer," she said. "If I were a member here, I'd never leave."

"It's no joke. It can get pretty crowded when the weather's nice, especially Friday afternoons. I'm surprised there's no one up here right now. I don't think I've ever seen it empty."

"That might be because it looks like it's going to rain." She gazed up at the cloudy sky, and when she tilted her head back she felt a little dizzy from the wine.

Just at that moment they heard a roar of thunder and the rain started coming down.

Hard.

The nearest shelter was a small awning hanging over the restrooms and a utility closet on the other side of the pool. They made a run for it—moving as fast as they could without spilling their drinks—then flattened themselves against the wall and watched the skies open up. The raindrops danced on the pool like tiny ball bearings.

They both started to laugh.

"Did you get wet?" Reid asked, just slightly out of breath.

"Not too much." Katrina watched the deluge with wide eyes. "I've never seen it rain this hard."

"Really? This is nothing."

She gaped at him. "You're joking."

"Not joking. You should go to Florida sometime. Ma'am, you ain't seen *nothin'* until you've been through a rainstorm in the South." He said the last part in an exaggerated southern drawl.

She laughed and stared out at the downpour in amazement. "I'm glad it's not too cold out here. It's actually much nicer than I thought it would be."

"At least we have drinks to keep us warm either way." He clinked his glass against hers.

The dance of the raindrops on the cement was mesmerizing. Katrina could hardly believe she was on the rooftop of a swish social club in New York City on a warm fall evening with the rain pounding down in silvery sheets all around her. She felt so free—so *alive*—that she soon realized she didn't want it to stop.

Was it the rain that made her feel that way?

She wasn't so sure.

The two of them stood side by side in silence for several moments, their backs pressed against the wall, their eyes fixed on the raindrops. Then Reid bent down to set his empty glass on the ground. When he stood up, he faced Katrina.

"This has been fun," he said. "*Again.*"

She smiled. "It has. Thanks for inviting me out, and for introducing me to your friends."

He cocked his head to one side. "You really are like Snow White, aren't you? So innocent, so . . . *pure.*"

Katrina was surprised at the comment, which—despite being true—gave her a sudden twinge of discomfort.

Before she could reply, he spoke again. "I don't want it to stop raining." His voice was noticeably softer now.

"Me neither." She looked up at the sky again. "It's so pretty."

"So are you."

She caught her breath.

He put a hand on her arm. "Is that wrong to say?"

She looked at the ground "I . . . I think I should probably go."

"Please don't." He didn't release her arm.

She swallowed and couldn't make eye contact with him. His hand was warm, and she felt her pulse quicken. She was grateful for the steady drumbeat of rain that concealed the sound of her shallow breathing. The last thing she wanted was for him to know how flustered she was.

"Kat . . ."

She still couldn't look at him.

This wasn't what she wanted.

She knew she was going to get drenched if she took even one step out from under the awning, but she forced herself to do it. "I really think I should go. Thanks for everything, Reid." She met his gaze for just a moment, then dashed through the streaming rain toward the stairwell.

* * *

"He really hit on you?" Deb asked.

"I think so."

"Are you sure he wasn't just being friendly? You know how naïve you can be about men. No offense, of course."

Katrina sighed and looked out of her bedroom window. It was still pouring nearly an hour after she'd left Soho House. "I don't know. Maybe I was reading him wrong, but I don't think so. I'm pretty sure if I hadn't bolted, he was going to kiss me."

"Did you want him to?"

Katrina hesitated before replying. "No. And yes. Does that make sense?"

"Of course it does. It makes perfect sense. It's a very gray area."

"I feel guilty, Deb."

"Why? *You're* not married. And you didn't even do anything."

"I know, but I feel guilty for even being in that situation."

"Don't. What woman our age hasn't had a questionable encounter with a married guy?"

Katrina sat up straight. "I haven't."

"Well, now you have. Welcome to the club."

"You've had an *encounter* with a married man?"

"Yes."

"When? And who?"

"Remember that cardiologist at Stanford Hospital a couple years ago?"

"Which one? I feel like you're always dating doctors."

"The cute one with the glasses? The one who conveniently wasn't wearing a wedding ring when I met him?"

Katrina nodded into the phone. "Oh my gosh, that's right, I totally forgot about him."

"Lucky you. I still haven't. So are you going to see this Reid guy again?"

"I don't think so. I mean, I sort of want to, but I don't think I should. I should just stay away from him, right?"

"I'm hardly the morality police, but that's probably a good idea. There are a billion other guys in New York anyway. Why get tangled up with one who's already taken?"

"That's what I've been telling myself, or at least *trying* to tell myself, even though the attention was just so . . . nice." Katrina sighed. She hated to admit it, but it had been a long time since a man had paid attention to her like that. Actually—if she were really honest with herself—no man had ever paid attention to her quite like that. The way he'd looked after her so considerately, especially when Ryder had been less than chivalrous. It made her feel . . . deserving.

"Attention can be deceiving. You never know what someone's motives are."

Katrina flopped back against the pillows. "You're right. Okay, enough about me. When are you going to come to visit?"

"Sounds like you're doing pretty well out there on your own."

"Very funny."

"I'm just saying it's nice to see you coming out of your shell, that's all."

Katrina gazed at the ceiling. "I still want you to come visit. It would be so much more fun if you were here."

"Ugh, don't remind me. You know if it were up to me I'd be there right now. But with this new territory I'm in charge of, I don't see it happening anytime soon. I'm leaving at the crack of dawn tomorrow for a meeting in Fresno, of all places. A Saturday meeting in Fresno. Fresno! Land of lowrider pickup trucks with tacky things written on the back window. Shoot me now, will you, please? And as you're standing over my dying body, remind me why I wanted this promotion in the first place."

Katrina laughed. "At least you're not melodramatic or anything. I thought you wanted the promotion so you could buy me an expensive thirtieth-birthday present."

"Oh, yes, of course. That must have slipped my mind. Sorry. Well, anyhow, it looks like I'm going to have to live vicariously through you for the time being."

"Like I'm exciting enough for *anyone* to want to live through vicariously," Katrina scoffed.

"Come on, don't sell yourself short. You've got the world by the tail right now, but you don't seem to see it. Just a few weeks ago you were hibernating in a cube in Mountain View, and tonight you almost kissed a married guy in Manhattan. By *anyone's* measure of excitement, that's progress."

Katrina couldn't help but smile. "Okay, you've got a point."

"It's definitely progress. You're Kat now, remember?"

"I guess I am. You think maybe Kat would kiss a married guy?"

"I doubt it. Although I do like this new attitude of yours. I hope you keep it up."

"Thanks. I'll try my best. I think I'm going to hit the hay now. I'm exhausted."

"Okay then, you hit it, girl."

"Don't go crazy in Fresno."

"Don't rub it in."

Katrina lay on her back and stared at the ceiling for a while, replaying the evening's events in her mind.

Had Reid been about to kiss her?

It doesn't matter if he was or not.

He's married.

Despite what might be going on in his relationship, despite the attention he'd showered her with, he was *married*.

Married.

Off the market.

Unavailable.

Period.

End of story.

She sat up and swung her legs off the bed. It was time for her nighttime ritual. She shuffled into the bathroom and got to work.

Remove eye makeup with cotton ball.

Wash face with gentle foaming cleanser.

Apply night cream.

Floss and brush teeth.

Back in bed, she turned off the light and closed her eyes and tried not to think about Reid anymore, but it was no good.

The truth was, at least in her limited experience, most guys were either good-looking or smart. The ones who were both were usually arrogant.

Or not interested in her.

Or all of the above.

She'd finally found one who seemed to break the mold—and he was already taken.

Her mind raced for a while, but eventually exhaustion won out and she fell asleep to the steady patter of rain against the window.

Chapter Seven

It was still raining when Katrina awoke early the next morning. She opened the drapes and peered out her bedroom window. The sun was up, but the sky was dark with storm clouds, the street quiet save for the sound of raindrops hitting the pavement. She turned to the clock on her nightstand. Although it was barely seven thirty, she was wide awake.

After a hot shower she gingerly pulled on a pair of jeans and a sweater, her sore muscles reminding her of the yoga class she'd taken. Then she went in search of an umbrella, an essential item she had somehow forgotten to pack. She figured there had to be at least one in the apartment, so she checked the hall closet first.

One had been an underestimate.

She picked up a crammed bucket from the far corner of the closet and counted the umbrellas. There were seven in all. Most of them looked pretty flimsy, if not broken, and she wondered how many of them had been purchased from the opportunistic merchants who had a knack for appearing out of nowhere with cheaply made yet overpriced protection at the ready, just at the onslaught of a storm. She'd seen men selling umbrellas on nearly every street corner during the cab ride home from Soho House.

At the thought of last night she shook her head and blinked a few times, as if that would jar the memories loose and send them on their way, out the door, never to return.

Oh, that it were that easy.

Ten minutes later, armed with the sturdiest umbrella she could find, she set off to buy a newspaper from the kiosk on the corner. She said a quick hello to the vendor, a slight, almost frail man with white hair who, despite his friendly expression, never said a word. Paper in hand, she thanked him and turned in the direction of the coffeehouse. The old man nodded and waved good-bye with a wordless smile. As she walked away, she wondered what his life was like outside of the little hut. New York was so diverse that it was almost impossible to picture people's pasts—who they were and how they had ended up here.

Aside from the steady din of the rain and the clamor of the occasional car driving by, the neighborhood was tranquil—more so than at any time since she'd arrived. She had never been one to rise with the sun, but she had a feeling that Saturday mornings might become her favorite part of the week in New York, a secret window of time she wouldn't have to share with countless others. She was already looking forward to leisurely reading the newspaper in the early morning calm.

The coffeehouse was deserted except for an elderly couple sitting at a table by the windows. Each had a cup of tea and a crossword puzzle spread out before them. The skinny young barista was behind the counter, looking as bored as ever. Katrina glanced up at the chalkboard menu behind him before ordering her usual blueberry scone and skim latte. She'd just paid when the door behind the counter opened. Justin walked through it carrying a large bag of coffee beans.

He set the bag on the floor and clapped coffee dust off his hands. Then he greeted Katrina with a warm smile. "Good morning. You're in early today, especially for a Saturday."

"I know. I couldn't sleep."

"Rain keep you up?"

"Something like that."

He gave her a look, then nodded with just the hint of a smile. "I get it. Don't worry, I won't pry."

The young barista smirked.

"Be nice, Peter," Justin said as he turned toward the back door, although it looked like he was chuckling a bit himself.

Katrina felt her cheeks flush as it dawned on her why they were amused. She'd clearly given the wrong impression about what she'd been up to all night, but, not knowing how to rectify it, she remained silent.

Peter handed her the latte and scone.

"Thanks, Peter." *So that's his name.*

"No problem."

She was still feeling embarrassed as she turned away from the counter, but she was also a tiny bit flattered that they'd both assumed she hadn't spent the night alone. At home, no one would ever assume that. She took a seat at an open table near the windows and settled into the newspaper, dimly aware of the rhythmic cadence of the rain peppering the glass.

It wasn't until she was halfway through the front section that she realized she'd never thanked Justin for his list of things to do in New York. She looked over at the counter but didn't see him. She glanced at her watch. It wasn't even eight thirty yet. Was he in the back room? She doubted he was already taking a break, but then again, he probably began his shift super early. She looked back at her newspaper and wondered what it would be like to work at a coffeehouse, especially one where the other employees looked like they were barely out of high school. She could imagine her mother shaking her head and saying something along the lines of *That's what happens when you don't get a degree.*

Then she thought of Ryder from last night. He had a high-profile job, made loads of money, and—in his own words—liked to get into trouble for fun. Mr. Get-into-Trouble-for-Fun probably had a huge bank account, but in her opinion, he didn't have half the warmth of Justin.

"So what's on the docket today? More exploring?"

The sound of a man's voice startled her out of her thoughts. She looked up and saw Justin standing there.

"Oh, hi. I thought you'd left." She felt as if she'd been caught with her hand in the cookie jar. If he only knew what she'd just been thinking.

He smiled. "On a Saturday? Rarely. Did you get my list?"

She flinched with shame at how rude she must seem. "Yes, thank you. I'm sorry for not coming back with my notepad. I got a little . . . distracted."

He held up his hands. "No worries. I told you, I'm not a private investigator. Just a native New Yorker who wants to make sure our guests enjoy the time they spend in our glorious city."

"Do you live nearby?" She pictured him and his wife in a tiny yet cozy place around the corner. Or maybe they had a bigger place in one of the other boroughs? *It must be hard to pay rent anywhere in New York City on a barista's salary*, she thought. She wondered what his wife did for a living, or if their parents helped them out like Shana's did.

"Not too far. I gather you're enjoying your time in New York so far?" He crossed his arms in front of him.

She swallowed, still embarrassed at how he thought she'd spent the night, and tried to redirect the tone of the conversation. "I am, thanks. Anyhow, I think I'm going to check out the Museum of Natural History today. Seems like a perfect way to spend a rainy day." She took a sip of her latte, suddenly energized at the prospect of the day she had planned.

"Hmm." He frowned.

She set down her cup. "Hmm what?"

"I hate to break it to you, but I fear the entire city might have the same idea, or at least the portion of the population with kids."

Her face fell. "You think so?"

"Unfortunately, I *know* so. That place is packed to the rim even when it's nice outside and there are a ton of other kid-friendly options. And today's Saturday to boot."

"Do you have kids?" she asked, then immediately regretted the question. It was too personal. Why had she asked him that?

He shook his head. "I just like museums. Studied a bit of art in college. I take it you don't have kids either? You don't strike me as the type to abandon your children to go live it up in New York."

She smiled. "I would hope not."

"Anyhow, if you *do* go to the Museum of Natural History today, brace yourself for a monster crowd. I mean sardine-style *packed*. Those dinosaur bones are quite a draw."

"How disappointing." Katrina really didn't like crowds. Not surprisingly, they made her anxious. "This throws a wrench into my plans."

"Don't stress. There are more than enough things to do in New York when the weather's not cooperating. And sometimes having a wrench thrown at you is a good thing."

She narrowed her eyes at him. "I hope you don't mean literally. And you're right—I'll just come up with a new game plan. Don't worry about me." She thought about the huge list sitting in her apartment, as well as the one he'd given her. There had to be something suitable for a rainy day.

"I'm not worried about you at all. You seem pretty spontaneous."

"I do?"

He arched an eyebrow. "You moved here, didn't you? If that's not spontaneous, I don't know what is."

"I guess I don't see myself that way."

"Well, I know we just met, but maybe I see something in you that you don't—at least not yet. Or maybe I've just had too much coffee today and I should keep my pop psychoanalysis to myself."

She smiled and kept her eyes on her plate, her shyness holding her back from looking up at him. How could he possibly know what a big deal it was for her to have someone regard her as spontaneous? First Shana, now Justin. If they only knew how much it rattled her to have to change plans at all, much less at the last minute.

Finally, she looked up. "Thanks, Justin. Actually, I did something a little spontaneous last night."

He gave her a look, and she felt her cheeks flush with embarrassment again.

"Or yesterday *early evening*, I mean. I went to my very first yoga class."

"Oh yeah? How did that go?"

She put her hands on her opposite arms. "Let's just say I'm feeling it today. Apparently, I've gone nearly thirty years without knowing that I have absolutely zero upper-body strength, not to mention zero lower-body strength. It was a humbling experience."

He laughed. "I'm more into basketball and weights to stay in shape, but I keep hearing good things about yoga. Maybe I should try it sometime."

"Not that I have anything to compare her to, but I thought the teacher was great. She really made me think about . . . getting out of my comfort zone." Katrina was surprised at her candor, but Justin didn't seem to think she was being overly forthcoming. Or if he did, he didn't let on.

He twisted his wedding ring. "Getting out of your comfort zone can be hard, but in my experience, it's usually a good thing."

Just then several patrons filed in all at once, the sound of the downpour outside nearly drowning out the soft jingle of the bells attached to the front door.

Justin glanced at the recent arrivals, then smiled at Katrina. "And so the weekend rush begins. I don't want to get into hot water with the boss, so I've gotta get back to work. Have a good day, Kat."

"You too, Justin. Thanks for the heads-up on the museum."

"My pleasure."

She watched him hurry to join Peter behind the counter. She'd been going to the same Starbucks in Mountain View for years and had never met a barista like him there. At Starbucks, they all had the same perky, borderline robotic demeanor, but in all her years as a regular customer, none of them had ever expressed any genuine interest in her, much less gone out of their way to make her feel so welcome. Justin was different. He seemed to truly want her to enjoy her time in his city. Maybe it was because he was older, but she still couldn't help wondering why he served coffee for a living, especially now that he'd mentioned college. Had he dropped out?

Perhaps he did have a degree and did something else on the side—maybe acting, the way Shana did? Or maybe he'd pursued something else that hadn't quite worked out? Although she was curious, she didn't know how to bring it up without offending him, something she feared she'd already done enough. Maybe he was content making lattes and chatting with customers. He was certainly good at it.

She looked down at her cup. Who was she to knock Justin for working in a coffeehouse? What right did she have to judge someone else's career choices? She'd spent eight years in a job she hated just to please her parents—and where had that gotten her?

Nowhere, she thought.

* * *

Shana's boyfriend was just leaving the building as Katrina approached the front steps.

"Good morning, Kat." He looked up at the dark sky and opened his umbrella. "Enjoying this lovely weather?"

"Hi, Josh. Yes, there's nothing like a deluge to brighten up a fall day."

"Looks like you've already been out and about. Brave girl . . . unless you're just getting home from last night?" He winked at her.

"Sorry to disappoint." She pointed down the street. "I went around the corner for coffee. Are you on your way home, or just out to do the same?"

"I wish I were going out for coffee, but unfortunately I'm headed to the office."

"Ouch. On a Saturday morning?"

He shrugged. "Par for the course at my firm, sad to say. At least when we're working on a big case, which lately has been . . . always."

No wonder Grace wanted to get out of there, Katrina thought.

"Is Shana still here?"

"Yes, but not for long. She's teaching a class at ten."

Katrina's ears perked up. Despite being sore from yesterday's session, it was a *good* sore, and she wanted to try yoga again. Plus after last night, she could use some internal reflection and wondered whether Shana might offer a little more wisdom before class.

She said good-bye to Josh, then hurried upstairs and knocked on Shana's door.

"Hi, neighbor. What's up?" Shana was dressed in yoga gear, holding a steaming mug of tea. There was jazz playing in the background in her studio apartment.

Katrina pointed her thumb over her shoulder. "I just ran into Josh, who said you were leaving soon to teach a class. Can I come with you?"

"Really? You want to take another class?"

"Yes. Obviously I'll pay this time."

Shana broke out into a huge smile. "So you really *did* enjoy it?"

Katrina pushed a lock of damp hair behind her ear. "I told you I did."

"I know, but people say that all the time. I never know if they really mean it, you know?"

It was such an earnest comment that Katrina was taken aback. How could Shana not see what a good instructor she was? For a moment she saw her own self-doubt reflected in Shana's blue eyes—and realized how unfortunate it was.

She nodded. "Admittedly, I'm feeling muscles I never knew I had before today, but I really enjoyed it. And it's high time I got in better shape, so count me in."

"All right, you're in. But you're not paying."

"I don't want you to have to pay for me."

Shana sipped her tea. "Maybe we'll square off on that painting sooner than I'd hoped. I'll put your name in the computer for a few comps, which I'm allowed as one of my rare perks. Deal?"

"Deal."

* * *

Twenty minutes later, Katrina and Shana were on their way to the yoga studio. When they were less than ten feet from the entrance, Katrina's phone began to ring.

"I'll meet you inside, okay?" Shana pointed to the door. "Blair's here today, and she gets upset when I'm late. And shut off your phone so it doesn't ring in there, promise? That *really* ticks her off."

"Promise." It was still raining cats and dogs, so Katrina stood under the awning and fished her phone out of her purse. She hoped it wasn't Reid calling—but also secretly hoped it was. Why was she thinking about him? She knew she shouldn't be thinking about him. She also knew she shouldn't be thinking about thinking about him.

She hesitated for a moment when she saw the name on the display, then took a deep breath and answered.

"Hi, Mom."

"Good morning, Katrina. I just thought I'd check in to see how things are going out there." As usual, her mother's voice revealed little emotion.

Katrina doubted she was referring to sightseeing. "Things are going really well so far. I've been doing a lot of exploring around the city . . . and I've even been painting a little bit."

Her mother ignored the revelation. "Is the apartment suitable?"

"It's fine. Nothing fancy, but it's nice enough. Very clean."

"I've heard horror stories about cheap New York apartments. Are you *sure* it's clean?"

"It's fine, really. And it's not that cheap, believe me."

"All right. If you say so, I'll have to take your word for it. It's just that your father and I know you're hardly in a position to be spending a lot of money, so we worry about your living conditions."

"It's perfectly acceptable, Mom."

"So have you sent out any résumés yet?"

Katrina sighed. There it was: the real reason for the call. "Mom, I've been here for less than a week."

"So?"

"So I barely know my way around my neighborhood yet."

"Katrina, just because you decided to take a vacation, it doesn't mean the world has stopped."

"I know that."

"If you don't get started on your job search now, you're going to fall way behind. Trust me. I know you may think we're being unreasonable about this, but your father and I only have your best interests in mind."

Katrina squeezed the handle of her umbrella. "Got it. Listen, I've really got to go now. I'm sorry. Will you please tell Dad I said hi?"

"What I *want* to tell him is that you're sending out some résumés this weekend. Can I tell him that?"

"Monday. Okay? I'll start Monday."

"Don't slack off on this, Katrina. You'll only be disappointing yourself."

"I won't, Mom. I promise."

"All right, then. Good-bye, Katrina."

"Bye, Mom."

She hung up the phone and squeezed her eyes shut for a moment, trying her best to believe her mom acted this way because she loved her.

* * *

When Katrina walked into the studio, the pale-skinned woman she'd passed on the way out the day before was sitting at the front desk. Her dark hair was again pulled into a severe bun.

"Name, please?"

Katrina hesitated, and the woman gave her a strange look.

Katrina swallowed. "Lynden . . . Katrina Lynden. It, um, might be in there as Kat."

The woman typed the name efficiently into the computer. It was obvious she wasn't thrilled when she realized Katrina wasn't paying for the session. She gave her a stiff nod and gestured for her to enter.

Once she had lit a candle and sat down in front of the class, Shana smiled at the group, and Katrina closed her eyes along with the others.

"Did any of you love cotton candy when you were a kid?" Shana asked. "I remember thinking it was the absolute *best* food in the world, that life would be perfect if I could eat cotton candy for breakfast, lunch, and dinner. In my mind, that was all I really needed to be happy. My parents disagreed, of course, so I only got to have it on special occasions. But for whatever reason, there was something about cotton candy that made me happy, and even now, just the *thought* of it makes me smile. Sometimes that's all I need when I'm feeling a little blue. I'll close my eyes and remember how simple life was back then, and it reminds me that I shouldn't take things so seriously now. Do you have a childhood memory that brings you joy? A toy? A food? A stuffed animal?"

Katrina shifted on her mat and remembered the paint set her grandmother had given her for Christmas in fourth grade. She'd loved it as a child but hadn't thought about it in ages.

She felt the hint of a smile form on her lips.

Shana continued. "For my brother, it's the game Stratego. He used to play it with our grandfather as a kid in Ohio. When he's down in the dumps, or stressed at work, he'll think about Stratego of all things, and it always makes him feel a little better. Isn't that wonderful? You may be skeptical, but it works because the positive memories associated with these things from our childhood are so strong. We all have to grow up, but we don't have to leave behind what makes us happy, right?"

Katrina opened her eyes and glanced at Shana. Was she referring to her painting?

Shana didn't seem to notice. "As a wise man once told me, we are responsible for our own happiness. So whether it's memories from yesterday or twenty years ago, I believe if we focus on the things that make us happy, then happiness will find us in return." She paused for a moment, then stood up and turned on the soft background music. "Now let's all meet in downward dog position."

As they began to move through the poses, Katrina felt a bit uncomfortable, as though Shana had been speaking directly to her, almost as though she could read her mind. But when she saw the blissed-out look on the other students' faces, she suspected she wasn't the only one who felt that way.

* * *

"Do you always tell a story before class?" Katrina asked Shana on their way out of the building an hour later.

Shana nodded. "Pretty much. I'm not even sure why I started doing it. One day I just jotted down a few thoughts to share before class, and then before I knew it, they became a regular thing."

"Where do you come up with the ideas?"

She shrugged. "It depends. Sometimes they're based on what's going on in my life, or how I'm feeling. But I don't always tell a story. Sometimes I recite a poem, or ask a simple question for the group to think about during class. Or if a *person* inspires me, like you did last night, I talk about that. Josh gives me a lot of inspiration too. He's the wise man I mentioned today."

"Josh is the wise man?"

"You'd be surprised. There's a lot going on underneath that preppy exterior. He's warm and inquisitive and supportive, and he'd do anything to make me smile. I love him as much as I love myself."

I love him as much as I love myself.

Katrina glanced at the ground, embarrassed to have no frame of reference for such a profound statement. "I'm impressed, Shana, really. You're so . . . insightful."

"You think so? Sometimes I wonder if I come across as a little too New Agey. Blair's not really a fan of my approach to teaching. She's more into the burn-as-many-calories-as-you-can style of yoga."

Yeah, but her skinniness certainly isn't making her any nicer, Katrina thought. "Well, just so you know, *I'm* a big fan." She wanted to let Shana know how much what she'd said in class had resonated with her, but she wasn't sure how to articulate it without sounding . . . New Agey. So she left it at that, hoping what she'd said was enough.

"Thanks. I'll tell Gracie that the next time she calls me hippie-dippie." Shana held her arm out to one side and watched the raindrops fall against her hand. "Ugh, I've had enough of this rain. Despite what I said last night about taking chances in life, I think I'm going to spend the rest of the day curled up with a trashy romance novel. How's that for insight?"

Katrina smiled and poked her head out from under her umbrella to look up at the dark sky. It wasn't even noon yet, but it felt like dusk. "That sounds like the perfect way to wait out the storm, and if I were home, I'd probably be doing the exact same thing. Given how limited my daylight hours are here, I can't justify staying in. Especially on a Saturday."

"Makes sense. So what are your plans?"

"I'm not sure yet. But I'm going to get out there to, as you said, *see the world.*"

Shana laughed. "Well, have fun, whatever you do. Hey, we're going to Ten Degrees tonight if you'd like to join us."

"Ten Degrees? What's that?"

"It's a wine bar on Saint Marks."

"Is ten degrees the temperature inside? If it is, I'm not going. I'm from California, remember?"

Shana smiled. "It's a cool place—and not in the temperature sense. I promise you'll like it. It's much nicer than that dive bar we went to the other night."

"You're going with Josh?"

"Maybe Gracie too." Shana unlocked her door. "So what do you think? Want to come along?"

"If I have enough steam after a day of sightseeing. But to be honest, I'll probably end up on the couch watching TV."

"I won't tell anyone if you do. But if you can make it out, we'd love to see you there."

Katrina smiled. "Thanks, Shana." *Maybe one day* Kat *will be joining you,* she thought, *but I have a feeling that tonight Katrina will be going to bed early.*

Chapter Eight

The next morning, freshly showered and with the hefty Sunday paper under her arm and a solid night's sleep under her belt, Katrina walked into the coffeehouse a little after eight thirty. It was about half full, so she set her newspaper and sweater down on her usual table, then walked over to the counter to order. Today Peter was there.

"You again?" He gave her a wry grin.

"Hi, Peter."

"You're becoming our best customer."

"I am?"

"One of them. We've got quite a few regulars in here. You want the usual?"

"You know my order?" She felt her face flush.

He gave her a look. "Blueberry scone and a skim latte? It's not that hard."

She laughed awkwardly, silently kicking herself for reacting that way. Why should she care if he knew her usual order? "I'm sorry. You're right. No Justin today?"

"He's usually at the other shop on Sundays."

"The other shop as in coffeehouse?"

He nodded.

"There's another one?"

He handed her the scone on a plate. "It's on the Upper West Side. You should check it out sometime. It's twice the size of this place."

"I'll try to do that." She nibbled on the scone until her latte was ready, then made her way back to her table. It wasn't until she sat down that she realized she didn't know the name of the place. The sign outside featured only a cup of coffee, and the chalkboard menu didn't have a visible name or logo. It was as if the place didn't have a name at all.

* * *

Nearly an hour later, Katrina's phone chimed. As she reached for her purse, she mentally went over her prepared response in case the text was from Reid.

Thank him for inviting me out Friday night.

Don't mention what did or did not almost happen between us.

Graciously decline additional contact.

She hoped he wouldn't think she was rude to cut off their budding friendship, but after mulling things over on Saturday, she decided it was for the best.

The message was from her mother, a reminder to e-mail her parents a current résumé so they could critique it.

Katrina sighed and tossed the phone back into her purse without responding. Did her mother really have nothing better to do on a Sunday morning? It wasn't even seven o'clock there yet!

She gathered her things, waved good-bye to Peter, and slowly walked back to her building. She had three possibilities for how to spend the day but still hadn't picked one. Now that it had finally stopped raining, the list of ways her Sunday could unfold had once again expanded . . . endlessly.

She was a block away when she spotted Shana, Josh, and Grace heading toward her, all three of them dressed in shorts and bright orange T-shirts. She stopped walking and squinted at them. Was Josh wearing . . . a white terry-cloth headband?

"There you are!" Shana skipped up to her. "We just knocked on your door."

"Any chance you're up for playing soccer right now?" Grace asked.

Katrina tried not to laugh out loud. "Soccer? Are you joking?"

"Usually, but not this time," Grace said.

"We're short a girl," Shana said. "Please?" Her shirt, like the ones Grace and Josh wore, said "NYC Soccer" on the front.

"I've never kicked a soccer ball in my life," Katrina said. "I don't have the right shoes or anything."

"We don't care," Josh said. "We suck anyway."

"Dude, we worse than suck," Grace said to him. "We suck at *sucking*."

Josh shrugged. "Semantics."

"Please, Kat?" Shana held her hands prayerfully. "We'd be so grateful."

"You really don't care that I don't even know how to play?"

Grace put a hand on her shoulder. "Kat, *Kitty* if I may, which part of *we suck* didn't you understand?"

Josh held out his arms. "Does this look like the finely tuned instrument of a skilled athlete?"

Katrina smiled at him. "I think you look great."

"Come on, Kat. It'll be fun." Shana's hands were still in prayer position. "Please? And you don't need soccer shoes. You can just wear sneakers. That's what Gracie and I wear."

Katrina swallowed. What if she tried to kick the ball and missed? What if she fell on her face? She had always hated doing things she wasn't good at. At home she would never say yes to something like this.

But that didn't mean she couldn't say yes *here*.

She gave them a nervous nod. "Okay, sure. Why not?"

"Yay!" Shana did a little jump and clapped her hands, then gave Katrina a quick hug. "Thank you so much. We totally owe you."

"Let's see how you feel about that after you see me play."

* * *

Twenty minutes later, the four of them were in a cab in Chinatown, slowly crawling across Canal Street. Katrina stared out the window at the crowds swarming the stores and kiosks lining both sides of the street. It was a two-pronged river of tourists, cheap souvenirs, and knockoff designer handbags. Compared to the eclectic shops of the East Village, every vendor here seemed to be selling the exact same merchandise.

"You play soccer *here*?" she asked. "How could there possibly be a soccer field *here*?"

Shana pointed south. "Three blocks that way. There's a little park."

"We're going to be late." Josh looked at his phone.

Grace patted him on the knee. "We're always late, pumpkin face. Don't fret your terry-cloth-covered head over it."

"Suck it, Gracie." Josh patted her knee in return.

"You two play nice now," Shana mock-scolded them.

They finally made it to the other side of the intersection, and a few minutes later the cab dropped them off at a park located smack in the middle of Chinatown. Nearly every storefront had signs in Chinese, and nearly all of them were restaurants or markets, although Katrina couldn't help noticing several bail-bond agencies, with signs in English, sprinkled among them. In the past ten minutes, she'd seen countless paper lanterns in an array of bright colors, bushel upon bushel of herbs, fruits, and nuts, and more chickens, pigs, and ducks—all hanging from hooks front and center in the windows— than she'd seen in all her years on earth.

And there were people absolutely everywhere.

The small, turf soccer field was flanked by a basketball court and a garden on one side, and a second garden and an ornate building resembling a temple on the other. The gardens and temple area were packed with people of all ages, most of whom were Chinese, either milling around or sitting on the many benches scattered about. The basketball court was packed with people who appeared to be doing a form of tai chi.

As Katrina and the others hurried toward the field, she began to feel nervous. She had never been especially coordinated or athletic, and from what little she knew about soccer, those were the two biggest requirements for playing it.

* * *

"Well, Team Rotten Oranges, here's to a game . . . played." Josh stood at the front of the picnic table and held up his plastic cup. The team was on the crowded back patio of Whiskey Tavern, a half block from the field and the only Irish pub in the neighborhood. They had lost twelve to zero. Katrina had only touched the ball a few times, but she was relieved she hadn't broken an ankle—hers or anyone else's.

"Maybe you guys should have put one of those big orange pylons out there in my place," she said to Shana. "It might have done more for the team."

Shana waved a hand in front of her. "Shush. You did great. Twelve to nothing isn't bad for us."

Katrina was beginning to doubt there could be anyone in all of New York who was nicer than Shana.

The bartender arrived with a pitcher of beer and a tray lined with shot glasses. As he began to pass out the shots, Katrina eyed them warily.

"What are those?" she whispered to Shana.

"Picklebacks."

"Pickle whats?"

"Picklebacks. It's a shot of whiskey followed by a shot of pickle juice. They're super yummy."

The guy across the table from her nodded. "I love 'em."

"Delicious," said the guy next to him.

"See there, Kitty?" Grace handed her two glasses. "You'll love it."

Katrina smiled and shook her head. "Oh, thanks, but I'm not much of a drinker."

"Oh please, be a man." Grace set the glasses in front of her.

"You ditched us last night, so you can drink with us today," Josh said.

"That's right. We missed you last night. Did the couch monster get you?" Shana asked.

Katrina gave them a sheepish look. "I was pretty beat. I'm sorry." She'd actually spent much of the evening working on her résumé and had also e-mailed those contacts her mother had passed along, but she didn't want to admit that was how she'd spent her Saturday night, especially not to this group.

"No worries, rookie. You can make it up right now." Grace held up both of her shot glasses and looked around the table. "You losers ready?"

Everyone nodded and held up their glasses. Katrina reluctantly followed suit.

"To the Rotten Oranges!" Gracie shouted.

"To the Rotten Oranges!" the rest of the team shouted back.

"*No one* can stink it up better than we can!"

"*No one* can stink it up better than we can!" they yelled back. Katrina got the impression it was their standard chant. Not surprising. They really *were* terrible at soccer, she thought. She doubted they would disagree with her—or even care. They clearly had a ball on and off the field.

At Grace's signal, everyone tossed back their Jameson's shots, Katrina included. She tried not to gag. As she struggled to finish, she watched them all reach for the pickle-juice chaser, which she finally did too—albeit long after everyone else.

Josh leaned across the table to pat Katrina on the shoulder. He also handed her a full beer. "Well done. What did you think?"

She scrunched up her nose and blinked a couple of times. "Brutal at the beginning, but by the end it wasn't half-bad. The pickle juice tasted sort of good, actually."

Grace put her arm around Katrina and gestured to the bartender. "That's my Kitty Kat! Let's get her another one."

* * *

An hour later, Katrina squinted across the table at Josh and hoped she wasn't stumbling over her words. "Did you really dump Shana?"

"Yes." Shana nodded.

Josh shook his head. "Revisionist history."

"What happened?" Katrina asked.

"Here we go again." Josh gestured for the waiter. "This requires another pitcher."

Shana laughed. "Stop it. It was a misunderstanding."

"How so?"

Grace touched Josh's shoulder. "Squishy here didn't believe that Shana could actually like *him* more than farm boy at home, so he folded." She turned and looked at Josh. "That about right, pumpkin? You got up, threw your cards on the table, and walked away."

He grimaced. "I saw a picture. He's a lot better-looking than I am. And bigger."

Katrina squinted at him again. "You mean bigger taller?"

"Cha!" Grace pumped her fist. "Kitty's calling chubs *out*."

Shana put her hand on Josh's head. "I was so sad when you folded. I really like chubs."

"And then you ran into each other two years later?" Katrina asked.

"Yeah. What are the odds?" Shana said with a smile. "It was very romantical."

Katrina made a confused face. "Romantical?"

Gracie held up her glass. "After a few drinks, farm girl tends to add *al* to random adjectives. You'll get used to it."

"For extra emphasis," Shana said. "Like italics. It's *italical*."

"*Romantical.* I think I like that," Katrina slurred and stared off into space.

Grace laughed. "My friends, it looks like the kitty is officially buzzed."

"Are you okay, Kat?" Shana asked.

Katrina nodded. "I'm not used to drinking like this. I'm having fun though."

"All the more reason to have another beer." Josh refilled her glass.

"What about you?" Katrina turned to Grace. "Are you dating anyone?"

"I have a pretend boyfriend. I call him Married Guy."

"He's married?"

"Long story. So hey, have you worn the necklace yet?"

Katrina sat up straight and smiled. "Yes! I wore it the same night you gave it to me, in fact. It's beautiful."

Grace slapped her tiny palm against the table. "Damn *right* it is. It's about time some buyers noticed it too. What the eff is wrong with them? Can't they see how fabulous my stuff is?"

"Your stuff is fantastical," Shana said with a heavy nod.

"And it's not even that expensive. Maybe that's my problem. I've been sucking up and hoping it will pay off, but maybe I need to raise my prices instead. Is that what needs to happen here?" Grace looked around the table.

Katrina nodded, but she wasn't thinking about jewelry. Right now she was fixated on something else.

Grace is involved with a married man?

Is it serious?

How long has it been going on?

Is he going to leave his wife?

Maybe Deb had been right about how common infidelity was. She wanted to ask Grace more about it, but her brain wasn't operating at regular speed, and before she could figure out how to bring it up without sounding intrusive, or worse yet, rude, Josh spoke again.

"Don't get Gracie started on her jewelry. She'll never shut up."

Grace pointed at him. "I'll shut *you* up, doughnut hole."

He winked at her. "I heart you too."

"Anybody want water?" Shana stood up. "I'll get a pitcher on the way back from the ladies' room."

Grace stood up too. "I'll go with you. Damn if it I don't need to urinate like a racehorse."

As they walked away, Katrina gave Josh a quizzical look. "How can someone that tiny have such a foul mouth?"

"You haven't heard anything yet. Just wait until she's drunk."

"She's not drunk?"

"None of us are. Not yet, at least."

Katrina tilted her head in amazement. "How can you not be drunk? I'm pretty sure I am."

He smiled. "We *live* here, Kat. We've had a lot more practice than you. Sunday Funday has barely begun for us."

"Huh?" Barely begun? She would be ready for a nap soon.

As Josh began chatting with the other guys on the team, Katrina reached for her purse to check the time. How long had they been there? It seemed like hours. Had the day really just gotten started? New Yorkers operated in a different gear. Could she ever get used to this pace?

When she pulled out her phone, she saw two new text messages.

The first was from Deb, complaining about all the mullets in Fresno.

The second was from Reid, asking what she was up to.

She squinted at the screen. His message was short and friendly and didn't say anything about what had happened at Soho House the other night.

Maybe she'd gotten it all wrong?

Had she blown it out of proportion?

Whatever it was, she was clearly overthinking it.

She squinted at the screen again and tried to remember her plan for responding to him.

What was the plan?

I had a plan. I know I had a plan.

What was the plan?

Her head fuzzy, her fingers slow and clumsy, she wrote back that she was at Whiskey Tavern with her new soccer team. Given her performance, she knew it was unlikely they would ever ask her to play again, but for today at least, it was fun to think of herself as part of a real team.

She hit *send* and put the phone down on the table. Reid answered immediately, asking if he could come join them for a drink.

She flinched and suddenly remembered that she'd decided not to see him again, that her plan was to cut off contact.

She stared at the phone.

No, she told herself.

Don't reply.

She deleted the text, tossed her phone back into her purse, and stood up, then wobbled toward the restroom, proud of having done the right thing. The line was six women deep. Katrina had never seen a bar at home this packed on a Sunday afternoon. Then again, she realized, she had never been to a bar at home on a Sunday afternoon.

Home.

Had she really been gone only a week? Mountain View seemed a lifetime ago.

She already felt so different.

So much . . . happier.

So much . . . lighter.

Except for her bladder, which felt uncomfortably full at the moment.

She watched the line inch closer to the door and wished it would move faster.

When she finally returned to the table, Josh had refilled her glass with cold beer, but Shana mercifully had set a fresh glass of water next to it. Josh had also ordered several platters of appetizers for the table, and they all dug into chicken fingers, buffalo wings, garlic fries, and onion rings.

Grace dipped a garlic fry into ranch dressing. "I'm going to smell so bad after eating all this crap, but it tastes freaking amazing."

"I shouldn't be eating any of it if I ever want to get another audition," Shana said. "My face might break out."

"All the more for me," Josh said.

Grace patted his stomach. "Like Uncle Josh needs any more fried food."

One of the teammates sitting across the table looked at Shana. "How's the stage stomach these days?" he asked.

Katrina looked up from her plate. "Stage stomach? What's that?"

Shana stuck out her tongue. "Blech. Let's just say I suffer from performance anxiety."

"That's an understatement," Grace said.

"I get stage fright pretty bad," Shana said to Katrina.

"Define *pretty bad*."

"Like throwing up bad."

"That sounds terrible," Katrina said.

"It's not good," Josh said. "It makes me worry about her."

Shana chomped on a chicken finger. "I get sick before every audition, every performance."

Katrina raised her eyebrows. "Throwing up sick?"

"Yep. Never during rehearsals though. Just anytime there's pressure. I've been like that since I was a kid."

"Isn't that hard on your system?"

"Really hard."

"She needs to stop," Josh said.

Shana picked up an onion ring. "That's why I started doing yoga. My doctor thought it would help with the anxiety—calm my nerves and all that. I never thought I'd become an instructor. It just sort of happened."

"Has it worked?"

She offered a weary smile. "I'm not sure. I haven't had an audition in months. It's my own fault though. I haven't been all that proactive lately."

"I think that's a good thing," Grace said. "Screw what your parents want."

"Like that's so easy to do," Shana said.

Grace rolled her eyes. "Dude, my mom could have written *Battle Hymn of the Tiger Mother*. There's no way your parents could be any worse."

Katrina was about to ask Grace if she had any siblings, but before she could say anything, she saw a man approaching their table.

She froze.

It was Reid.

What is he doing here?

"Hey, Snow White," he said with a grin. "Can I join you?"

* * *

Half the table looked from him to Katrina. The other half was facing the other direction, their eyes glued to an NFL game on a big screen.

Katrina felt her face get hot. "Everyone, this is my friend Reid. Reid, this is, um, everyone."

"Hi, Reid," said those who had noticed his arrival.

Grace squeezed Katrina's knee under the table, then stood up and sat next to Josh on the opposite bench to make room for Reid. As he took a seat between her and Shana, Katrina wondered what had compelled her to tell him where she was. Why hadn't she just said she was at a bar, if anything at all? Then again, she hardly thought he would come looking for her. That sort of thing didn't happen in her life.

"Can I pour you a beer?" Josh held up the pitcher.

Reid grinned again. "You can't pour one fast enough."

Josh passed a full glass to him across the table, then turned back around to watch the game. If anyone thought it was inappropriate for Reid to be there, no one was acting like it.

"So you were all playing soccer?" Reid asked Katrina and gestured to the group.

"We got killed," Shana said with her usual smile. "I'm Shana."

"We suck," Grace said. "I'm Grace. So how do you know Kat?"

"Through a mutual friend," Reid said. "She introduced us right when Kat moved to town."

Grace narrowed her eyes at Katrina. "You have other friends here? I gotta say, I'm a little hurt by this information."

"Not many." Katrina reached across the table and put a hand on Grace's tiny head. "Don't worry. I'm not very popular."

Grace picked up an onion ring and pointed it at Reid. "Well, *Reid*, I'm sure you're very nice, but just so you know, *no one* is as fun as we are. Or as I am."

"Duly noted," he said with a laugh.

Josh turned around to grab an onion ring, then elbowed Grace. "Did you hear what you just said? That was sort of high up on the cockiness scale, even for you."

She nodded. "I heard myself, and I liked it."

"I'm not sure how to respond to that," Josh said.

"Shana and Grace live in my building," Katrina said to Reid. "Josh is Shana's boyfriend. The rest of the team I just met today."

Grace waved another onion ring at Reid. "You're cute, but you're wearing a wedding ring. What's your story? Where's your wife? Why are you here with us right now?"

"Gracie!" Shana laughed.

"I'm buzzed, I say things," Grace said. "So sue me."

"It's okay," Reid said. "I hope to be buzzed soon too."

Grace nodded at him. "I like your attitude." She turned in the direction of the waiter. "Let's get this man a pickleback."

Katrina couldn't help but notice how Reid had deflected the questions. Where *was* his wife? Why *was* he here with them?

* * *

By the time they finally left Whiskey Tavern, it was getting dark. Although Katrina had long ago switched to water, there was no sugar coating her lingering state of intoxication. The others were also drunk by then, thanks to many more pitchers of beer and several rounds of picklebacks. The group filed out of the front door and congregated on the sidewalk.

"Which way are you headed?" Josh asked Reid. "We can cram you into our cab if you need a ride near the East Village. We'll probably do one more beer somewhere on Second or Third."

Reid looked at Katrina. "You up for one more?"

She shook her head. "I can't drink another drop."

"Come on, Kitty, tomorrow's a holiday," Grace said, putting her arm around her. "One more beer won't kill you."

"Tomorrow's a holiday?" Katrina said.

"For me it is," Grace said. "I'm calling it No More Sucking-Up Day. I think it might go viral."

Josh put his hand over Grace's mouth. "Okay then. I say we head over to Finnerty's." He looked at Reid. "You in?"

Reid grinned. "Why not?"

"I want one of him," Grace said to Shana—and not in a quiet voice.

No you don't, Katrina thought. Didn't *any*one care about his wedding ring? She was too drunk to think clearly, but she still knew the best thing for her to do at that point was to say good-bye to everyone and put herself to bed.

They piled into a cab and headed back to the East Village. The driver pulled over in front of Finnerty's, but when Grace saw the crowd milling around outside the entrance, she raised a hand in the air, commander style.

"Everyone here looks twelve years old. I'm calling an audible. How about we go to The 13th Step?"

Josh rolled his eyes. "*You* look twelve years old."

She pointed at him. "Choose your next words carefully, Uncle Josh. So who's in for The 13th Step?"

Josh raised his hand. "I second the motion."

"Motion granted." She turned toward the driver. "Change of plans. Will you drop us down at Tenth instead?"

Shana tapped Grace on the arm. "How is two out of five a majority?"

Grace pushed her hand away. "I'm Asian. Don't question my math skills."

"If you guys are headed south, I think I'm going to get out here and walk home," Katrina said, opening the door. "Sorry, everyone, but I'm hitting a wall."

"To be honest, I can't believe you made it this long," Josh said. "I'm impressed."

"Me too," Grace said. "I thought your embarrassingly low tolerance for alcohol would have sent you packing hours ago."

"I'll walk you home," Reid said to Katrina, following her out of the taxi.

"Be sure to drink lots of water," Shana said with a wave as the cab pulled away.

Katrina and Reid slowly began walking north on Second Avenue. "You okay there, soccer girl?" He put a hand on her shoulder.

She hiccupped. "I'm not much of a drinker."

He chuckled. "I've noticed."

"I'm also not much of a soccer player. But it was so much fun to try something new, even if I was terrible. I hope I'm not too sore tomorrow."

"That might be the least of your troubles tomorrow."

She looked at him. "Hangover?"

"Probably."

"Am I slurring my words?"

"A little bit."

She looked straight ahead and shook her head. "I'm so pathetic."

"No you're not. You're adorable. To be honest, it's a refreshing change to run across someone who *doesn't* drink like a fish. You don't find that too much in this city, at least in the circles I run in."

She felt a little guilty for it, but she couldn't deny that it made her feel good to have a handsome man like Reid call her *adorable*, regardless of how inappropriate it was.

They walked in companionable silence for a while, and soon reached Katrina's block. It was dark and quiet here, in stark contrast to the chaos of Second Avenue. As they approached her building, she found herself getting nervous. When she'd left for the soccer game hours earlier, this was hardly the way she'd expected to come back. And it was light-years removed from her carefully thought-out plan not to see him anymore.

Yet here they were.

And then there were two.

They walked up the steps of the brownstone in silence. When they reached the top, she dug in her purse for her keys, then forced herself to look at him, her pulse quickening.

"Well, thanks for walking me home. I hope you had fun with my friends."

"Are you crazy? How could I not? I had a fantastic time."

She swallowed. "Good. Okay then, I guess I'm going in now. It was very kind of you to walk me home."

"It's easy to be kind to someone like you." He leaned close and kissed her on the cheek, but once he'd done so, he didn't move. Instead, he lingered there, and she felt the heat of his breath against her neck.

"Can I walk you up?" he whispered.

She shook her head. "I don't think that's a good idea."

"You're so beautiful." He lightly kissed her neck.

"Reid, please don't," she whispered back.

Leaning his body against hers, he put a hand behind her head and began to smooth her hair. "Please? I've never met anyone like you before."

She closed her eyes. His touch felt so warm, but she couldn't let him walk her upstairs.

"I can't."

"Why not?"

"Do I really have to say it?" She kept her eyes closed.

"I'm so attracted to you, I can't help myself. You're driving me crazy." He kissed her neck again, and she tried not to think about how good it felt to be treated like this.

She opened her eyes and looked at him. "Why do you like me, Reid?"

He laughed. "I don't know, there's just something about you. Is that so hard to believe? I haven't been able to stop thinking about you, Kat. From the first night we met."

I haven't been able to stop thinking about you. For as long as Katrina could remember, she'd wished someone would say those words to her. And now someone had.

Someone smart.

And interesting.

And attractive.

And married.

Why did he have to be married?

He spoke softly into her ear. "You're sweet and innocent and kind, and by coming to New York like you did, you've reminded me what it's like to be spontaneous and just have *fun,* to let loose and enjoy life. Is that so wrong?"

She shook her head slowly.

"Please . . ." he said again. He slipped his hands around her lower back and pulled her against him.

Brittany's words rang in her ears. *Poor guy is miserable*, she'd said.

He was kissing her neck again, breathing heavily now.

Was he really serious about being unable to stop thinking about her? About enjoying life again because of *her*?

She couldn't get involved with a married man, but maybe he was planning to leave his wife.

Was that what was going on?

Finally, she kissed him back. When their lips met she felt a jolt of heat spread through her body, and her knees almost buckled.

Stop! a voice in the back of her head yelled, yanking her to her senses.

She forced herself to push him away. "I'm sorry. I can't do this. Not yet."

"Yes, you can."

"I think you should go now."

"I'm crazy about you," he whispered. "Please don't make me go home."

"It's wrong . . . I can't."

He nuzzled her neck again. She felt another spark at the contact.

"I'm sorry. I . . . I can't . . . I have to go inside. Good-bye, Reid." She unlocked the door, then hurried inside and ran up the stairs without looking back.

Chapter Nine

"Oh my God, Deb, I kissed him."

"The married guy?"

"Yes."

"When?"

Katrina pressed a palm against her forehead as she walked along the waterfront. "Last night. I totally kissed him. Am I a horrible person? Oh my God, I'm a horrible person." She glanced around to make sure no one could hear her.

"Calm down, calm down. What happened exactly?"

Katrina relayed the day's events: the soccer game, the pickle-backs, the kiss at the front stoop, everything.

"Wait a minute. *You* played soccer?"

She kicked a pebble. "Yes. I can barely move today. But yes."

"Wow. You really are a different person out there, aren't you? First changing your name and then painting, and now playing sports and kissing married men. I can hardly keep up with the new you."

"Are you trying to be funny? I'm stressing out here, you know." She looked out at the Hudson River and wondered how cold the water was.

"Relax. You just kissed him. It's not like you're sleeping with him. You don't plan to do *that*, do you?"

Katrina shook her head. "*No*. Definitely not. I don't even want to see him again."

"Then stop beating yourself up. You had too many drinks and you kissed someone you shouldn't have kissed. We've all done that. It hardly makes you a horrible person."

"Are you sure? I feel pretty awful right now."

"Believe me, you're not. You're a good person, Katrina . . . or Kat, or whoever the hell you are."

Katrina couldn't help but laugh. "Maybe I should go back to Katrina. *Kat* is getting me into trouble."

"The Kat thing is working fine for me. Just tell her to watch her alcohol intake."

"Believe me, I will."

"Hey, I've got to run now. Have a conference call in a half hour that I'm woefully unprepared for. Talk to you later?"

"Sure. Thanks, Deb."

"Anytime, *Kat*."

Katrina tucked her phone into her pocket, then began pumping her arms to step up her pace. Regardless of how she was feeling inside, it was a beautiful day outside, so despite her aching muscles she'd decided to go for a walk on the west side of town. She'd just checked out Chelsea Piers on the West Side Highway esplanade and was now making her way toward the High Line, an abandoned elevated train track that had been converted into a public park.

When she reached the entrance, she climbed the stairs and headed south along the walkway. She wasn't moving very fast, but it felt good to loosen up her sore legs. She was eager to see the bustling streets of Manhattan from a different angle, hoping a new perspective might help her come to terms with her conflicted emotions. She'd spent last night tossing and turning, glad she'd sent Reid home but feeling terrible about having kissed him, however fleetingly.

She also felt terrible about how *good* the kiss had felt.

How good the attention had felt.

She briefly covered her eyes with her hand and sighed.

Yes, she knew it could have been worse—much, much worse—but still, she shouldn't have done anything at all.

I feel so guilty.

Although I'm not married, right?

Is guilty even the right word?

Whatever she was feeling, it wasn't good.

Life can get so complicated.

As she watched the scenery unfold beneath her feet, each block revealing a secret window into life on the streets below, she pushed Reid from her mind and began to focus on the week ahead. There were so many things she wanted to see, and with each passing day the list only seemed to grow.

She'd also decided to paint more.

After a visit to the Tenement Museum Saturday afternoon, she'd stumbled upon a tiny art gallery tucked between two hole-in-the wall restaurants on the Lower East Side. In the window hung a small painting of a single vibrant yellow tulip sprouting from a chipped clay flowerpot. It was a simple image, but she had been struck by the contrast of old and new—and found it beautiful, much like the church she'd seen next to Stuyvesant Square. As she peered through the window, she'd felt a pang of longing and thought *I could paint that.* Deep down, she'd always wondered what it would feel like to see her own artwork on display in a gallery, out there for anyone to enjoy—or critique—a tiny piece of herself to be shared with the universe.

Then another thought had occurred to her.

If that were ever going to happen, she'd have to actually *paint something.*

* * *

Nearly an hour later, Katrina was two blocks from home, her hands on her hips, her breath a little uneven from all the exercise. She hadn't eaten anything before leaving her apartment, and when her stomach began to growl, she was glad she'd tucked a twenty-dollar bill into her pocket. She bought a newspaper from the old man at the kiosk, then walked over to the coffeehouse.

Justin was alone behind the counter when she entered.

"Hey, Kat. Working out again?" He jogged in place.

She held up her arms and pretended to show off her biceps. "Yeah, can you believe it? I played soccer for the first time yesterday, and now I just went on a brisk walk. Toss in two yoga classes since Friday, and that's more exercise than I've had in the past year. I can't believe I'm still in one piece."

"It suits you. You've got a nice rosy glow going on."

She put her hands up to her cheeks, which felt hot, and did a little curtsy. "Why, thank you."

"Skim latte and a blueberry scone?" he asked.

"Actually, I was thinking I might do something different today."

He raised his eyebrows. "Really?"

She looked up at the chalkboard. "I was thinking about going for something a little more on the hearty side. Maybe one of your breakfast sandwiches."

"Hearty? You looking to beef up now that you've become an athlete?"

"I've got a bit of a hangover. I thought that might help."

"Big night last night?"

"Big afternoon. Beers after the soccer game turned into an all-day affair. My neighbors are crazy. Shots, pitchers, the whole deal. I couldn't keep up with them. I hope I didn't say anything I'm going to regret."

"Too much truth serum?"

She laughed. "I've never heard it called that before, but it sounds pretty accurate." If he only knew how her day had ended.

He scratched the back of his head. "I can't do the marathon-drinking thing anymore. When I was in my twenties, I could go all night, but somewhere along the way, I lost the talent for going non-stop. I can *go*, but now I have to *stop* pretty soon thereafter."

"I never had that talent at all." She pressed her palms against her temples. "I wish I hadn't caved to the peer pressure. My head would be feeling so much better right now." She also wouldn't feel so tormented by that kiss, which she was quite sure never would have happened if she'd been sober.

"I learned a long time ago to ignore peer pressure. Too danger-ous." He gestured around the room. "I can't be dragging if I want to keep growing my businesses."

She titled her head to one side. "Your businesses?"

He tapped his palm on the counter. "This one, for example."

"You manage this place?"

"I own it."

"You *own* this place?"

"Sure do."

She was stunned. And embarrassed. "Do you . . . own the other one too?"

"Which one?"

"The one on the Upper West Side."

He nodded. "Yep."

"Gosh. I had no idea, Justin. You once said something about get-ting in trouble with the boss, so I just assumed . . ."

He gave her a sly smile. "I was probably just kidding around when I said that. So all this time you've thought I was a career barista, slogging aimlessly through life?"

She felt her cheeks turning red. "Hey now, don't go putting thoughts into my head. *Slogging* is a pretty strong word. Is it even a word?"

He laughed. "It's okay. If I were you, I probably would have thought the same thing at the sight of a thirty-seven-year-old man making cappuccinos day after day. Or, in your case, skim lattes. The truth is, I have an MBA, but I didn't like wearing a suit and tie every day, so I chose a career in which that's not required. Now what can I get you?"

She began to read the chalkboard but stopped halfway up and looked at him.

"Wait a minute. You asked me *which one.*"

"Huh?"

"When I asked if you owned the other coffeehouse, you said *which one.* Do you own others too?"

"Other coffeehouses? No."

"Do you own other businesses?"

He pointed back up at the chalkboard. "We can talk about that another time. Now are you going to order a breakfast sandwich or what?"

Before she could reply, he twisted his wedding ring, then nodded toward the back door. "Listen, I've got to run out to an appointment. April will take care of you, okay?" He pointed toward a barista Katrina had never seen before. She looked about the same age as Peter.

"Okay, sure. Thanks, Justin."

"Congratulations, by the way," he said.

"Congratulations?"

"On changing your order. I know that wasn't easy for you."

He smiled, then turned and walked out the back door.

Katrina couldn't help but wonder where he was going.

Chapter Ten

Katrina spent the next two weeks immersed in a frenzy of sightseeing—and studiously avoiding both her job search *and* a conversation with her mother. She also didn't hear from Reid, which allowed her to focus on wholeheartedly embracing her inner tourist. She dutifully crossed many of the *must-sees* off her list.

Empire State Building, check.

Museum of Modern Art, check.

Times Square, check.

Rockefeller Center, check.

She also managed to plow through a number of Justin's suggestions, which—if she were honest with herself—she enjoyed more than the standard guidebook fare. It surprised her to realize that when she ventured into lesser-known territory—be it for a slice of pizza in Queens or a stroll through an obscure museum in Harlem—she felt as though she had been given access to the *real* New York, the side most visitors never see, and she loved that. Plus she kept stumbling upon hidden gems all on her own, which she found just as exhilarating. A tiny art gallery here, a used bookstore there, a mom-and-pop ice-cream shop around the corner—it was all magical to her.

One of her favorite spots turned out to be Chelsea Market, where she found a vintage black cocktail dress and enjoyed the best peanut-butter cookie she'd ever tasted. As she walked home that day, carrying her shopping bag like a real New Yorker on her way home from work, she felt like pinching herself to make sure this was really her life.

Her fitness was improving too. She had attended several more of Shana's evening yoga classes, and one day she rented a bike and pedaled up the West Side Highway to the Cloisters museum—though her legs were so tired by the time she got there that she ended up riding the subway home, bike in tow. She even went for a thirty-minute walk/jog, although it was about twenty minutes of walk and only ten minutes of jog. Still, she was proud of those ten minutes. The regular exercise was beginning to make her feel stronger and healthier—and it gave her the stamina to keep plowing through her list—her endless list—of things to see and do in New York.

She also continued to paint. Every few days she found herself inspired by something she'd seen during one of her walks or sightseeing ventures, and she'd often return later with her easel and a fresh canvas. Before she knew it, she'd completed three more paintings. When she lined them up against the blank wall of her bedroom one evening, she immediately noticed a pattern she hadn't intended: none of the images included a well-known building or monument, and all of them featured a contrast of some sort.

A shiny pair of pink galoshes on a dusty front stoop.

A crisp stack of newspapers neatly tucked against the chipped paint of a kiosk.

Bright-white curtains peeking out of a rain-splattered windowpane.

Katrina didn't know why she was drawn to this approach, or what it meant, but she tried not to think too much about it. Instead, she did her best to follow her artistic intuition and enjoy the new-found feeling of stimulation that came with it.

She was painting!

What she *wasn't* doing was working on her résumé. Or her LinkedIn profile. Or her job search. The acquaintances her mother had suggested she contact hadn't replied to her e-mails yet, and while she knew she should reach out again, she just . . . didn't.

One Thursday evening, after a marathon outing during which she'd ridden the ferry to and from Staten Island, seen the Wall Street bull, visited the 9/11 Memorial, *and* covered what felt like a dozen miles on foot, popping in and out of art galleries and boutiques, she arrived home exhausted. As she peeled off her shirt and tossed it in the general direction of the hamper, she looked around the bedroom and realized she hadn't cleaned the apartment in more than a week. At home, she scrubbed her place every Sunday afternoon, whether it needed it or not. Part of her was upset that she had let things slide without even noticing—but a bigger part of her wasn't.

She glanced at the hamper, which was surrounded by a small pile of clothes that had somehow missed their target.

She smiled to herself.

It was just a pile of clothes.

But it was also more than that.

Her phone rang from the living room. When she went to pick it up, she grimaced at the name on the display.

Mom.

She debated whether or not to answer. She'd already answered an earlier text her mother had sent requesting an update on the job search—in that reply, she'd promised to send an update "soon," without being more specific than that. Katrina could tell by the tone of her mother's texts that she was disappointed in her daughter's recent lack of effort. In her mother's mind, Katrina was being selfish and letting both her parents down, and she wasn't hiding how she felt.

Katrina set down the phone without answering it and walked back into the bedroom. She glanced at her laptop on the desk but didn't approach it. Instead, she opened a drawer and pulled out some workout clothes, suddenly in the mood to take a yoga class despite her fatigue.

On the way out the door, she took one last look at her laptop and decided she'd e-mail those women again when she got home.

And work on her résumé.

And perhaps tidy up the apartment.

Then, maybe, she'd get back to her mother.

* * *

"Hey, lady," Shana whispered as Katrina entered the studio. "Gracie and I are going for a bite after class. Want to join us?"

Katrina looked around the room. "Grace is taking a yoga class?"

Shana stifled a laugh. "Now *that* would be a sight: Grace 'I hate yoga' Fong finally joining me for a session. No, she's meeting me afterward at Beyond Sushi on Fourteenth. You should come with us."

Katrina felt her shoulders stiffen. "I'd like to, but I've got to work on my job search tonight. I've been neglecting it, and it's catching up with me."

"Are you sure? Gracie finally got her first retail order today, so we're going to celebrate."

"She did? That's wonderful."

"Isn't it? I'm thrilled for her. Are you sure you can't join us? I know it would mean a lot to her. Plus this place has super-yummy spider rolls."

Katrina frowned. "My mom is sort of on my back for slacking off, and now I'm feeling really guilty. I'm sorry."

"I understand."

"You do?"

"More than you know." Shana squeezed Katrina's shoulder and smiled, then walked to the front of the room. She lit a candle and sat down cross-legged on her mat.

Katrina closed her eyes and tried to relax as Shana began to speak.

"I was on the Lower East Side the other day and came upon some construction that was blocking the sidewalk. I wasn't really in a hurry but was still slightly annoyed to have to make a detour, which I imagine is a pretty typical response for a New Yorker, even a yoga teacher. But when I switched to the other side of the street, the most amazing thing happened. I saw this tiny little storefront I'd never noticed before."

Katrina nodded slightly as she thought of how much she enjoyed stumbling upon little stores and boutiques not found in any guidebook, of how much she'd come to treasure the list Justin had written for her.

Shana continued. "The shop was adorable, but I'd never noticed it because for some reason I never walk on that side of the street when I'm in that neighborhood. And until then, I hadn't even realized I had a routine in that neighborhood. The windows were decorated with pretty lace curtains and a gorgeous display of candles and crystals, so I decided to go inside. The owner immediately approached me to welcome me to her store. She was this tiny old woman who wanted to know all about me, and when I told her I was a yoga instructor, you should have seen her eyes light up. She said she'd once been a yoga teacher as well. Then she put her arm around me and led me to the back of the store. She handed me a CD to play in class and refused any kind of payment. When I asked why, she said it was her gift to *me* for sharing *my* gift with my students, and that she was honored I'd chosen to visit her shop."

Katrina felt a little shiver down her spine.

"I didn't have the heart to tell her I'd stumbled across her store by accident, and I certainly didn't feel right leaving without buying something, so I bought the candle I'm burning right now. Then, when I got home later, I listened to the CD, not sure what to expect." Shana giggled. "The music was so gentle, so soothing, so *perfect* for me that it almost made me cry. I'm going to play it during class today, and I hope you will enjoy it as much as I did." She stood up and walked over to the stereo. "That little old lady's simple act of kindness had a profound impact on me, and I only met her because I took a tiny detour across the street. So today I'd like you to think about how *wonderful* things can result from the slightest changes in our routines, the result of the smallest wrinkles in our plans. Now let's meet in downward dog pose."

As she moved into downward dog and began to stretch her legs, Katrina thought of her own routines.

Her lists.

Her structure.

Her expectations.

After class, Katrina sat quietly by herself until the other students had left, then rolled up her mat and walked over to where Shana was putting away the candle. She tapped her on the shoulder.

"I've changed my mind about sushi. Count me in."

Shana's eyes brightened. "Nice!"

"Shana, you went over again." The sound of a woman's voice made them both turn their heads. Blair, in her standard black yoga gear and bun, was standing at the door. Her thin arms were crossed in front of her, a frown on her face.

Shana closed the cabinet door and hurried over to the broom closet. "I'm so sorry, Blair. I'll get the floor swept right away."

* * *

"Do you even *want* to be an accountant again when you go home?" Shana asked Katrina as she dipped a pot sticker in soy sauce.

"It's more complicated than that," Katrina said.

"No it's not." Grace stabbed a piece of spider roll with a chopstick and popped it into her mouth.

Shana pointed at the chopstick. "Are you *ever* going to learn how to use those?"

Grace shrugged as she chomped. "I'm a disgrace to my Chinese heritage. What can I say?"

"The thing is, I don't know how to do anything else," Katrina said.

"So?" Grace said. "You could learn."

"But I don't know what else I'd even *want* to do."

"What about painting?" Shana said. "You seem to really love that."

Katrina smiled weakly. "I do, but I'm not very good at it."

"Yes you are, Kat," Shana said. "You're *very* good at it."

"Thanks for saying that, but I don't know the first thing about how to sell paintings. Like zero."

Grace speared another spider roll. "You think I know a damned thing about how to sell jewelry? I'm literally flying by the seat of my pants."

"And I've only been teaching yoga for like a year," Shana said. "I waitressed before that. And my degree was in drama."

"You two make it sound so easy," Katrina said. "But you don't know my mother."

"We've already been down the demanding-mother road," Grace said. "I beat you." She tapped her temple with a chopstick. "It's all up here. *That's* what's holding you back, Kitty Kat."

Shana put a finger to her chin. "Hmm . . . I like that. I may have to use it in one of my classes."

"Don't forget to cite me as the source. Chinese wisdom, you know." Grace bowed her head.

Katrina sighed. "Do you think I could put you two on the phone the next time my mother calls?"

"I don't pick up when mine calls," Grace said. "That works just fine for me."

Katrina didn't feel like talking—or even thinking—any more about her mother right then, so she redirected the conversation. "You were right about that Blair," she said to Shana. "She's kind of scary."

"I know, right?" Shana's shoulders slumped just slightly. "Kind of an energy vampire."

"Who's Blair?" Grace asked.

"The owner of the studio," Shana said.

"Oh, you mean Cruella de Vil?" Grace stuck out her tongue. "Total witch."

Katrina nearly choked on her salmon roll. "Oh my gosh, she *does* look a little like Cruella de Vil! I feel so mean for saying so, but it's true."

"From the stories I've heard, *I* sure as hell don't feel mean for saying so," Grace said. "After sweeping up the studio, that woman could fly out of there on her own broom."

Shana put a hand on Grace's arm. "Be nice, Gracie. That's my boss you're talking about."

"Since when are bosses off limits? Besides, that woman is horrible to you. I don't know why you still work for her."

"What else am I supposed to do? Go back to waitressing? The theater thing clearly isn't working out, and I need to pay my bills somehow. It's not like I have a lot of options right now."

Grace pointed a fork at her. "Too bad you don't have any *stock* options. Then you could tell that bag of bones what to do with her scrawny ass."

Katrina laughed and gestured to Grace. "I still can't wrap my head around how such vulgar comments come out of someone who looks like a porcelain doll."

Grace shrugged. "You should hear my sister. I'm the nice one."

* * *

When Katrina got home later that night, she sat down at her laptop to follow up with her mother's contacts. Regardless of where her heart lay, she had to be practical and plant some seeds. She hoped that sending out some résumés, maybe even setting up a couple of phone interviews, would ease the creeping sense of anxiety she'd begun to feel whenever she thought about the future. Like Shana, she knew it was important to have options.

Chapter Eleven

Before Katrina knew it, another Saturday morning had rolled around. She got up early, bought her *New York Times* from the little man at the kiosk, and walked over to the coffeehouse. The weather had grown noticeably colder, and she wished she'd worn a scarf. Maybe she'd take a stroll through the Village later and buy a cute knitted one from a street vendor.

Inside the coffeehouse, she didn't see Justin or Peter anywhere. April was behind the counter, playing with her phone. Though she greeted Katrina with a friendly smile as she approached, she didn't seem interested in chitchatting.

"Good morning. What can I get you?"

Katrina looked up at the menu board, then glanced at the glass canisters on the counter. She pointed to a tray of muffins topped by a glass cover. "Are those good?"

April smiled. "Delicious. They're chock full of fat, but they're to die for, especially the poppy-seed ones."

"Okay, I'll try one. And I think I'll have a hot chocolate too. Large, please."

"Sure thing."

As April rang up her order, Katrina smiled to herself.

It's amazing how good little changes can feel.

She took the muffin and hot chocolate to her favorite table and began reading the paper. Soon she was swept away in a story about yet another corruption case in New York's state government, which seemed to produce an endless supply of scandals from both sides of the political aisle. Self-proclaimed righteous candidates who rode into office on promises of reform . . . then were tossed out on their backsides, facing bribery charges.

Katrina frowned at the paper.

They all pretend to be something they're not.

"Penny for your thoughts?"

She looked up and saw Justin standing there. "Huh?" She blinked.

"Wow. You were really gone there, and scowling a bit as well." He took a seat. "You okay?"

She blinked again. Had she been scowling? "Just have a lot on my mind, I guess."

He chuckled. "Talk about stating the obvious. Anything you'd like to talk about?"

She didn't reply.

He waved a hand in front of her. "Earth to Katrina . . ."

She took a deep breath, then looked him in the eye. "Was it hard for you to . . . um . . . pursue a nontraditional career?"

"Hard for me how?"

She swallowed. "I mean, it's clearly worked out for you, but were your parents ever disappointed that you didn't take the safe road? You know, do the corporate thing?"

He laughed. "My dad's a cardiologist and my mom's a partner in a law firm. What do *you* think?"

"So I can take that as a yes?"

"You can take that as a yes."

"How did you deal with it?"

He shrugged. "To be honest, I didn't feel like I had a choice. After business school, I got a good job at a management consulting firm, but despite all the perks, from the minute I walked into my office, I knew that life wasn't for me. It was just too . . . confining. And every time I met with a big client to discuss how to grow their business, I felt like a phony because I wanted to be building something of my *own*, not helping some faceless organization figure out how to make more millions. And I didn't want to have to wear a suit to do it. One day I remember thinking I was either going to suffocate in my tie or hang myself with it. I didn't last long in corporate America after that."

"Well, I for one am glad you didn't hang yourself. I wish I had your conviction."

"You're a smart cookie. You'll figure it out. I'm not worried about you."

"Thanks, Justin. I really appreciate how nice you always are to me."

"It's my pleasure. You're good people, and I like good people."

She blushed. "Thank you."

"I like good people, and I'm also good at *reading* people, and you looked like you needed to talk, so here we are, talking." He discreetly cocked his head in the direction of a woman seated at a table across the room and lowered his voice. "For example, I can read *her* too."

Katrina lowered her voice too. "Her *what*?"

"Every time she comes in here, she orders a cappuccino. Today, however, she ordered a *skim* cappuccino. From that, I'm inferring she's trying to lose a few pounds."

Katrina wrinkled her nose. The woman looked at least thirty pounds overweight, if not more. "That fairly obvious observation makes you good at reading people?"

Justin smiled and scratched the top of his head. "If it gets you to tell me what's bothering you, then yes."

She narrowed her eyes at him. "Are you this nice to all your customers?"

"No."

"You're lying."

"Yes."

She laughed. "Okay, okay. If you must know, I'm a little anxious about my job search."

"You're looking for work?"

"In theory, yes."

He cocked his head toward the counter. "Ever made a latte?"

She smiled. "I'm more of a numbers person."

"What kind of job are you looking for?"

"Accounting."

"You don't sound very excited about it. I believe I just heard a sigh."

"Excited about accounting, or about looking for a job?"

"Both of the above."

She made a sheepish face. "Is it that obvious?"

"You want an honest answer?"

"Of course."

"Judging by how you're acting right now, I think you'd be happier making lattes."

She frowned. "I fear you might be right, but I don't have much of a choice."

He stood up and squeezed her shoulder. "You always have a choice, Kat."

* * *

Later that morning, Katrina was on her way to Shana's ten o'clock class when her phone rang. She caught her breath when she saw the name on the display.

Reid.

She hadn't heard from him in weeks.

She didn't think she'd ever hear from him again.

She looked up at the darkening sky, then answered—with zero plan, this time, for how to act.

"Hi, Reid."

"Hey, stranger. How are you doing?"

"I'm doing well, thanks." She knew her voice sounded strained, but she couldn't help it.

"Still breaking hearts all over town?"

She didn't respond.

What should she say to that?

What *could* she say?

"Kat, you still there?" he said.

"Still here. I'm about to go to a yoga class."

"What are you doing after yoga? Do you have plans you can't break?"

She glanced up at the sky again. It was definitely going to rain. "Why do you ask?"

"Can I interest you in a matinee later?"

"A movie?" She hadn't thought about going to a movie, but a theater would be nice and dry, that was for sure. But she didn't want to go to a movie with Reid—that was also for sure. She didn't want to go anywhere with Reid.

"I was thinking more like *The Book of Mormon*."

She stopped walking. "*The Book of Mormon*? As in in the smash Broadway musical?"

"Yep. You interested?"

She hesitated.

"Do you have tickets? Isn't that show sold out like forever?" she asked.

"I have two incredible seats if I want them. I have a connection through work. The window is closing though. I need to get back to him by eleven or he's giving them to someone else."

She thought about it for a moment. She knew she shouldn't even be considering seeing him, but seeing *The Book of Mormon* with him was another story. And seeing a Broadway show was certainly on her to-do list. How could she turn this down? It was nearly impossible to get tickets, and those that were available were way out of her budget.

"I don't know, Reid."

"Just say yes. We'll have a blast."

She didn't respond.

"Snow White?" he said.

"Why don't you go with your wife?"

"Don't ask me that. Will you come?"

She squeezed her eyes shut. Why did it have to be so complicated?

"Can I think about it?"

"How long do you need?"

"My class starts in a few minutes. Can I let you know afterward?"

"Sure."

* * *

Shana smiled as she lit a candle, then sat down in the front of the room and inhaled deeply. She briefly pressed her palms together, then began to read from a small notebook as the students closed their eyes.

"From when we're little kids, we learn how important it is to say *no*. No to drugs. No to cigarettes. No to strangers. No, no, no. But what about learning to say *yes*?"

Katrina opened her eyes. Had Shana been reading her mind?

Shana continued. "I had a roommate in college who always assumed the worst about people. I could never understand why, but from the get-go, she would think they were trying to con her, or cheat her, or take advantage of her in some way. She was a nice person, a *kind* person, but it took forever to earn her trust, and as a result, she had few friends. She worked hard in school and has a good job now, but she doesn't have much joy in her life. She's very good at saying *no*, but she never learned how to say *yes*. Yes to new experiences. Yes to friendly yet unfamiliar faces. Yes to leaving Ohio. Yes to the *unknown*. She's built a safe little world for herself, and she's *existing* just fine, but in my opinion she's not really *living*. And for that I feel sorry for her."

Katrina shifted on her mat. How did Shana do it? How did she always know?

"I'm not saying we need to jump blindly into every opportunity that comes our way, but I think it's important to have an open mind. Don't judge a person or a situation on its face, because you just might be wrong. And if you're wrong, you might be missing out on something amazing."

Shana closed her notebook and set it on the small table beside her.

"Now let's all meet in downward-facing dog."

* * *

After class, as she waited outside the studio for Shana, Katrina called Reid.

"I'll go."

"Excellent. I'll pick you up in a cab at one thirty."

"Okay, see you then."

"You'll see who when?"

As she clicked off her phone, Katrina saw Shana walking up to her.

"Reid. Remember the guy who met us at Whiskey Tavern after soccer?"

"Oh yes, of course. How's he doing?"

"He's good, I guess. Haven't seen him in a while. He just invited me to the matinee of *The Book of Mormon*."

Shana's face tightened for a split second at the mention of the show, but her grimace was quickly replaced by a smile, albeit a stiff one. "That sounds fun. I've heard it's an amazing production."

Katrina put a hand on Shana's arm. "I'm sure you'll get your big break one day."

"I think that ship may have sailed, but thanks, Kat. It's nice of you to say it."

"I truly think your day will come. How could it not? You're a natural in front of an audience."

"That's in a yoga class. On a big stage . . . let's just say it's a different story. Want to grab a bite? I'm starving." Shana started walking.

"Sure. Where should we go?"

"There's this great coffeehouse not too far from our place. You'll love it."

Katrina looked sideways at her. "That place with the big cup on the sign but no name?"

"You know it?"

"I'm sort of a regular there. I stumbled across it when I first got here, and I've been in there nearly every day since. I had breakfast there this morning. I still don't know what it's called though."

Shana shrugged. "I just call it the coffeehouse. Josh and I go there all the time. I love their scones."

"Blueberry?'

Shana shook her head. "Plain. Always plain."

By the time they reached the coffeehouse, it had begun to rain. They hurried inside and got in line.

"So what's the deal with this Reid?" Shana asked.

Katrina looked at her. "What do you mean?"

"I *mean*, what's the deal? He's married, right?"

"Yes."

"But you like him?"

"Sort of. Is it that obvious?"

"A little. He's very cute. Is he happily married?"

"I don't think so. But it shouldn't matter, should it? He's *married*."

Shana squeezed her hand. "I'm sorry, Kat."

"Thanks. We're going to be friends. It's fine. Just a little awkward at the moment."

"Sometimes life is just . . . *complicated*, isn't it?"

"I'm learning that."

"Hey, speaking of complicated, we're taking Gracie to Molly's tonight if you want to join us."

"Who's Molly?"

"Molly's is a pub over on Third."

"Oh. Is that why it's complicated? Because it sounds like a person's apartment?"

Shana shook her head. "It's complicated because Gracie and her pretend boyfriend sort of broke up, so we're taking her out for drinks to cheer her up."

"Pretend boyfriend? You mean the married guy?"

"Huh?" Shana looked confused.

"That's what she called him."

"He's not married."

"He's not?" Now Katrina looked confused.

"No. I'll let her tell you the story. Anyhow, Josh and I are taking her out to keep her spirits up, especially since she's having such a rough time with her jewelry. Things have stalled a bit since that first order came through."

"That's nice of you."

"It's the least I can do. She's been there for me after many a failed audition, tissues in hand. She acts tough, but she's a softy underneath."

Katrina nodded. "Yeah. She gave me one of her necklaces the day after I met her. I was so surprised."

"Yep, that's Gracie. So anyhow, I hope you can meet up with us tonight."

"I can't promise anything, but I'll do my best."

A man's voice interrupted their conversation. "Well, if it isn't two of my favorite customers, one of them back for the second time before noon. You two know each other?"

Katrina and Shana turned to face the counter.

"Hi, Justin," Shana said. "You know Kat?"

Justin smiled. "I know everyone who comes in here. Hi again, Kat." He gave her a friendly nod. "It never fails—a city of eight million people, and yet it somehow feels like a small town."

"We live in the same building," Shana said. "She's been taking my classes."

"Ah, yes, yoga. She's told me how much she likes her teacher. I didn't realize she was talking about you though."

Shana looked at Katrina. "You told him about me?"

Katrina blushed. "Maybe."

"You're so sweet."

"What can I get you both?" Justin asked.

"Just a large orange juice for me," Katrina said.

"I'll have my usual," Shana said.

"One large orange juice, one plain scone and a chai tea coming right up," Justin said.

Shana nudged Katrina and pointed to a table by the window. "Want to grab that one over there?"

Katrina nodded toward the exit. "Do you mind if I get mine to go? I need to get a move on for that matinee."

"Sure, no problem."

"Big plans today?" Justin asked Katrina.

Shana laughed. "Let's just say that it's . . . complicated."

* * *

Right on time, Reid swung by in a cab to pick up Katrina. "Get wet much?" he asked as he held the door open for her from inside.

After a full week of sunshine, it was pouring again.

"This is crazy!" Katrina closed her umbrella, then ducked inside and pulled the door shut behind her. "Does it always rain this hard here? I think I ruined my new boots." She laid the umbrella at her feet, water dripping all over the plastic floor covering.

"They say it's supposed to clear up tonight, but they always say that. There's a reason everyone in New York has ten umbrellas and at least one pair of galoshes."

"I'm learning that."

"Thanks for coming. It's really good to see you again," Reid said with what she now thought of as his trademark grin. He gave her a quick kiss on the cheek, and she nearly gasped when she saw his left hand.

It was bare.

Oh my gosh.

He's not wearing his wedding ring.

"Are you okay?" he asked. "You look startled."

"Oh no . . . I mean yes, I'm fine."

"It really is good to see you again."

She gave him a weak smile, stunned.

Does this mean what I think it means?

The cab dropped them off at the Eugene O'Neill Theatre on Forty-Ninth and Broadway. A long line snaked all the way down the block, dozens of umbrellas creating a makeshift, multicolored tent with no sides. The crowd was buzzing with energy, and no one seemed the least bit bothered by the weather.

As they made their way to the back of the line, Katrina glanced over at Reid, "Do you like the rain?"

He shrugged. "I don't mind it. I think it's pretty, actually. And I like the sound of it. I find it relaxing."

"What about snow? Do you like snow?"

He shook his head. "Now snow I could do without. Snow ain't so pretty."

"Really? But it's so beautiful in the movies." Katrina had never lived in a place where it snowed, and she'd always wanted to.

"When it first comes down, yes, it's gorgeous. And from a bird's-eye view, it always looks perfect. But when you get up close and see all the dirt, it's not so nice. Once it turns to slush and gets covered with mud and exhaust, it can be downright ugly. The distance hides the reality."

She gave him a curious look.

Was he talking about snow? Or was he talking about his marriage?

She turned her gaze to the street and watched the raindrops dance on the cement before trailing away. The movement was so simple and pure yet hypnotic.

"Kat?" Reid asked.

She looked at him. "I'm sorry. Did you say something?"

He pointed to the line in front of them, which had just started moving toward the theater.

"You ready to do this?"

She smiled. "I am."

* * *

"So what did you think?" Reid asked as they exited the theater.

Katrina lifted three fingers, then switched to just one. "Third best overall musical I've ever seen, but first overall comedy performance."

"You've already positioned it in two categories?"

She nodded, then raised one finger before switching to two. "Best overall was *Les Misérables*. Second was *Phantom of the Opera*. I saw them both in San Francisco. They didn't make me laugh like this one did though. Did you hear that lady behind us snorting?"

He pretended to cough. "I think the whole theater did. I'm surprised no one called security."

"Can you imagine having a laugh like that? I'd be mortified."

"I'm sure her poor husband is. Hey, do you want to grab something to eat? I'm pretty hungry."

Katrina looked at her watch. It was just after four o'clock. "That sounds great. I'm starving. I didn't really eat after yoga." She couldn't bring herself to tell him why, which was that her stomach had been in knots at the prospect of seeing him again. She was dying to know why he wasn't wearing his wedding ring, but she forced herself to be patient. He would tell her when he was ready.

"Do you like seafood? Have you been to Marea?"

She held up four fingers. "I love lobster, crab, mussels, and scallops."

"You like holding up fingers, don't you?"

"I guess I do. I'm a numbers person, remember. But today's the first time I've ever done it."

"Well, I find it very endearing. And there's a first time for everything, right? Let me see if I can get us in for an early dinner on such short notice."

"Is it fancy?"

"Sort of."

"Am I dressed okay?" Under her coat she was wearing a sleeveless black-and-white-striped dress with a pair of knee-high black boots, both of which she'd found at a tiny vintage clothing store on East Seventh. She'd accessorized with a pair of teardrop silver earrings she'd bought from Grace. The outfit was bolder than anything else in her closet, but she loved it.

"You look stunning, as always. You're the fairest one of all, remember?"

As Reid pulled out his phone, she once again noticed his bare ring finger.

Questions fluttered inside her.

Is he really splitting up with his wife?

Is it because of me?

Could he really be my Prince Charming?

She looked up at the bright lights of Broadway all around, soft and hazy in the mist. It had stopped raining, but the sky was still filled with dark storm clouds, waiting to open up again at any moment. It was still afternoon, but it already felt like evening.

Reid hung up and put his phone back in his pocket. "Okay, we're in, but not until five thirty."

"Did you use more connections to get us that reservation?"

"You could say that."

She narrowed her eyes. "Are you in the Mafia?"

He shrugged. "Manhattan is a banker's town. What can I say?"

"It's so different from Silicon Valley. Nearly everyone there works in technology. All you hear when you go out for dinner is people talking about this hot app or that hot start-up, or the latest billionaire CEO who isn't even old enough to rent a car. Nearly everyone here seems to be doing their own thing. I really like that."

"There's a lot to like about New York."

"So I'm learning."

"You said you wanted adventure, right?"

She nodded. "Indeed I did."

"Well, that's what I'm here to provide. Why don't we grab a drink before dinner? I know a good little spot on the way. We could walk there."

"Sure." Despite her wish to be spontaneous, not to mention the giddiness she was feeling at the thought of Reid's being single, she wasn't thrilled about the idea of drinking on an empty stomach. Maybe she would just order a soda. Or would that look too unsophisticated?

He pointed east on Forty-Ninth. "This way, my lady." He put his hand on the small of her back, and though deep down she knew she should push it away, she didn't.

* * *

Marea was located on Central Park South, directly across the street from the park. Katrina tried not to gawk as they entered, but it wasn't easy. Down a step or two to the right was an elegant dining area, with tables covered with crisp white cloths, and dark hardwood floors encircled by an orderly lineup of bold red lamps on shelves set at regular intervals along the walls. The effect was lavish—even magical—but it was the left side of the room that really caught Katrina's attention. Carved out of iridescent, honey-colored onyx, the bar seemed to glow, as if illuminating the room in soft light. The back bar, also onyx, was even more stunning. Etched with thick, wavy lines all the way across, it resembled a gigantic, spectacular golden seashell.

"Wow," Katrina whispered in awe. There weren't many places like this in Mountain View, at least not that she'd had the pleasure of patronizing.

Reid spoke briefly with the hostess. "Table's almost ready. How about a drink while we wait?"

"Sure. That sounds nice." She'd stuck to her guns and ordered a Sprite at the bar they'd just come from, so she figured it would be okay to have a glass of wine, especially at a bar that looked like this one.

Once they'd settled in, the bartender handed each of them a drink menu, then retreated to allow them to peruse their options.

"What's your poison?" Reid asked.

Katrina hesitated, unsure what to order. "What are you having?"

"Scotch on the rocks, my signature." He'd had two of those at the other bar.

She swallowed. Scotch definitely didn't sound like a good idea.

"I think I'll have a glass of wine." She scanned the list for a vintage she recognized, or at least one she could pronounce, but didn't see either. She felt out of her depth. She was back at Soho House all over again.

"Anything catch your eye?" he asked.

She forced a smile and tried to conceal her unease. "Anything white is fine. Why don't you choose one for me? I'm just going to run to the ladies' room."

"You should try the seventy-seven d'Yquem. It's amazing."

She did her best to look confident despite having absolutely no idea what that was. "That sounds lovely, thank you." As she walked toward the restrooms she observed the well-heeled clientele and felt a pang of longing for the low-key ambience of the East Village. Would she ever feel comfortable dining in places like this? Would New York help her grow into that type of person?

Did she want it to?

When she returned a few minutes later, Reid was chatting with the bartender. As she took a seat, he handed her a goblet of wine, then pointed to his own nearly empty glass, indicating that he was ready for another. The bartender nodded and moved away to fix him a fresh drink.

Reid grinned at her. "I love Lagavulin."

"You love what?"

"Lagavulin. It's a single-malt scotch."

She smiled and nodded, insecurity continuing to nip at her heels. She'd never heard of Lagavulin, yet more evidence of her lack of sophistication. "As you can probably guess, I'm not very familiar with scotch." She took a sip of her wine and willed herself to stop feeling so self-conscious.

Reid finished his drink and set the empty glass on the bar. "That's because you're new in town. As I'm sure you've observed, that's what people do in New York. We drink. It's how life works here."

"What do you mean?"

He reached for the full glass and began using it as a prop. "Allow me to explain. In the winter, when it's too freezing to go outside, everyone hunkers down in a bar and bitches about the cold weather—*and drinks*. Then in the summer, when it's crazy humid out, everyone hunkers down in a bar and bitches about the hot weather—*and drinks*. And then when it's nice in the fall and the spring, when it's beautiful outside, everyone wants to sit in the sun and enjoy the fabulous weather—*over a drink*."

She couldn't help but laugh. "Is that so?"

"Oh it is very much so. You've only been here a few weeks, but you'll see. We'll get you yet."

She wasn't sure how to respond, so she just nodded. She couldn't deny that a lot of her new friends spent much of their free time in bars, but that couldn't possibly hold true for everyone, could it?

Would she ever get used to the New York way of doing things?

The hostess appeared and gestured toward the dining room. "Mr. Hanson, your table is ready." She pointed at Katrina's nearly full wineglass. "Let me carry that for you."

Reid polished off his scotch in one smooth swig and set the empty glass on the bar. Then he slipped his hand around Katrina's waist and led her to their table.

* * *

Their dinner conversation provided Katrina with a glimpse into life in the upper echelons of Manhattan. Reid was a great storyteller and enjoyed sharing the shenanigans of his outrageously wealthy colleagues, especially the drunken antics of Ryder from Soho House. Exclusive parties, strip clubs, high-stakes poker games, private jets. Luxury and extravagance dripping from the walls, illicit activity tucked around every corner. Reid was clearly in his element revealing the dark underbelly of the investment banking world to a wide-eyed outsider.

"He really flew all of his friends to Barbados for his thirtieth birthday? I can't imagine how much that must have cost." Katrina was awed but also overwhelmed by the world he was describing. His life was so different from her own, like something she'd seen only in movies.

Reid shrugged. "It was a drop in the bucket for him. His wife probably spends more than that each year on jewelry." He sipped his scotch and gave Katrina an inquisitive look. "What about you? Did you have any interesting coworkers at the advertising agency? Is it anything like *Mad Men*?"

She scooped a bite of panna cotta with her spoon and shook her head. "Our firm was nothing like that show, not even close. I wouldn't last a week in an office like that."

"So no three-martini lunches?"

She smiled. "Not in the accounting department, that's for sure."

"Damn. No chain smoking either?"

"Not allowed in the building."

"No dirty deeds in the break room? Or getting busy with the hot secretary on the desk? Give me *something*, please."

Katrina laughed and reached for her water glass. "Sorry, but no. Besides, no one has a secretary anymore."

"You're killing me." He looked disappointed. "So what have you been up to since we last hung out? I feel like I haven't seen you in ages."

"Sightseeing, mostly. I'll probably never get through my list, but I'm doing my best. I've also been doing a lot of aimless exploring . . . and painting."

He raised his eyebrows. "Painting?"

She took a sip of wine and nodded. "I used to paint when I was younger, but then for some reason I just . . . stopped. And now I guess I've started again." She smiled as she realized how good it felt to say the words out loud. When it came down to it, it really was that simple. She'd stopped, and now she'd started again.

"What do you paint?"

"Nothing too complicated, and not what I would have expected, given that I'm in New York City. I've found myself drawn to subjects a little . . . off the beaten path, you could say."

"I like to think *I'm* a little off your beaten path."

She blushed and looked down. "Maybe."

"I love what you're doing with your life right now. I wish I had that freedom."

She kept her eyes on the table. The way he was talking to her, the way he seemed so *interested* in her, it made her feel as if . . . as if he really cared about her.

Just as she'd felt that night at Soho House.

She closed her eyes for a moment.

It was almost as if . . . as if he weren't married.

Is this really happening?

"You okay there, Snow White?"

She opened her eyes. He was giving her a strange look.

"I'm fine, thanks. I think I'm just a little tired."

"There's no time to be tired in New York, and especially not on a Saturday night. It's still early."

Katrina swallowed, suddenly nervous about what might happen later. She looked around the room and decided to change the subject. "This restaurant is gorgeous. Do you come here a lot?"

Reid shrugged. "Often enough. We rarely go anywhere but downtown for dinner, but if we have to come this way, Marea is the place to be."

She flinched at his use of *we*. All day she'd been wondering why he wasn't wearing his wedding ring. He'd just cracked the door with that comment, so now seemed like as good a time as any to push it open.

Emboldened by the wine, she decided to be direct.

"Where's your wife today?"

"She's visiting her sister in Boston."

"When is she coming back?"

Reid hesitated for a moment, then intensified his gaze as he replied, "I'm not sure yet."

Katrina felt her stomach flip.

"Oh," she whispered.

They're really splitting up.

This is really happening.

Just then the waiter approached to clear their dessert plates. Katrina was grateful for the interruption.

She needed time to think. She excused herself to visit the ladies' room.

As she washed her hands, she had a silent conversation with her reflection in the mirror.

What happens now?

Do I let him kiss me this time?

Or should I just go home?

Maybe I should relax and see how it plays out.

She was thrilled and terrified at the same time. Though she was wildly hopeful about what lay ahead, she wanted to avoid being tormented by any more guilt until there was greater clarity regarding his marital status. So, tempted though she was to succumb to the attraction, she knew the smart thing to do was to say good-night at the end of the evening.

Reid was signing the bill when she returned.

"Hey there. Ready to go?" He finished the last of his drink and grinned at her.

"Sounds good."

As they walked outside, Katrina was surprised to see that the weather had turned pleasant. Maybe she would rally to meet up with Shana and company at the bar after all. Not that she needed any more to drink, but it would be nice to see her friends. It would also be good for her to spend the rest of such a pretty evening somewhere other than her apartment—and with someone other than Reid.

At least for now.

"How about a nightcap?" Reid said.

She felt her body tense.

"Hello? Anyone there?" he said.

She blinked. "I'm sorry. I got lost in my head for a minute."

"So what do you think? Nightcap sound good?"

She knew she should leave.

"I'm supposed to meet my friends in the East Village. I'm sorry."

"You sure? We could grab a quick drink right around the corner. One of the many things I love about this city is that you can't toss a quarter without hitting a bar." He pointed toward Columbus Circle.

Katrina's eyes followed. The streets were bustling and bright, everyone out and about, living it up on a beautiful Saturday night.

She was having fun too, a *lot* of fun.

"Come on," Reid said. "Just one drink?"

She held her breath for a moment. Shana's words from class rang in her ears.

Don't judge a person or a situation on its face, because you just might be wrong. And if you're wrong, you might be missing out on something amazing.

She smiled. "Okay . . . sure. One drink would be nice."

* * *

After another half glass of wine, Katrina was officially tipsy. And Reid was becoming more and more friendly.

"I don't believe it," he said.

"It's true."

He lifted his drink and shook his head. "How could someone so pretty not have a boyfriend?"

She pointed to his drink. "I think that's the scotch talking."

"Come on now, give yourself some credit. You're a very attractive woman."

She felt her neck get hot at the compliment, then glanced around the bar to avoid looking him in the eye. They were at an Irish pub called D. J. Reynolds on Fifty-Seventh, and the crowd ranged wildly in age. She spotted at least a dozen patrons who looked to be in their seventies, plus another handful who looked barely old enough to drink. The fashion statements ran the gamut from tweed jackets and ascots to flat-rimmed baseball hats and baggy jeans.

It was unlike any bar she'd seen at home.

It was . . . perfect.

"Everyone fits in here, don't they?" she said, still taking in the surroundings.

"You mean New York?"

She nodded. "It seems like no matter how old you are, or how you're dressed, or what you do, you can pop into any bar—whether it's a dive reeking of stale beer and popcorn or a swanky lounge serving top-shelf liquor—and no one cares. In Silicon Valley, it's just not like that."

"How so?"

"I mean everyone is so *similar* there, at least the people I seem to come across. Similar in dress, similar in age, similar in education. There are some cool bars near my apartment, but they're mostly filled with clusters of techy guys in polo shirts with their company logos, chattering about a new video game or their fantasy football team."

Reid laughed. "Remind me never to move to Mountain View."

She looked around the room. "I don't think I've ever been in a bar I could imagine my parents strolling into for a drink."

"Speaking of a drink, can I get you another?"

She covered her glass with her hand. "I'm good, thanks. Actually, I think it's about time I headed out."

"You sure?" He looked disappointed.

"Yes, but thanks so much for everything. The show, dinner, all of it has been so much fun. I feel like today has been the quintessential New York experience."

"You're off to meet your friends now?"

She shook her head. "I don't think I'm going to make it. It's been a long day, and I'm pretty beat, sad as that sounds."

"You're hardly sad, fairest one. Let's blow this Popsicle stand." He stood up and gestured for the bill.

As Katrina reached down to pick up her purse, she felt a little dizzy. She wished she hadn't had that third glass of wine.

As they walked outside, Reid stepped into the street to hail a cab. "I'll drop you off."

She touched her cheek and realized it felt a little numb. While her grasp of Manhattan geography was still rudimentary, she knew the East Village was *not* on the way to Tribeca. But before she could say anything, a cab had pulled over. Reid opened the door, and she climbed in and turned to say good-bye to him, but he was already getting in after her.

"Oh, thanks so much, but I'm okay getting home on my own, really."

"Nonsense. This way I can pay your fare. Now move over."

Not wanting to be rude, she slid across the seat, and he sat down next to her.

"Twenty-Second and Third?" he asked her.

"Yes." She closed her eyes to think for a moment, then opened them and recited the exact address of her building.

Reid looked ahead to the front seat. "Did you get that?"

The driver nodded and pulled into traffic. Katrina leaned back against the seat and exhaled. "I'm sleepy."

"New York will do that to you."

They rode in silence for a few minutes, winding their way through the crowded streets of Midtown. Then Reid spoke. "What's been your favorite part of your time here so far?"

"That's a good question, especially given the sightseeing rampage I went on last week. But if you put a gun to my head, I'd have to say it was . . . seeing *The Book of Mormon.*" *With you,* she thought silently. And it was true. Yes, it was complicated, but it was so nice being with a man who made her feel so . . . *special.*

He touched her cheek. "I could never put a gun to your head. I much prefer it intact."

As they headed south away from Midtown, the skyscrapers gave way to apartment buildings, pubs, and restaurants. Every other car on the road seemed to be a yellow cab, and nearly every one of them was full. Katrina wondered where everyone was going, and with whom. It was a sea of strangers all sharing the same city streets before disappearing into their separate lives.

Eventually the driver turned onto Katrina's street and began to slow down. When he stopped in front of her building, she reached for her purse and turned to Reid.

"Thanks again for everything. I had a really nice time."

He had his hand on her cheek again. "You sure you want to go home? It's still early."

"I'm sure."

"We could go meet your friends for that drink."

"Thanks, but I'm beat."

He shrugged. "If you say so. I'll walk you in."

She shook her head. "Oh, you don't have to do that."

"Yes, I do."

Before she could say anything more, he was paying the driver and opening the door. He stepped out and held a hand for her to follow.

"Come on, I insist. I'll catch another cab in a few minutes."

She took his hand and followed him out, and together they walked up the steps of the building. She reached into her purse for her keys, then held them up and smiled. "I guess this is good-bye then."

He nodded toward the door. "I'll walk you upstairs to make sure you get in safe."

She waved a hand in front of her. "Oh, I'll be fine. You don't have to do that."

"I want to."

"Really, I'm fine. It's okay."

He softened his voice. "Kat, just let me walk you up, okay?"

She sighed. "Okay. But then you really need to leave. Promise?"

He held up three fingers. "Scout's honor."

She struggled briefly with the lock on the front door, then experienced a similar problem with the second door, the wine and nerves teaming up to impair her motor skills. Finally, they were inside the building, the noise of the street below barely audible now.

"I'm on the third floor." She spoke in a whisper, although she wasn't sure why. It wasn't even nine o'clock.

"Show me the way." He grinned, half-whispering himself, and an odd thought struck Katrina.

He looks like the Cheshire cat.

She kept one hand on the railing to balance herself as she headed upstairs, acutely aware of Reid following close behind her. When they reached her door, she turned and forced herself to look at him. She cleared her throat and managed an awkward smile.

"So here I am, safe and sound."

He stepped close to her and put his hand on her lower back. "So you are."

She swallowed. "Okay then, well . . . I guess I'll . . . see you soon."

He slowly shook his head. "No, you won't," he whispered.

"I won't see you soon?"

He shook his head again. "You'll see me . . . now." He leaned toward her, then softly kissed her. This time she didn't resist. His lips pressed gently against hers. She closed her eyes and gave in to the warm sensation filling her body.

Instinctively, she leaned into him. In response, he immediately put his other hand on the small of her back and pulled her closer. As their kiss deepened, her body continued to heat up and her breath quickened.

No one had *ever* kissed her like this before.

"You're so beautiful," he whispered, moving his lips to her neck. "I want you so much."

She kept her eyes closed, not able to think about anything except how good it felt to be touched like this.

"Let's go inside," he whispered.

She swallowed.

She wanted to say yes—she was aching to say yes—but she knew they had to wait. First he had to make a clean break from his wife. Move out, at least.

Or maybe he already had?

"I can't," she whispered. "Not yet."

He nuzzled her neck, then grazed her earlobe with his fingertips. "Please . . . Kat . . . please. You have no idea how much I want you."

She wanted him too, but she wanted him the right way.

She wrapped her arms around his waist and buried her face in his chest. "I'm sorry, Reid. I can't. Not yet."

"Yes you can," he said, nuzzling her ear again. "Please say yes."

"I can't."

"You know you want to," he whispered.

"I do, but I just . . . can't. Maybe when it's official, but I wouldn't feel right before then."

His body stiffened. He removed her arms from his waist and straightened up.

"When what's official?"

"Your separation."

"What are you talking about?"

She pointed to his bare ring finger. "Your separation. I know a divorce takes a long time, but—"

He took a step backward. "You think I'm getting divorced?"

"Aren't you?"

"Hell no."

She felt like she'd been punched in the gut.

"But . . . but you're not wearing . . . then why . . ." She looked at his left hand.

He held up the hand. "You think because I'm not wearing my wedding ring I'm getting a divorce?"

She nodded slightly.

The friendly glint in his eyes disappeared, switched off like a light. "For Christ's sake, Kat, will you stop being such a tease?"

She caught her breath. "What?"

He raised his voice. "You heard me. A *tease*. Stop the act, will you?"

"Stop what act?"

"The I'm-so-innocent act. It was cute at first, but it's getting old."

Suddenly she felt like she was going to cry.

He pressed his palms against his temples. "*No*, I'm not getting divorced, and *yes*, occasionally I cheat on my wife. Don't pretend you didn't know that."

She stared at him. "I . . . I . . . I don't understand what you want from me." She could barely get out the words.

He sighed. "I don't want *anything* from you, okay? I just want to sleep with you. What's so hard to understand about that?"

She opened her mouth, but no words came out.

"What?" he asked. "What?"

"I . . ."

"Look at you: the sexy dress, the boots. Don't act like you didn't know what was going on here."

She glanced down at her outfit, the one she'd planned so painstakingly. "I thought . . . I thought . . . this was special . . ." she whispered.

"Special? Why would you think this was special?"

"Because I thought you . . . I thought we—"

"Well, you thought wrong. I'm sorry if I gave you the wrong impression, but it's pretty cut-and-dried. I'm married, and I plan to stay married. I never said otherwise."

"But you called me Snow White . . ." she whispered. *The fairest one of all.*

"So?"

"And you're not wearing a ring . . ."

He looked at his hand and shrugged. "I took it off to go to the gym this morning and forgot to put it back on. That's all."

She could feel tears building up behind her eyes. She wanted to run, to escape from the reality of the situation, but she felt paralyzed, her mind reeling at what he was saying.

He sighed again, more heavily this time, and began to button up his coat. "Listen, I think I've been straightforward all along, but it's obvious we're not on the same page. This was never going to be some fairy tale where we rode off into the sunset together. It was about two consenting adults having sex. And that clearly isn't going to happen, so I think it's best if I take off now."

She nodded, her head in a daze. "Okay."

He took a couple of steps down the stairs before stopping and looking up at her. "It was nice meeting you, Kat. No hard feelings. Enjoy your time in New York."

"Bye, Reid," she whispered.

He disappeared down the staircase.

She stood there, stunned, until she heard the front door of the building bang shut.

Then she started to cry.

Chapter Twelve

Katrina sat on the edge of the bed, tears streaming down her cheeks. She covered her face with her hands and choked back the sobs, shaking with humiliation.

How did that just happen?

Why am I so stupid?

What is wrong with me?

She curled her legs up against her chest, then placed her chin on top of her knees. A maelstrom of emotions coursed through her.

Shame.

Guilt.

Anger.

Sadness.

Heartache.

I'm such a fool.

A stupid, stupid fool.

She thought back to the first night she'd met Reid, and how he'd acted each time they'd been together. As she dissected each conversation to the extent her memory would allow, she realized the red flags had always been there, but that she'd chosen to ignore them.

He'd never said he was unhappily married.

He'd never said he planned to leave his wife.

He'd never talked about the future, or with whom he planned to spend it, in any way, shape, or form.

All he'd done was pay her a lot of compliments and *not* mention his marriage in any of their conversations. Instead of seeing that for what it was, instead of seeing the *truth*, she'd been so grateful for the attention that she'd taken the partial picture he presented of his life and eagerly filled in the blanks with what she *wanted* to be there.

The *fairy tale* she'd wanted.

He'd made her feel attractive and interesting and *special*, and because of that she'd projected her own fantasy onto the canvas of their relationship, painting a picture of a romance that was never going to be.

It's all my fault.

She pressed her palms against her forehead, cringing with horror as Reid's words played over and over in her head.

Don't act like you didn't know what was going on here.

Why would you think this was special?

I'm married, and I plan to stay married. I never said otherwise.

She slipped off her boots and pulled back the covers on her bed, still wearing her new dress, about to curl up into a ball and try to tune out the wretchedness and humiliation of the night.

Perhaps she'd been wrong about being able to change her life. Maybe the cards were already laid out for her, and she should just accept it. She was clearly out of her depth in New York, too naïve to navigate this sleek, sophisticated world where everything—and *everyone*—was so different from what she was used to.

Maybe her parents were right.

She would never fit in here.

She should just go home and get a job.

Her mother's words echoed in her head.

You need to get your head out of the clouds, Katrina.

You can't expect a man to come along and rescue you, Katrina.

You need to be able to support yourself, Katrina.

She sighed. It was time to go home.

Just as she was about to turn off the light, she stopped.

No.

I can't just give up.

I don't want go back to that life.

I don't want to be that person anymore.

She swung her legs onto the hardwood floor, pushed herself off the bed, and headed into the bathroom to fix her makeup.

She was going back out.

* * *

"Oh my gosh, look who made it!" Shana, noticeably wobbly, got off her stool and waved at Katrina.

"Here, kitty kitty." Grace wiggled her fingers at her.

Katrina approached the bar. "Here I am. Can you believe it?"

"I love that outfit! You look beautiful. Have a glass of wine. Do you like Malbec?"

Katrina frowned. "I have no idea. I know nothing about wine."

I'm unsophisticated. I'm a fool.

Though she was about to automatically decline, she realized that some wine sounded perfect just then.

Why not?

"I'll have some though," she said with a shrug.

"It's yummy. You'll love it." Shana put a hand on Josh's arm. "Get her a glass, would you, sweets?"

Josh flagged down the bartender. "Coming right up."

Grace clumsily tapped Josh's shoulder. "Hey, big man, I could use a refill too while you're at it." She lifted her nearly empty wine-glass toward Katrina in a toast. "Give the Kitty props for staying out past her bedtime."

"I didn't think you were going to make it," Shana said. "How was the show?"

Katrina forced a smile. "It was nice."

Grace narrowed her eyes. "Wusswrong?"

"Was that English?" Katrina asked.

"We've been here for a while," Shana said. "She asked what's wrong."

Grace nodded. "I'm hammered. So wusswrong?"

Katrina tried to keep smiling. "What do you mean?"

Grace waved a tiny hand in front of Katrina's face. "What do I *mean*? You look like a freaking clown with that scary fake grin, that's what I *mean*. What's wrong with you?"

"Are you okay, Kat? Did something happen?" Shana asked.

The smile faded, and Katrina's shoulders slumped. "You don't want to know."

Grace rubbed her tiny hands together. "Oooh, now I *really* want to know. Come on, Kitty, spill it."

Katrina could feel the tears coming again and hoped she could keep them at bay. Just then Josh handed her a glass of wine.

He also pointed to a pickleback shot sitting on the bar.

Katrina shook her head. "Oh, thank you, Josh, but I don't think I could do a shot. I've already had a few drinks tonight."

"You clearly need more," Grace slurred.

"Come on, catch up with us," Josh said.

Katrina looked at the shot. Reid's harshest words ricocheted through her head.

Will you stop being such a tease?

This isn't some fairy tale.

I don't want anything from you. I just want to sleep with you.

"You in?" Josh held up the glass.

Katrina swallowed, then nodded. "I'm in."

Shana put her arm around Katrina's shoulders. "Do you want to talk about it?"

"Don't give her a choice," Grace said. "Tell her she *has* to talk about it. It's not good to bottle things up. You'll turn into a cold, angry woman, like the one who gave birth to me."

Katrina looked at both of them and felt the tears welling up. "Why are you two always so nice to me?"

"Thassa really weird question." Grace squinted at her.

"Because we're your *friends*," Shana said.

"It's just that . . . I've just never been very good at . . . making friends," Katrina said.

"Nonsense," Grace said. "Wussnot to like? You've made friends with *me*, for chrissake. I can scare away the best of them."

"Kat, don't be so hard on yourself." Shana rubbed Katrina's upper back. "What happened tonight, sweetie?"

"Business first." Josh handed Katrina the shot and chaser, which she choked down as slowly as—and no more elegantly than—the one after the soccer game.

She coughed for about ten seconds, then relayed the night's events to her friends.

* * *

"What a dick," Grace slurred.

Katrina hiccupped. "I thought he really liked me. I feel so stupid."

"You not stupid. *He* stupid," Grace said. "Men stupid."

"I'm standing right here," Josh said.

Grace rolled her eyes. "You don't count."

"I'm not sure how to take that," Josh said.

It was an hour and several drinks later, and Katrina was officially drunk.

"Men suck," Grace said.

"Still standing here," Josh said.

Grace poked him in the chest. "Are you sure you're standing, little man? Because you kind of look like you're sitting."

Josh chuckled. "Look who's talking. Didn't you once tell me you have to sit on a phone book to be able to drive a car?"

"I may have mentioned that," Grace said.

"I need to pee." Shana wobbled off to the restroom.

"Who needs another drink?" Josh asked.

"Hit me." Grace gave a thumbs-up sign.

"I don't think I can stand up," Katrina said.

"That's another yes." Grace gave a thumbs-up again.

Katrina put her hand on Grace's arm. "I'm sorry we've spent so much time talking about me tonight. Shana told me that you and your boyfriend broke up. I'm really sorry."

"He sucks. All men suck."

"Still here," Josh said without turning around.

"What happened?" Katrina asked. "I thought you said he was married, but Shana said he isn't. Is he separated?"

Grace laughed. "He's not married. He's never been married."

"Then why did you . . . ?"

"I just call him *married guy* because he's married to his *job*. I'm in love with the man, but the man is in love with his freaking *job*."

"What's his job?"

"He's an IT manager at a dumbass software company in Jersey City. Stupid New Jersey."

"So you broke up with him because you didn't feel like a priority? Or because he was always working?"

Grace pointed to herself. "*He* dumped *me*. Little Chinese prick. He said he has feelings for me but has zero time left for a personal life right now, so for *my* sake we should just stay friends. Prick."

"He said for *your* sake you should just stay friends?"

She nodded. "Like I'm supposed to believe that load of crap. Just man up and tell me you're not into me, you know? Don't wuss out and blame it on your freaking *job*."

Katrina frowned. "I'm sorry, Grace. You deserve better than that. I agree, the truth is always the best policy."

"He's a coward. All men are cowards."

"Thank you for that," Josh said.

"*Dude*, I already told you, you don't count." Grace held up the silver pendant dangling at the end of the chain around her neck.

"Who needs him anyway? Now I can focus on my jewelry, which is what I should have been doing all along anyway. My jewelry's kick-ass, right, Uncle Josh?"

"It's the best," he said with a cough. "And you know how much I know about women's jewelry."

"Damn, I'm hammered," Grace said out of nowhere. "Like a nail into a wall."

Katrina looked at Josh. "Are you guys really playing soccer again tomorrow?"

He nodded. "Thank God the game's not until three. It's gonna be ugly."

"*So* ugly. Although we normally stink so bad that I doubt the other team will even notice we're on our deathbeds," Grace said.

"Do you want to play?" Josh asked as he handed Katrina her glass of wine, which she feared she might drop. "I think our other girl's back in town, but if you're up for it, we could always use a sub."

"Are you that desperate?" Katrina asked.

"Hey now, you're better than I am," Grace said. "I mean, you stink too, but you're still better."

Katrina laughed. "I was planning to go to the Met tomorrow."

"Go in the morning," Josh said.

"I have a feeling I'll be sleeping in tomorrow. Or in a coma."

"Hey, everyone, look who I ran into." Shana appeared through the crowd, her arm intertwined with a tall man wearing a flannel shirt and jeans.

It was Justin.

"Well, hello there, handsome." Grace pointed to his shirt. "Rocking the sexy lumberjack look as usual, I see."

"Hi, Grace. Hi, Josh. Hi, Kat."

Katrina was surprised. "Justin, hi. What are you doing here?"

"You mean, why am I on this side of the counter?"

"No, of course not." She felt her ears get hot, embarrassed at her faux pas, suddenly well aware of how drunk she was despite being so . . . drunk.

He smiled. "Relax, I'm just teasing you."

"Can I buy you a drink?" Josh asked.

"A Newcastle would be great, thanks."

"One Newcastle coming right up. How about a pickleback on top?"

Justin shook his head. "No thanks. I don't do shots anymore."

Grace squinted at him. "Then why the hell are you here?"

Shana laughed. "Gracie, don't be rude."

"I can't help it. I *am* rude." Grace shrugged. "Sorry, Justin. No offense."

Justin chuckled. "It's okay. I know you're rude. No offense taken."

"Anyone else need a drink?" Josh asked.

"I could use a glass of water," Katrina said. "A huge one. Or maybe a hose."

Justin gave Katrina a concerned look. "You doing okay? You look a little woozy."

"She's schnockered," Grace said.

Katrina nodded. "I'm . . . schnockered."

Grace started laughing. "God, we're a shit show tonight."

"I think I need to visit the ladies' room." Katrina stood up, steadied herself, and cocked her head toward the back of the bar. "I'll be right back."

Shana nudged Justin's arm. "You should go with her to make sure she's okay."

"Kitty's a serious lightweight. She might end up in a gutter," Grace said.

Josh pointed at her. "Rude."

Grace pointed back. "Midget."

Katrina began slogging her way through the crowd, Justin a step or two behind her.

"You sure you're okay?" He put a hand on her arm as they reached the unisex restroom. Two women stood in line ahead of them. "You really don't look so great."

She yanked her arm away from him. "I'm fine. Why should you care anyway?"

"What?"

"Stop being so nice to me, Justin. What is it with you, anyway?"

"What is it with me? What are you talking about?"

She glared at him, tears in her eyes. "Yes, you. Men. *Married* men. All of you. What is it with you?"

"What do you mean?"

"I mean where's *your* wife, Justin?"

He seemed taken aback at the question. "What?"

"Your *wife*. Where is she? It's Saturday night. Why are you here, talking to me? Being so nice to me? What's wrong with you? Shouldn't you be with *her* right now?"

"That's not fair."

She narrowed her eyes. "You think that's not fair? I'll tell you what's not fair. You're *married*, yet here you are, on a Saturday night, at a *bar*, your wife nowhere to be found, being nice to *me*, taking care of *me*. *That's* not fair, Justin."

He shook his head. "You're drunk, Kat."

"So what? Just because I'm drunk I can't speak the truth? Isn't alcohol supposed to make you honest? Didn't *you* tell me that?"

"You don't know what you're talking about."

She poked him in the chest. "I don't? So it's not true that you've been flirting with me since we first met? That you've gone out of your way to talk to me every time I came into the coffeehouse? That you've made me feel like you actually give a damn about me?"

He stared at her, a confused look in his eyes. Or was it a look of hurt?

She kept talking. "I know what you've been doing. Being nice to me, buttering me up so I'll believe you actually *like* me? All because you're just waiting for the chance to cheat on your wife, right?" She wasn't yelling, but her voice was louder than necessary.

"Kat, please, stop."

A few tears slid down the sides of her face. But she didn't care.

"It's not . . . fair," she said, her shoulders slumping.

It's not fair.

Justin gestured to the vacant restroom, his voice low, a strained look on his face. "It's your turn, Kat."

"It's not . . . fair," she said again. She wiped a tear from her eye, then pushed past him and opened the door.

Inside the restroom, she studied her face in the mirror as she washed and dried her hands, then clumsily reapplied her lip gloss.

Grace is right.

Men aren't worth it.

They'll only hurt you.

It's better to focus on yourself.

When she came back out a few moments later, Justin was gone. She awkwardly maneuvered her way back through the crowd toward the bar, where Grace and Josh now perched on bar stools. Shana was doing tree pose, one foot propped against the inner thigh of her standing leg, both hands above her head in prayer position.

Katrina scanned the room, looking for any sign of Justin.

"Dude, you know the grass *is* always greener," Grace said to Josh.

Josh picked up his glass. "I disagree. Sometimes you have to give it the old college try."

Grace shrugged. "I guess you do only live once. I'd hate to throw in the towel before the fat lady sings."

Josh nodded. "You can't count those chickens before they hatch."

Shana giggled, her tree wobbling to one side. "You two are nuts."

"What are they doing?" Katrina asked Shana as she pointed to Josh and Grace.

Shana put down her leg. "They're having a conversation in clichés. First one to break has to do a shot."

"Are they always this competitive with each other?"

Shana's eyes got big. "You have no idea. Last year for Josh's birthday we had a little Ping-Pong tournament at this fun bar called SPiN that has a bunch of tables, and I thought one of these two was going to end up needing stitches."

Grace tapped Josh on the shoulder. "Uncle Josh, maybe you're right. Maybe I *should* put the pedal to the metal. An ounce of prevention is worth a pound of cure, you know."

Josh held up his glass in a toast. "I think you should do that. Money doesn't grow on trees."

"How long is this going to go on?" Katrina asked Shana.

Shana shrugged. "Until Tuesday, maybe."

"Where did Justin go?"

"He's not with you?"

Katrina shook her head.

"Then I have no idea."

"It's true. A penny saved is a penny earned," Grace said.

"I think he's mad at me," Katrina whispered to Shana.

"Mad at you? Why would he be mad at you?"

Katrina frowned. "Because I think I was just mean to him."

"You can do it," Josh said to Grace. "Just remember that the early bird gets the worm."

Shana gave Katrina a strange look. "Why would you be mean to Justin? I can't imagine you being mean to anyone."

"I don't know. I think I was . . . projecting." She stumbled over the word.

"Projecting?"

"But I'd have to be careful." Grace frowned. "As you know, when the cat's away the mice will play."

"What did you say to him?" Shana asked.

Katrina pushed a few strands of hair away from her eyes. "I can't remember exactly. I think I got on his case for coming here tonight, instead of spending the evening with his wife, which he should be doing on a Saturday night, right? I think I accused him of cheating. Or wanting to cheat. It's all kind of fuzzy." She pressed a palm against her forehead. "I've had too much to drink."

Shana shook her head slowly. "Oh, Kat . . ."

"I know—it was dumb. I'm stupid. I was just taking things out on him because of what happened with Reid, because of Grace's boyfriend, because of all of them."

"True, but then again, a watched pot never boils," Josh said.

Shana made a pained face. "You really yelled at him?"

Katrina nodded. "But maybe he deserved it. I mean, what *is* he doing at a bar on a Saturday night without his wife? What's he doing being so sweet to *me* when he should be home with *her*?"

"I guess you could kill two birds with one stone," Josh said.

Shana shook her head. "Kat, you've got it all wrong."

Katrina squinted, trying to focus her eyes. "What do you mean?"

"Dude, you're not beating around the bush," Grace said.

Shana put a hand on Katrina's shoulder and leaned close to her. "*I* invited Justin here tonight."

"You did? Why?"

"Well, love conquers all, doesn't it, Gracie?" Josh said.

"Because I thought *you* might be here."

"Me? Why?"

Shana hiccupped. "I thought it would be fun for you two to run into each other outside of the coffeehouse. Sort of coincidentical, but on purpose."

"What are you talking about?"

"You two are so natural together. It's cute."

"He's *married*, Shana."

Shana leaned closer to Katrina and hiccupped again, then whispered into her ear.

"His wife left him."

Katrina caught her breath. "What?"

"She ran off with another man. I think it was a friend of his too."

Katrina covered her mouth. "Oh my gosh. His *friend*?"

"Very bad of both of them. *Very* disloyalcal." Shana stamped her foot.

"But he wears a wedding ring," Katrina said.

"Probably hard to let go. It's a tragical situation."

"I win!" Josh stood up and lifted his fist overhead. "You broke!"

"Dammit, you do win." Grace stood up and steadied herself, then wobbled away toward the restroom, followed by Shana.

"Champion again." Josh lightly pounded his chest.

Katrina tried to wrap her mind around what she'd just learned. Justin's wife had cheated on *him*?

Things suddenly became less fuzzy, and she heard her own words from just a few minutes ago in a new light.

I mean where's your wife, Justin?

Shouldn't you be with her right now?

What's wrong with you?

She cringed at the thought of how cruel she had been, how her words must have sounded.

She closed her eyes.

I'm an idiot.

Chapter Thirteen

The next morning, Katrina woke up with a monster headache, but the memory of the previous night's events hurt much worse than the throbbing in her temples.

I'm never drinking like that again.

Her mind replayed it all like a slow-motion movie. How had what had begun as such a pleasant afternoon unraveled into . . . into such a monstrous, tangled mess?

The matinee.

Drinks with Reid.

Dinner.

The romantic cab ride back to the brownstone.

The horrible incident at her door.

Then tears.

And indignation.

And wine.

And more wine.

Then the drunken conversation with Justin in the bathroom line, followed by Shana's revelation.

Reid openly cheats on his wife but won't leave her?

Justin's wife cheated on him with his friend then left him?

One potential romance, one budding friendship, both blown to bits in the span of a couple of hours.

Why can't I see things for what they really are?

I'm never drinking like that again.

I'm never flirting with a man again—married, single, or anything in between.

I need aspirin now.

She tossed off the covers and sat up in bed, then pressed her hands over her eyes.

Maybe a hot shower would help.

She slowly padded into the bathroom and stripped, tossing her tank top and shorts onto the floor instead of carefully looping them over the hook on the back of the door like she usually did. She turned on the water as hot as she could stand it, then stepped inside and hoped it would melt away the awful feelings ricocheting inside her heart.

* * *

"Hey, Kat, how're you doing today?"

Katrina removed her sunglasses and grimaced. "Hi, Peter, I've been better. Is Justin here?"

He shook his head. "He's at the Upper West Side shop on Sundays, remember?"

Katrina snapped her fingers. "That's right, I totally forgot. Where exactly is that?"

Peter gave her a sly smile. "You going to visit him?"

"Maybe."

He jotted down the address on a sticky note and handed it to her. "Tell him I said hi."

"Thanks. What's the place called?"

"Same as here."

"What's *this* place called?"

"You don't know?" He looked amused. "You come in here like five times a day."

Katrina smiled. "I keep meaning to ask but always forget. And for the record, I only come here once a day, sometimes twice."

He chuckled. "The official business license says A Place for Coffee, and yes, that was meant as a generic equivalent, and yes, I know the sign out front doesn't say anything."

"That's really the name?"

"Yes, ma'am. Justin said that's how he wanted it."

"Why?"

He shrugged. "You'll have to ask him. He's the boss."

"Got it. Thanks, Peter." She turned to leave.

"That's it? No skim latte and blueberry scone?"

She shook her head and put her sunglasses back on. "Not today."

* * *

By the time Katrina made it to the Upper West Side, it was nearly noon. She walked into the coffeehouse and removed her sunglasses, then scanned the room. The place was similar in design and character to the one in her neighborhood, and even featured the same friendly chimes on the front door, but it was much more spacious.

After looking everywhere but directly behind the counter, she finally turned in that direction, ashamed to face Justin but knowing she had to.

There was a long queue of people waiting to order.

Justin was standing at the cash register.

She took a place in line and stared at the floor, suddenly feeling more nervous than hungover.

What should I say to him?

Why was I so awful to him?

He'd been nothing but kind to her, and she'd lashed out at him for no reason other than the fact that he was married.

And apparently that wasn't even true.

The line inched forward. She scanned the Sunday paper as she waited, not really reading any particular story. She just couldn't focus.

Finally, the people in front of her stepped to one side, and there he was.

"Hi, Justin." She smiled weakly.

He looked surprised. "Kat, hi. What are you doing here?"

She pointed in the direction of downtown. "I stopped by the other place, and Peter said you were here. I . . . I wanted to talk to you."

He glanced behind her, and she turned to see a half-dozen people in line behind her. "I'm kind of busy right now," he said.

She swallowed. "Yes, of course. I understand. I just wanted to tell you how sorry I am for last night." It came out as a whisper, and suddenly she began to cry. She felt a lump form in her stomach as the reality of what she'd done hit her. She'd treated him horribly, and no matter how many times she apologized, she could never take that back. She hoped things could go back to the way they had been. She'd be crushed if she'd ruined things permanently.

He turned toward a woman wiping down one of the espresso machines. "Hey, Karen, can you cover the register for a few minutes?"

She put down the rag and hustled over. "Sure thing, Justin. I got it."

He nodded toward the far end of the counter, and Katrina followed him. When they reached it, he stopped and handed her a napkin.

"Are you okay?" he said.

She nodded and dabbed her eyes, but she wasn't okay. Tears slipped down her cheeks. "I'm so sorry."

"Look, Kat, I appreciate that you came all the way up here, but you don't owe me any apologies. It's not worth crying over."

"I *do*. And it *is*." She blew her nose. "I was really out of line, and you didn't deserve any of it. I don't know why I behaved like that. That wasn't like me at all."

He shrugged. "It happens."

"Not to me, it doesn't. I'm not like that, and I don't want you to think I am. It's just that I'd been out earlier with this guy . . . and things hadn't gone so well . . . and I took it out on you."

He held up a hand to stop her. "I get it. It's okay, really."

"I don't usually drink like that." She'd stopped crying now.

He laughed. "Clearly. You were quite a sight."

She tossed the napkin into the trash and covered her face with her hands. "I'm so embarrassed. Honestly, I don't even remember what I said to you. I just know it wasn't nice, and I hate that I did it."

"It's no big deal. People say stupid things when they're drunk. Why do you think I don't drink much anymore? Believe me, I've put my foot in my mouth many a time."

She peeked out at him from between her fingers. "I still feel like a horrible person."

He smiled. "Please. You're hardly a horrible person. We all do things we regret sometimes."

She flinched. She knew he was talking about more than just how she'd treated him. She couldn't remember exactly what she'd said about Reid, but she knew it was enough. Justin was no dummy.

She decided to nudge the conversation in another direction.

"Thanks for being so understanding. And Shana told me about your wife. I'm so sorry, Justin."

"Thanks. I'll be fine. I'm . . . dealing with it."

"Has it, um, been a long time since . . . ?" She wondered again why he was still wearing his wedding ring but thought it would be impolite to ask.

"Since she left me?"

Katrina nodded slightly. *Was that a rude question to ask?* The last thing she wanted was to come across as rude when she'd come to make amends.

"It'll be six months next week." He cleared his throat. "So how's the head feeling today?"

He clearly wanted to change the subject, so she dropped it. "Oh my gosh, you have no idea. I never knew what a true hangover was before I woke up this morning. I thought I was going to die." She pressed her palms against her temples.

"I know the feeling—that's why I do all I can to avoid it."

"I've learned my lesson. Never again."

He gestured around the room. "So what do you think? It's bigger than the one in the East Village, but I like to think it has the same vibe."

"I love it. Hey, that reminds me. I keep forgetting to ask you about the name of this place."

"Ask me what?"

"Peter said you intentionally have no signage and gave it a generic name. Is that true?"

"Yes, ma'am."

"Why?"

"I want people to name it themselves, depending on how it fits into their lives."

"What do you mean?"

"What do *you* call it?"

"The coffeehouse."

"Exactly. A lot of people refer to it as the scone place."

"They do? Really?"

He nodded. "And I've noticed older people tend to call it the coffee *shop*, not the coffeehouse. A small difference, but notable in its consistency."

"Interesting."

"I think so too. A lot of the college students in this neighborhood call it the breakfast sandwich place. It's all about people seeing what they want to see, sort of a blank canvas they can paint on themselves." He pointed at the chalkboard behind the cash register. "Speaking of breakfast sandwiches, what can I get you for that hangover? The egg sandwich and grilled cheese are both favorites with the postparty crowd. Unless you're going back to your usual?"

She tapped a finger against her chin. "I think it's definitely time for something new."

Chapter Fourteen

"Well, hello there. Aren't *you* looking lovely for a Sunday afternoon? I'm digging that scarf-jewelry combination you've got going on." Brittany made a figure eight with her index finger.

Katrina adjusted the slim swath of silk, this one a dark green, then lightly touched the silver hoop earrings Grace had recently given her in exchange for a painting she'd done of the High Line above a sea of taxicabs. After apologizing to Justin, she'd spent a good chunk of the afternoon at the Met, then chatted on the phone with Deb on the way home to shower and change before meeting up with Brittany for an early drink.

She'd been tempted to cancel, given how wrecked she still felt from the night before, but she knew there was a good chance this would be the last time she'd get to see Brittany before her time in New York came to an end. She'd briefly considered suggesting some kind of meeting place other than a bar, but since she wasn't familiar with the area where Brittany lived, she'd just deferred to her.

She smiled. "Thanks, Brittany. You look great too, although you *always* do. I wish I had your style."

"Ha. You should see me in the morning. Trust me, it ain't pretty. So how have you enjoyed your time in New York? Have a seat and tell me all about what you've been up to in the past few weeks." Brittany patted the empty bar stool next to her.

"I've got to say, New York has been—"

"Wait, hold that thought." Brittany held up a finger, then turned to flag down the bartender. "Excuse me, kind sir. Can you please bring over a glass of sangria for my friend here?"

Katrina shook her head. "I'm okay with just a soda tonight."

"Are you sure? The sangria here is to die for."

"Thanks, but I'm sure. Could you order me a Sprite, please? I'm just going to run to the ladies' room."

Brittany turned toward the bartender. "Did you hear that, hon?"

He winked at her. "Got it."

"Have you slept with *him* too?" Katrina whispered to Brittany.

"Not yet," Brittany whispered back. "*Yet* being the operative word."

When Katrina returned to the bar a few minutes later, Brittany tapped the empty stool next to her. "Now fill me in. What have you been up to since I last saw you?"

Katrina gave her a weary smile. "I've done a ridiculous amount of sightseeing, as you can imagine. It's been sort of exhausting, actually. Somehow I still have a ton of things to check off my list, which only seems to get longer every day."

Brittany rolled her eyes. "Sightseeing is boring. Making lists is boring. Please tell me you've been doing more than that."

"I have. I've been painting some, and I've also been taking yoga classes." She stiffened slightly. *And kissing married men.*

Brittany smiled. "Good for you! Very New York of you. So are you loving it here? Aren't you *so* glad you came?"

"Yes. And I am. It just hasn't exactly been . . . what I expected."

"What do you mean?"

Katrina shifted on the stool and frowned. All afternoon she'd debated whether or not to tell Brittany about Reid, and finally, she'd decided it was best for Brittany to hear it from her. "Well, it's just that something . . . something sort of happened with Reid."

"What do you mean?"

Katrina took a deep breath. "I mean . . . he hit on me."

"Of course he did." The look in Brittany's eyes was matter-of-fact.

"No, I mean, *he tried to sleep with me.*"

"So?"

Katrina's jaw dropped. "You're not surprised?"

Brittany shook her head. "Not at all. Why do you think I asked him to come meet us at Super Linda that night?"

"What are you saying?"

Brittany took a sip of her sangria. "I'm saying that it was clear you were in need of some attention of the male persuasion, so I hooked you up."

"You *planned* that?"

Brittany gave her a strange look. "Am I not being clear enough? *Yes,* I teed one up for you. Reid is hot. I thought you'd want to hit that for sure."

"But why would you think . . . I mean . . . he's *married.*"

"So?"

"*So?*"

Brittany took another sip of her drink. "Yes, *so.* What's the big deal? I told you his deal. It's not like he's happily married and you'd be getting in the way of something. Believe me, he knows exactly what he's doing."

"Yes, but . . ."

"But what?"

"But I didn't think . . . I mean . . . I thought . . . I thought he really liked me."

"I'm sure he *does* like you. What's not to like?"

"No, I mean . . . I thought he was . . . planning to leave her," she whispered.

Brittany choked back a laugh. "You thought he would leave his wife for you?"

Katrina swallowed. "Not *for* me. But yes, I thought maybe that was in his plans. . . . He just seemed to like me so much . . . that maybe it planted a seed in his mind. . . ." She felt a small tear trickle down her cheek.

Brittany put a hand on Katrina's shoulder. "Oh, hon."

Katrina interlaced her hands in her lap and looked down. "I'm an idiot."

Brittany gave her a sympathetic smile. "*Please.* You're hardly an idiot. You're just like you were in the dorms: so book smart, so sweet, but as socially naïve as a country bumpkin. Didn't you listen to a word I said about married bankers? They're *pigs.*"

Katrina wiped away a tear. "I heard you. I did . . . but I guess I just thought . . ." She felt her head begin to ache again.

"You thought he was different?"

Katrina sighed, more tears forming in the corners of her eyes. She knew she was talking in circles, that her logic didn't make sense. "He just paid so much attention to me. I'm not used to that."

Brittany sighed. "Listen, hon, I'm really sorry for putting you in that position. I didn't realize you didn't get what was happening. But can I give you a piece of advice?"

Katrina nodded.

"I know this may sound harsh, but you need to learn how to *open your eyes*, at least if you want to survive in New York."

Katrina forced a smile. "I'm trying."

* * *

Katrina took the subway to First Avenue, then called Deb on the slow walk back to her apartment. Although she'd told her all about the debacle with Reid earlier in the day, she was confused by Brittany's advice and needed to hear her friend's voice again.

As the phone rang, Brittany's words echoed in her head:

You need to learn how to open your eyes, at least if you want to survive in New York.

Open her eyes to what?

Infidelity?

Deception?

Giving up the hope of ever finding real love?

If that's what opening her eyes meant, maybe coming to New York *had* been a mistake.

Could that really be the case?

"Hey," Deb said. "I'm on my way out the door."

Katrina sighed. "Maybe I should just come home."

"What? Why?"

"I don't think I'm cut out for New York."

"Don't think like that. You're doing great."

"You're just saying that."

"I'm not just saying that."

Katrina kicked a pebble on the sidewalk. "Maybe this mess with Reid is the universe's way of telling me I don't have what it takes to survive in the big city, that I should just pack my bags and go home."

"You're being ridiculous."

"I'm afraid this place is going to eat me alive, Deb."

"Only if you let it. Don't let it."

"Easy for you to say."

"Don't be so melodramatic. We talked about this ad nauseam earlier today. So Reid's a player. So what? Learn from it and move on. Don't let him define your experience there. It sounds to me like you've met some great people. Haven't you?"

Katrina glanced behind her in the direction of The HorseBox, the pub she'd gone to her very first night in town. "Okay. You have a point. I *have*." Shana, Grace, Josh, Justin. They were all true friends now, no doubt about it.

"See? Screw Reid. Focus on the positive."

Katrina laughed weakly. "You sound like my yoga teacher."

"She sounds like a wise woman. And since when do you do yoga?"

"I've sort of picked it up since I've been here."

"See? You *are* doing great there. So stop dwelling on the negative."

"You're right."

"Of course I'm right. But I'm also late, so I've gotta run. Be strong, my friend."

"I'm trying to, I promise. And I think I know just what I need right now to help with that."

"A stiff drink?"

"Ha! Hardly."

Katrina said good-bye to Deb and hung up the phone, then quickened her pace. If she hustled, she could make Shana's Sunday-evening class.

* * *

"Hi, Kat. What a nice surprise!" Shana kept her voice hushed, in keeping with yoga studio etiquette, but she was clearly delighted to see Katrina.

"I thought I could use some exercise tonight, not to mention one of your stories."

"Still recovering from last night?"

Katrina nodded. "That, and I'm feeling a little lost right now, like New York is too much for me to handle."

Shana put a hand on her shoulder. "This is just a rough patch. You'll get through it."

"You don't think I should pack up and go home early?"

Shana laughed quietly. "Now *that* is ridiculous." She pointed to an open spot in the front corner of the room. "We can talk after class, okay?"

"Okay."

As Katrina rolled out a mat and sat down, Shana dimmed the lights and lit a candle. She inhaled deeply, then smiled at the students. "If it's all right, tonight I'd like to ask a favor of you. I'd like each of you to share why you practice yoga, what keeps you coming back when there are so many other ways you could spend your precious free time. We have a small group, so it shouldn't take long. This is something I've wanted to do for a while, not for my benefit but for yours. We all get something different from yoga, and in my opinion that's what makes it so beautiful, so *powerful*. It's the diversity of perspective that brings us all together, and that is truly special. You can keep your eyes closed, and I'll walk around the room. When I place my hand on your head, feel free to share your thoughts with the class. If you prefer not to participate, that's fine, and no one will know. Just remain silent, and I'll move on to the next student."

Katrina tensed. What would she say when it was her turn?

Shana stood up and lightly tapped her chest. "I'll begin with my own reasons. I practice yoga because it makes me feel calm and centered, and I *teach* yoga because it brings me joy and makes me feel like I have a purpose in life."

She began to wander through the room, and the responses followed.

"I love coming to yoga because it's an escape from the chaos of my life. I love my husband and kids, but sometimes I need some time just for me."

"Coming to your class makes me remember how lucky I am to be healthy, and that it's okay to have ice cream for dinner sometimes." *(Laughter)*

"Don't judge me for saying this, but I like how it keeps my arms and butt toned." *(More laughter)*

"Yoga gives me the peace of mind to follow my own path in life, and a healthy body to do it in, although I'll never look as good as Shana does in yoga pants." *(More laughter)*

"I never used to be able to touch my toes. I love that I can touch my toes now. Is that a silly reason?" *(More laughter)*

"When I'm on a packed subway train and hating everyone around me, sometimes I close my eyes and breathe deeply, and it calms me down. I learned that here, and I love it."

Katrina heard footsteps approaching her, then felt the soft touch of Shana's hand on her head. No longer so concerned about what the others would think of her answer, she smiled and spoke directly from her heart.

"Coming to yoga class makes me feel . . . strong."

Shana gave Katrina's head a gentle squeeze, then returned to the front of the class and pressed her palms together. "Thank you *so* much for sharing those wonderful insights with me and your fellow students. I'm grateful to have you all in my class *and* in my life. Now let's meet in downward-facing dog."

After class, which had been more strenuous than any Katrina had attended, she stepped outside and called Deb again while waiting for Shana to get her things together.

"Three calls in one day? You're starting to scare me," Deb said. "You hanging in there?"

"I don't think I should come home."

Deb laughed. "That's my girl. Of course you shouldn't. I told you that like two hours ago. And three hours before that."

"Well, you were right."

"Of course I was right. I'm also about to step into a movie theater, so I've got to go. Talk soon?"

"Okay. Love you."

"You love who?" Shana asked as she walked out of the studio.

"Oh, that was my friend Deb from home."

"The one who was supposed to come here with you?"

Katrina nodded.

"You're feeling a little homesick?"

"I don't know if *homesick* is the right word. More . . . out of sorts."

"Well, in my humble opinion, leaving for good isn't the answer. But maybe leaving for just a couple days wouldn't be such a bad idea.

It might help you clear your head. There are tons of cute places to visit around here."

Katrina raised her eyebrows. That wasn't such a bad idea. Having tackled New York, the prospect of a couple of days alone somewhere didn't faze her a bit.

The realization delighted her.

"Where do you think I should go?"

Shana put a finger on her chin. "Hmm . . . maybe the Hamptons? High season is over now, so it shouldn't be too hard to find a place to stay."

"You think so? I've always heard how swanky the Hamptons are. You don't think they'd be too flashy for me?"

"East Hampton is sort of glitzy, but not Southampton. It's super quaint, and even though things will be winding down, there should be a decent number of people still out there. You should totally go."

"Is it far? Would I need to rent a car?"

Shana shook her head. "Take the Jitney. There's a stop not too far from our building. It only takes a couple of hours."

"Take the *what*?"

"The Hampton Jitney."

"What's that?"

"A bus."

"You mean like a Greyhound?"

Shana nodded.

"Why do they call it a jitney?"

"Probably because it sounds fancier. I think they give you snacks and a newspaper. And there's free Wi-Fi."

"But otherwise it's just a bus?"

Shana shrugged. "Pretty much. But you know what they say about the power of good packaging, right?"

"That sounds like something you'd talk about in one of your classes."

Shana laughed. "Good idea. I should write that down." She reached over and gave Katrina's shoulder a squeeze. "And speaking of my classes, you *are* strong, Kat."

Chapter Fifteen

There was a light drizzle in the air early the next afternoon when Katrina boarded the Hampton Jitney. It was Monday, and a few weeks into the off-season, so she was surrounded by empty seats as the driver pulled away from the curb. A complimentary *New York Times* on her lap, she pressed her forehead against the window and peered down at the busy sidewalks below. Once they emerged from the Midtown Tunnel and the skyscrapers of Manhattan began to fade into the distance, she finally relaxed and soon was asleep.

When she woke up, the Jitney was rolling quietly along a one-lane road. She glanced at her watch. They'd been traveling for less than an hour and a half, but it looked like they'd reached another planet. After a stretch of farmland, signs of civilization began to appear. A fruit stand here, a vegetable stand there, and multiple sod farms dotted the road. The most unexpected nod to modern times that Katrina noticed—and immediately adored—was a scraggly old man on the side of the road who appeared to be selling hot dogs out of a run-down RV. She hoped the Jitney driver would pull over, curious to find out what a hot dog sold on the side of a road tasted like, as well as what the man selling them would *be* like.

She chastised herself for forgetting to bring a canvas and her paints on the trip. She would have loved to paint the rickety, dusty RV juxtaposed against the swish-looking Hamptons Jitney. For all anyone knew, both vehicles could have been made by the same manufacturer, but everyone knew they would forever operate in different worlds.

After stopping briefly in Manorville, the driver pulled into Southampton. As she stepped off the bus, Katrina immediately understood why people invariably used the word *quaint* to describe the hamlet. The main street—which was actually called *Main Street*—looked as if it had been lifted from another, more genteel era. Lined with leafy trees and antique lampposts, the sidewalks were punctuated by the crisp striped awnings of clothing boutiques, jewelry stores, stationery shops, antique stores, and sandwich places, each one bright and inviting.

She'd made a reservation at a small bed-and-breakfast right past Main Street. It hadn't taken her long to choose the place—she fell for it as soon as she saw the website's photo of the classic colonial-style yellow house, complete with white plantation shutters, surrounded by a lush green lawn and a white picket fence. It had looked so . . . peaceful. As she rolled her carry-on suitcase down the pristine sidewalk toward the inn, she smiled and silently thanked Shana for the suggestion to come here. Though she'd been in town for only a few minutes, she could already tell Southampton was going to offer her just the respite she needed from the big city.

As the innkeeper handed her the key, she realized she had never stayed in a hotel alone before, and she felt a stirring of pride.

I'm staying in a bed-and-breakfast.

By myself.

I'm a grown-up.

With a hint of a smile on her lips, she climbed the stairs to the second floor.

The room wasn't big, but what it lacked in size, it made up for in charm. The queen-size bed was covered by a light-yellow canopy and topped by a fluffy down duvet swathed in a crisp white cover. An oak armoire and a dark-green velvet chair occupied one side of the room, and the white wallpaper was dotted with tiny green flowers. The plush, dark-green carpet looked as though it had just been shampooed. Warm afternoon sunlight bathed the entire room in a soft glow. The overall effect was soothing but not fussy. She also noticed how quiet it was. There was a stillness she hadn't experienced since she'd arrived in Manhattan.

After unpacking her things, she decided to take a stroll through town. She was just locking her door when she heard her phone chime. It was a text from her mother, who wanted to know if she'd set up any phone interviews yet.

Katrina deleted the message without responding, then opened the door and tossed the phone on the bed. As she descended the stairs, the innkeeper, a short, pudgy gray-haired woman who Katrina guessed was in her sixties, looked up from her desk with a warm smile.

"Get settled in okay?" she asked. Light jazz played in the background.

Katrina smiled back. "Yes, ma'am. Thank you. The room is lovely."

"You're in one of my favorites. If you haven't already, be sure to check out the view of our English garden in the back. It's just splendid, especially in the early afternoon sunlight." She spoke with a twinkle in her eye that reminded Katrina of Mrs. Claus.

"I'll be sure to do that. I was thinking of going for a walk along the beach before dinner. Is there a particular route you'd recommend I take to get there?"

The innkeeper shook her head and smiled again. "My dear, you can't go wrong in Southampton. Just see where the wind takes you, and enjoy the scenery along the way."

* * *

The innkeeper hadn't been exaggerating. Katrina found Southampton downright enchanting, especially when compared to the gritty East Village. Adding to the charm were the picturesque residential blocks surrounding Main Street. The houses were immaculate, the lawns manicured, the leaves raked, the window boxes bursting with bright flowers. She spotted a handful of old-fashioned bikes with wicker baskets propped here and there, as well as a number of people riding bikes or strolling. Most wore cable-knit sweaters tied loosely around their shoulders, and many had tiny dogs in tow. It was hard to believe it was all real—it seemed like a perfectly choreographed stage set.

Every person she saw greeted her with a smile.

She spent nearly an hour wandering the streets and window-shopping, then headed out to Cooper's Beach, a ten-minute walk from the bed-and-breakfast. She took off her shoes and held them in one hand as she strolled along the shore, enjoying the sensation of warm, soft sand crunching between her toes. Despite California's reputation for sun, a stroll along its northern beaches typically involved shoes and socks, not to mention a warm coat—and oftentimes a hat. She thought of Half Moon Bay, the closest beach to Mountain View, where the water was so frigid that even die-hard surfers wore wet suits.

The Southampton coastline boasted an imposing lineup of classic country homes, most of which were white brick finished with cedar shakes. Katrina knew that many of them had been passed down through the generations, and she tried to imagine the families gathering for tennis-and-martini-filled summer weekends over the years. Each house was separated from the shore by an iron gate to keep unwelcome gawkers at bay. Despite a few gaudy McMansions—which created a somewhat jarring contrast of old and new money—the overall effect remained undeniably charming.

Turning her gaze to the waves rolling gently onto the beach, Katrina reflected on how much her life had changed in just a few short weeks. Here she was, literally standing on the opposite end of the United States, three thousand miles from the only home she'd ever known.

In a place where she knew absolutely no one.

And she'd come here all by herself.

Everything about her life right now was unfamiliar, every experience new. Yet somehow—maybe for the first time ever—she felt comfortable in her own skin.

She felt a breeze swirl up around her, and as she reached inside her purse for a hair tie, she suddenly remembered the windy night she'd arrived in New York City. She'd been so nervous waiting in that taxi line, so afraid she wouldn't be able to do it without Deb.

Deb, who had convinced her to change her life before it was too late.

Deb, who had pushed her to go to New York on her own.

Deb, who had seen something in her that she wasn't able to see herself.

Until now.

She wandered another half mile along the beach, savoring the beauty from all sides: the deep-blue water, the white sand, the rolling dunes sprinkled with beach grass, the storybook scenery framed by a towering windmill in the distance. When the sun's rays began dancing across the waves, marking dusk's arrival, she could no longer ignore her growling stomach. Reluctantly, she turned around and made her way back to Southampton Village.

Shana had suggested she have dinner at a place that used to be called James On Main but now had a new name she couldn't remember. "I think everyone still calls it James On Main," Shana had said. After consulting with a friendly passerby, Katrina discovered it was now officially called Lori Restaurant, but judging from the woman's reaction, Shana was correct. Apparently everyone still called it James On Main. She wondered what the new owner thought of that.

She wandered down Main Street to number seventy-five, and took a peek inside. The space was much larger than it appeared from the sidewalk, its high ceilings furthering the cavernous effect. It was about half full, mostly of small groups of women, along with a few older couples. The bar was dotted with solo patrons, some of whom were also having dinner. She decided to follow their lead and eat there. She'd never felt comfortable dining alone, especially when she'd forgotten to bring something to read—as she had tonight—but she was starving, and the place looked cozy.

The bartender approached as soon as she took a seat.

"Hello there. What can I get you tonight?"

"A menu would be nice, thank you. And a Sprite, please."

"Coming right up."

Seconds later, an attractive man with salt-and-pepper hair walked up and stopped at the bar stool to her right.

"Is this seat taken?"

"Oh, no, I don't think so." Her eyes darted to his left hand. No wedding ring.

He set his drink on the bar, then took off his jacket and hung it on the back of the stool. "First time in Southampton?" he said with a smile.

She laughed. "Is it that obvious?"

"You have that look about you."

"And what look is that?"

"Wide-eyed, sincere. It's alluring."

The bartender reappeared and set down her Sprite, along with a menu. "Let me know if you have any questions. The specials are in the front," he said before disappearing again.

The man pointed to Katrina's glass. "That's all you're drinking?"

Katrina nodded.

"Can I buy you a real drink . . . what's your name?"

"Kat . . . er, Katrina," she said. "Katrina's fine."

"Well, Katrina, it's nice to meet you. I'm Preston. Now will you indulge me? I hate to drink alone."

She looked at him for a moment. He looked friendly enough, but something wasn't right. She wasn't sure why or how, but something just felt . . . off.

"Can I ask you a question, Preston?"

He smiled. "Of course."

"Are you married?"

He looked surprised. "Am I married?"

"It's not a trick question."

He hesitated for just a moment.

Just long enough.

"Good-bye, *Preston*." She picked up her drink and walked to the other side of the bar.

* * *

After a deluxe breakfast of scrambled eggs and homemade pumpkin bread early the next morning, Katrina spent nearly an hour reading the newspaper before changing into exercise clothes and heading out on a combination walk/jog around town. She was feeling noticeably stronger and, even more importantly, she was proud of herself for having made the effort.

When she got back to the bed-and-breakfast, the innkeeper was cleaning up the kitchen area.

"Well, hello there. Have a good run?"

Katrina smiled. "Calling it a *run* would be a stretch, but it was nice to get the blood pumping a little bit."

The woman put her hands on her waist. "You're in such good shape—I'm jealous."

Katrina was startled by the woman's comment. "Thank you. I'm working on it." *In such good shape?* In her entire life, she had never thought of herself as being in shape.

The innkeeper sighed. "I keep telling myself I need to exercise but never seem to get around to it. I'd love to have your discipline. Would be good for the self-confidence, you know?"

Katrina nodded. *In her eyes, I'm confident,* she thought. *Confident, disciplined, and in good shape.*

She thought about how different her life looked to her now from when she'd first arrived in New York.

Perspective really is everything.

And everyone's perspective is different.

* * *

Katrina spent the afternoon wandering in and out of the myriad boutiques and jewelry stores in Southampton Village. She couldn't really afford anything, but it was fun to look. She came close to buying a pair of strappy heels that were 60 percent off but decided against it. That she'd even considered purchasing them was victory enough for her.

After stopping for coffee, she stumbled across a boutique with a stylish pink dress in the window. She immediately thought that Grace's jewelry would be a perfect fit there, and wondered if the owner was on site. Maybe she could get a business card and have Grace get in touch. Going door-to-door to convince shop owners to carry her jewelry sounded like an incredible amount of work, and she didn't envy Grace for having to do it.

She pushed open the door and hadn't even set a foot inside when a voice barked at her from the back of the empty store.

"Can't bring that in here."

Katrina froze, then looked at the coffee cup in her hand. "This?"

A well-dressed woman appeared from behind a mannequin and nodded. "Sorry." She pointed out the door. "There's a trash receptacle right outside."

"Oh, okay. Sorry about that." She backed out of the door, embarrassed. But the latte was brand-new, and she wasn't going to toss it.

Maybe she'd stop by for that business card later.

* * *

That afternoon, Katrina did something she hadn't done since she'd arrived in New York.

She took a nap.

A long, glorious, lazy nap.

And she didn't feel guilty about it.

When she woke up, she momentarily forgot where she was. As her eyes adjusted to the dimness, it came back to her.

I'm in Southampton, New York.

On a Tuesday.

By myself.

She smiled.

There was no denying it anymore.

She was different now.

And she was happy.

That evening, she did something else she'd never done before. She went to a movie by herself.

It wasn't until she was on the Jitney back to Manhattan late the next afternoon that she realized she'd forgotten to swing by that boutique for a business card to give to Grace. Maybe she could find a similar shop in the city? She wanted to help Grace, but she was intimidated at the prospect of approaching another icy owner who didn't want coffee in her store.

Justin would never bark at a customer like that, she thought.

Then again, Justin *sold* coffee.

The warm thought of Justin was quickly squelched by the sour memory of how she'd lashed out at him after her night out with Reid. She knew he'd forgiven her for how she'd treated him, but she still hadn't forgiven herself. That would take time.

The Jitney rolled along, and as the skyline of Manhattan came into view, Katrina remembered that first taxicab ride into town, how anxious she'd been, her stomach in knots, terrified of being there without Deb. Watching the skyscrapers grow larger—many of them familiar to her—she realized how different the city felt to her now. No longer a daunting, impenetrable fortress, New York was now a familiar place where she had an apartment, and friends, and a life.

She was returning . . . home.

When she logged into her e-mail account that evening, she had a new message through LinkedIn.

It was from a recruiter, asking if she'd be interested in a senior accountant position at a software company in Sunnyvale.

Start date: December 1.

Chapter Sixteen

"Hey, look who's back. How were the Hamptons?" Justin spread his hands on the counter.

Katrina gave him a curious look as she approached. "How'd you know I was in the Hamptons?"

"Shana was in here yesterday. Plain scone and chai tea—her usual. Did you have a nice time? What can I get you?" He pointed at the chalkboard behind him. "Peter came up with a couple of new specials."

"I think I'll have my usual as well."

"Skim latte and a blueberry scone?"

"Yep. I've missed that." She patted the *New York Times* under her arm. "Thought I'd go back to my routine this morning."

"Sometimes it's good to go back to your routine. What did you do out there? Take in a couple of lawn parties, maybe play some croquet?" He squinted at her. "Although now that I think about it, I can't really picture you in an oversized hat."

She smiled. "I did remarkably little, actually. Just wandered around, went to the beach, did a lot of thinking."

"Thinking about what?"

She shrugged. "Nothing in particular, just life, I guess."

"Always a good subject in my book."

"When I got back last night I found out about a job possibility back home."

"In accounting?"

She nodded. "Senior accountant at a software company. I'd start right after I get back."

He scratched the back of his head. "Hmm . . . given the pronounced lack of enthusiasm in your voice, is a *good luck* in order?"

She shrugged. "It's a good opportunity."

"Well then, congratulations, Kat." He didn't look convinced, but, to be fair, neither was she.

"Thanks." She glanced around the room. "I know I haven't been here very long, but I'm really going to miss this place."

He tapped the counter with his palms. "This place *here*, or this place New York?"

She smiled. "Both."

He handed her the scone on a plate. "Well, for what it's worth, this place will miss you too. So, no wild nights out on the town in the Hamptons then?"

She laughed. "Oh, well, of *course*. That's a given with me, you know. I barely slept, with the clubbing and all."

He tilted his head slightly to the side. "You look different."

"I do? How so?" She put a hand on her neck and ran her fingers over her necklace. It was the one Grace had given her, with two interlocking circles.

"I'm not sure. It's like you're the same but different."

"I hope that's a good thing."

"It is." He glanced over her shoulder at the growing line behind her. "I'm sorry, Kat. I've got to get moving here. Peter will bring you that latte, okay?"

"Sounds good." She took a small bite of the scone. "Wow. I'd forgotten how yummy these are."

"Best in town. That's how to build a business, you know."

"Making amazing scones?"

He smiled. "By offering something people want before they even know they want it."

Chapter Seventeen

It had been only three days since her last yoga class, but Katrina couldn't wait to get back to the mat that evening.

She'd had an initial call with the recruiter about the accounting position, and it had gone well—extremely well, actually. It had surprised her, but for the first time she could hear self-confidence in her own voice when speaking about her knowledge and professional experience, conviction in how qualified she was for the job. Next up was a phone interview on Monday afternoon with the company's HR director. The position would be a significant step up from her job at the advertising agency, with a higher salary and more responsibility, of course. And if she took it, she'd be able to finish out her trip in New York without the constant pressure of *what comes next?* looming over her shoulder.

Granted, it wasn't her dream job. Far from it, in fact. But at least she was keeping her options open, which would keep her parents momentarily satisfied.

She might as well do the phone interview.

No harm in that, right?

As she sat down on her mat, she tried to convince herself the answer to that question was *yes*.

She closed her eyes as Shana lit a candle and began to speak to the group.

"I'm not much of a sports person, but the other day my boyfriend and I were at a bar, watching a football game. There were only a few seconds left, and one of the teams was lining up to kick a field goal to win the game. Everyone was going crazy, and I couldn't help but think how strange it was that in a few seconds one of the teams and all its fans were going to be *elated*, and the other team and all its fans *devastated*, simply because of a number on a scoreboard. I mean, when you really think about it, isn't that *silly*?" She giggled. "I guess that's why I'm not a sports person."

Katrina smiled to herself.

Shana continued. "After the game, I kept thinking about the concept of *keeping score*. While of course it's a part of professional sports, so many people keep score of their own lives by comparing themselves to others, and that is destructive. They marry the wrong person because all their friends are getting married. They buy a car they can't afford because all their friends drive nice cars. They work at a job they hate because the title sounds impressive at cocktail parties. In *your* life, it shouldn't matter what anyone else is doing, or what anyone else thinks. *You* are the only person keeping score of your life. All that should matter to you is what is important to *you*. If you make major life choices based on what other people expect from you, or what will earn the approval of others, you'll never be happy."

Katrina flinched. How did Shana *always* know?

Shana stood up. "Remember, *you're* the only referee in your life. Now let's all meet in downward dog."

Chapter Eighteen

The phone interview Monday afternoon went smoothly, as did two more after that, and before she knew it, Katrina had a formal job offer in hand . . . or at least in her in-box.

And she didn't have much time left in New York. How had it gone by so fast? She'd worked diligently through her list of things to see and do, but for each item she checked off, she had added a new one. She'd finally accepted the fact that she was never going to get through her list before she left and settled into a comfortable daily routine that began with a visit to the coffeehouse each morning.

After reading the paper there, she'd set out on foot to see the sights—some famous, some less so. Interspersed with the memorials and monuments was aimless, delicious wandering, her guidebook tucked away in her purse. By now the sites had largely become an excuse to wander the streets, watching life unfold around her. Her enchantment with the city and its streets grew stronger with each hidden park, gallery, boutique, deli, or corner store she happened upon.

She continued to paint, and had nearly covered the once-bare walls of her bedroom with her own artwork. She'd also bartered with both Grace and Shana for jewelry and yoga sessions. Shana's favorite painting was of a young girl in a Catholic school uniform doing tree pose in the middle of a park. Grace's was of a tilting stack of cardboard coasters on a shiny wooden bar.

She had no plan for what to do with the rest of the paintings when it was time to move back to California.

Yet.

One afternoon, after a long walk around Lower Manhattan and the South Street Seaport, she sat down at her computer and read the offer letter again.

Better salary, check.

More responsibility, check.

Good benefits, check.

Satisfied parents, check.

She furrowed her brow, trying to come to terms with the fact that soon she'd have to face real life again.

Then she made her decision.

It was time to move forward.

* * *

Later that week, at Justin's urging, Katrina planned to spend most of the day walking across the Brooklyn Bridge and visiting the Transit Museum. Both had been on her list for ages, but she had yet to get to them.

The list . . . the endless list.

Despite having to navigate her way through throngs of tourists who also thought it was the perfect day to walk across the Brooklyn Bridge, Katrina was glad she'd followed Justin's suggestion. She'd seen the famous bridge many times from afar, but up close it was truly stunning, the stone towers soaring majestically into the sky, the entire structure enveloped by hundreds of wire cables spread diagonally from the summits to the deck in a protective web.

And that was just the bridge itself. The views it offered of Manhattan and Brooklyn, the Statue of Liberty, Governors Island,

and the neighboring Manhattan Bridge, just up the East River, were some of the prettiest she'd seen during her entire time in New York. And to think it had taken her this long to get here.

She stopped walking and gazed back at Lower Manhattan, studying the iconic skyline. It was her first look from outside the city since her ride back from the Hamptons, and her first ever on foot. There was no doubting the city's grandeur, but it was fantastic for her to realize that it no longer intimidated her.

When she reached the Brooklyn side, she followed the pedestrian exit and made her way east, grateful that the bulk of the camera-wielding tourists seemed to be turning around to head back across the span. She wandered through Cadman Plaza Park, which led to the steps of the venerable Kings County Courts building. She peered behind the pillars and wondered who was inside, standing in front of a judge right then, possibly awaiting a decision that would forever alter the path of his or her life.

She meandered south for a few blocks, stopping several times along Court Street to check out the sidewalk vendors and their wobbly card tables, which featured everything from trench coats and cheap sunglasses to Bibles and decorative cell phone cases. When she reached Schermerhorn Street she turned left and descended the steps marking the entrance of the Transit Museum, which she imagined must frequently be mistaken for a working subway station.

After spending a couple of hours learning about the history of the cavernous tunnels running beneath New York City, she asked a security guard to point her in the direction of the Brooklyn Promenade. Justin had insisted she check it out, calling it one of the prettiest spots in the entire city. She hadn't heard of it, but by now she realized that didn't mean a thing. She felt a twinge of insider's pride, a sort of kinship with the locals, who knew that the neighborhoods offered more interesting discoveries than many of the tourist destinations.

And Justin hadn't let her down yet.

Ten minutes later, she decided he was right.

Located at the west end of a historic neighborhood called Brooklyn Heights, the Brooklyn Promenade offered a spectacular view of Lower Manhattan—framed by the Brooklyn Bridge on one end and the Statue of Liberty on the other—that could have been pulled straight from a movie set. The towering buildings clustered on the other side of the East River, which she'd just passed through the day before on her way to the South Street Seaport, were now at least a mile away, but somehow they looked close enough to reach out and touch. The illusion was striking.

And profound.

And beautiful.

She thought about how much this view must have changed over the years, gradually shifting as Manhattan grew denser, the buildings taller, the skyline fuller. Although it was—and would always be—Manhattan, it was always changing.

The same, yet different.

She stared across the river and thought about how scared she'd been of New York just a few short weeks ago. Where had that fear gone? And what had taken its place?

She was the same person, yet different.

And soon she would be leaving all this behind.

For financial security.

For professional stability.

For an office.

It's okay. I'll be okay.

She thought of the offer letter, now printed out and sitting on her desk.

It was signed, sealed, and ready to be mailed.

Before she knew it, she'd be back in California.

It had been a tough decision, but it was for the best.

It's for the best.

She balled her hands into fists, trying to ignore the churning feeling in her stomach, trying to convince herself that accepting the job was the right thing to do. She *had* to go back to Mountain View. If she didn't, what would she do here? As much as she loved exploring the city, she couldn't afford to do that forever. Her time here had felt like a dream, but this particular dream had to come to an end.

I can always come back to visit, right?

As she looked back across the East River, she suddenly wanted to capture the conflicting emotions she was feeling by painting the view in front of her. But her supplies were back at her apartment, and it would take her a good hour if not longer to bring them back. By that time it would be getting dark, so she'd have to come back another day.

Which reminded her of how few of them she had left.

On the way to the subway, she wandered through Brooklyn Heights, admiring the picturesque brownstones lining the quiet streets. Each one was prettier than the one before it. Unlike her neighborhood, which was a motley blend of pristine and downright dirty, this area was uniformly well manicured. It was exactly what she'd envisioned when she thought of what living in New York City could be like, back when the idea of living a more fulfilling life was just a fantasy.

She turned onto Montague Street, which was clearly the neighborhood's main drag, and drank in the small-town feel of it. Though she spotted a few chain stores, most of the establishments seemed to be of the mom-and-pop variety, including a small hardware store that looked as if it were straight out of the 1950s. The space next door to it was boarded up, with a "For Lease" sign taped up on the front window. Katrina wondered what had been there before, and why it had failed, or whether it had failed at all. Maybe the owners had just decided to move on? Try something different?

Maybe they'd packed up and moved to the West Coast for an adventure . . . or a new beginning.

Just before she reached the subway, she felt the urge for coffee and ducked into a Starbucks. It was the first time she'd been inside one since she'd left California. While she waited for her drink, she had a flashback to her former life at home, to picking up her coffee at Starbucks every morning, to bringing it to her quiet cubicle in the office.

"Nonfat latte for Kat!" the barista called out.

Katrina turned around, momentarily surprised to hear herself referred to as *Kat*. She'd never ordered a drink at Starbucks as Kat before. In fact, she'd never referred to herself as Kat at all. She didn't mind when her friends in New York called her that, but she hadn't yet made the transition herself . . . until she'd ordered this latte.

The next time she visited a Starbucks, it would most likely be in Mountain View.

Would she become *Katrina* again there?

What would happen to Kat?

She looked at the name on her cup and realized how much she didn't want to lose her.

It was just a name written in pen on a coffee cup, but it was so much more than that.

It was a different life.

Kat's life.

She sipped her latte and thought about Shana—kind, gentle Shana, who had made Katrina feel welcome from the moment they met. And Grace, of course. What would things be like without spunky Grace around? And sweet, good-natured Josh. She was going to miss him too.

She thought about the coffeehouse, and how much she was going to miss having a friendly place to sit quietly and read the newspaper before tackling the day. And talking to Justin, who always made her feel good about herself, no matter what. She was going to miss that. She was going to miss *him*.

She'd even miss Peter.

Though she hadn't known them for long, she felt more connected to this group of friends than to anyone except Deb at home. She wasn't sure how or why it had happened, but they knew a side of her that others back in California didn't—and she feared never would.

And the yoga studio. She was going to miss having a place to collect her thoughts, to reflect on what was important to her. To feel healthy inside and out.

And her walks.

The aimless wandering.

The boundless learning.

She was going to miss all of it.

She left Starbucks and slowly began walking to the subway. Her legs were heavy, her head a bit fuzzy. She was distracted, almost sluggish.

She was . . . sad.

Sad at the thought of what her life would soon be like again. Back in Mountain View, back in a place where . . .

Halfway to the subway stop she froze.

Back in a place where . . .

Oh my gosh!

She turned around and looked back down Montague Street.

She had an idea.

A big idea.

She had to talk to Shana and Grace.

But first she had to talk to Justin.

She tossed the rest of the latte into a trash can, then quickened her pace and descended into the subway station. As she was about to swipe her MetroCard, she heard the unmistakable sound of an approaching train. She hurried through the turnstile and toward the platform just as a Manhattan-bound train pulled to a stop. She stepped inside and took a seat as the doors closed behind her, already mentally mapping out what to tell Justin.

She'd reached the subway at just the right moment. She hoped that was a good sign.

* * *

Twenty minutes later, Katrina resurfaced in the East Village and made her way toward the coffeehouse, her mind racing as she walked.

Opening observation about your New York experience.

Main statement and supporting points.

Closing expression of optimism for the future.

Just before she reached the entrance, she stopped walking and closed her eyes. If Justin liked her idea, her life would change on a dime. Was she ready for that?

She balled her hands into fists.

It's time to stop being afraid.

You can do this!

She took a deep breath and pushed the door open, the now-familiar chimes announcing her arrival.

The place was about half full. She scanned the room for Justin but didn't see him. Peter was behind the counter, chatting with an elderly male customer. As soon as Peter handed the man his coffee and the gentleman walked away, Katrina stepped forward.

"Hi, Peter. Is Justin here?"

He pointed over his shoulder. "He's in the back."

"You think I could go talk to him?"

Peter shook his head. "I don't think that would be a good idea."

"Are you sure? It's sort of important."

"He's talking to his wife."

Katrina's eyes opened wide. "Really?"

Peter nodded.

"Why?"

He shrugged. "She came in here to speak to him about something, I'm not sure what. He didn't want to do it out here, so they went in the back."

"Does she come to see him often?"

"She used to. You know, before they split up. Since then, I haven't seen her much."

Katrina stared at the closed door and wondered what they were talking about. Were they getting back together?

"You want something to drink while you wait?" Peter asked.

She looked at him. "You think I should wait?"

"Are you in a hurry?"

"Not really."

"Then why not stick around? I'm sure he'll be out soon."

Katrina stiffened. She was anxious to talk to Justin about her idea, but the queasy sensation rolling through her told her she was feeling more than anxiety.

The thought of seeing him with his wife made her uneasy, even nervous.

But that wasn't all.

The thought of seeing Justin with his wife also made her . . . jealous.

She caught her breath.

Oh no.

"Katrina?" Peter eyed her with concern. "You okay?"

She blinked. "I'm sorry. Yes, sure. I'll have a skim latte. Thanks, Peter."

"No blueberry scone? Aren't you leaving town soon? You won't have many more chances to get 'em warm like they are right now."

She laughed. "Okay, sure. Why not?"

He pointed to her purse. "You've got your *New York Times* in there?"

"Always."

He nodded toward her favorite table. "Go have a seat and read. I'll bring over your order in a minute."

"Okay. Thanks, Peter."

"My pleasure." He glanced briefly at the closed door, then lowered his voice and gave Katrina a look she hadn't seen before. "Between you and me, I never liked her anyway."

* * *

Fifteen minutes later, Katrina heard the click of a door. She glanced up from her newspaper and saw Justin emerge from the back room, followed by his wife, who didn't look anything like Katrina had expected. She was tall and slender, with straight, nearly white blonde hair cut into a sharp bob. She wore a fitted black pantsuit and a single strand of pearls. Though she was undeniably beautiful, her eyes were cold.

Katrina turned away and forced herself to stare at her newspaper until she heard the chime of the front door. She read the same sentence six times, not grasping a single word.

Her foot began to tap under the table.

What were they talking about?

Why am I so nervous?

She touched the bridge of her nose and pictured the freckles there. She hadn't gotten a close look, but she bet Justin's wife didn't have freckles. She looked too chic to have freckles.

"Hey, Kat. I heard you wanted to talk to me."

She looked up and saw Justin standing there, a strained expression on his face.

"Are you okay?" She yanked her hand away from her face.

He frowned. "When I got married, I never dreamed that one day I'd be reviewing divorce papers."

"You're getting divorced?" Her foot stopped tapping, and her nerves began to calm, now that it was just the two of them.

"Looks like it."

"Oh my gosh, I'm so sorry, Justin." She gestured to the empty chair at her table. "Do you want to talk about it?"

He took a seat but shook his head. "Not really."

"It might make you feel better to talk about it. Isn't that what you always tell me?"

He smiled. "I appreciate that, but right now I'd rather talk about *anything* other than this."

She didn't reply. What could she say to a man whose wife had just officially left him?

Finally, he spoke. "So what did you want to see me about?"

She stood up to leave. "Maybe I should come back another time. I feel like I'm intruding."

He reached out to squeeze her arm. "Kat, sit down. I could use the distraction. *And* the friendly face."

She slowly sat back down, trying not to notice how warm his hand felt on her arm. "Are you sure? I don't want to bother you."

"I'm sure. And you could never bother me. Now, what did you want to talk to me about?"

She took a deep breath and went over her talking points in her head.

Opening observation about your New York experience.

Main statement and supporting points.

Closing expression of hope for the future.

She closed her eyes.

You can do this.

"Kat?" Justin asked. "You there?"

She opened her eyes, then sat up straight and pressed her hands together. "Okay. Well, as you know, I'm supposed to be leaving soon but have really grown to love New York . . ."

Chapter Nineteen

Grace narrowed her eyes at Katrina. "So why all the secrecy? You're like the freaking CIA all of a sudden."

"What's going on, Kat?" Shana asked. "You have me curious."

"First, let me buy each of you a drink. What would you like?" They were seated at a table at Headless Horseman in Union Square.

"The lightweight's buying drinks? Now I'm *really* curious," Grace said. "I'll take a Stoli and soda."

"I'll have the same," Shana said.

After Katrina had ordered the cocktails and a Sprite for herself, she turned to face her friends. She spread her palms on the table and took a deep breath, then began her prepared remarks, which she'd practiced all afternoon.

"You know how much I've enjoyed getting to know you both, right? And how much I appreciate the way you took me under your wing, no questions asked, even though I was a little, um . . . reserved."

Grace coughed. "A little? Dude, a fully booked restaurant was less reserved."

"Be nice, Gracie." Shana smiled at Katrina. "You've really blossomed since then, Kat."

"I know I have, and I owe a lot of that to you two. With the exception of Deb, you've become my best friends, even though I will never be able to go drinking properly with you."

"You're tragic at drinking," Grace said. "It's truly embarrassing."

"Gracie . . ." Shana said.

"That's okay. It's true. I'm a terrible drinker. But it's fine, because while I've always known that booze isn't my thing, now I'm fine with just *saying* so, as opposed to avoiding social situations altogether. But what I'm getting at is that you two mean a lot to me now, and while I know it sounds really cheesy, I couldn't imagine my life without both of you in it."

Grace reached a tiny arm behind her own shoulder and patted herself on the back. "I tend to have that effect on people."

Katrina looked at Shana. "You know how much I've loved taking your classes, right? And especially how wonderful I think your stories are, despite what Blair says about them."

Shana nodded.

Katrina turned to Grace. "And you know I'm crazy about your jewelry, right? How I think that any buyer who wouldn't snap it up is foolish?"

Grace narrowed her eyes again. "Where are you going with this? Is this the part where you tell us you're really a millionaire CEO? Or a man?" She looked up and around the room. "Are we on camera right now?"

Shana patted Grace's head. "You really need to stop watching so much reality TV."

"*Anyhow*," Katrina said, continuing with her script, "since I've been in New York, I've changed a lot, and I've realized that much of that change has to do with how I look at things now, and that a new perspective can completely alter how you experience something. Like seeing Manhattan from the Brooklyn Promenade, for example." She looked at Shana. "Or new packaging, like the Hampton Jitney."

Grace gave her a strange look. "Say what? Dude, are you okay?"

Katrina nodded. "I'm fine. What I'm trying to say—in a rather roundabout way, I admit —is this: I have an idea." She shifted in her seat and took another deep breath, then looked at Shana. "First, I've been doing a lot of thinking about you. I don't think you realize how special your yoga classes are, Shana. You have a real gift for connecting with people."

Shana smiled. "I do?"

"She does?" Grace said.

"*Yes*, she does." Katrina put a hand on Shana's arm. "Your talks are so insightful. When I listen to them, I always feel like you're talking directly to me, as though you know just what I need to hear, exactly when I need to hear it, before I even know I need to hear it."

Grace held up her palms. "This is getting a little too touchy-feely for me."

Katrina laughed. "What I mean is, I think your talks probably have that effect on all your students, that everyone gets what they need out of them, however it applies to their own life."

Shana's face broke into a grin. "You mean like . . . a horoscope? That's how I think about them when I write them."

"Yes! That's exactly what I was thinking. It's all about your own perspective."

"As you well know, Blair thinks I should focus more on making people sweat," Shana said.

"Blair doesn't know what she's talking about," Katrina said.

"Is this going anywhere?" Grace sipped her drink and pretended to nod off.

Katrina nodded. "I think Shana probably already knows this, but I suspect her heart isn't in the Broadway thing anymore, if it ever was. I think—however unexpectedly—she's found her heart's now in teaching yoga." She looked at Shana. "Am I wrong about that?"

Shana looked down. "You're not wrong. Josh says the same thing."

Katrina turned to Grace and began the next section of her speech. "And I've also been thinking about you."

Grace fluttered her eyelashes. "*Moi*? That's my favorite subject."

"Yes, *you*. I love your jewelry, and I know how you've been beating your head against the wall trying to find stores willing to sell it."

"True. Lame-ass finicky buyers."

"And then there's me." Katrina put a hand on her chest. "I've never really said it out loud, but deep down . . . I've always dreamed about having a place to show my paintings."

"As you should! How many times have I told you I love your paintings?" Shana said.

Grace checked the time on her phone. "Are we going to get to hear this big idea before I'm old and gray? My mom and her sister both went gray prematurely, so I don't have a lot of time."

"Let her talk, Gracie," Shana said.

Katrina took one last deep breath, then exhaled. "Okay, here it is. I'd like to open a new kind of multifaceted studio . . . and I'd like you two to help me."

"Say what?" Grace said.

"What do you mean by *new kind*?" Shana asked.

Katrina looked at Shana. "Remember the other day in class, when you asked us to share why we do yoga, and we all had a different response?"

"That made me so happy."

"Well, that's what I'm thinking this place would offer—something unique and special for everyone. It would be a yoga studio, but not just *any* yoga studio. I envision a beautiful, welcoming space where you can teach more classes—and inspire others—as you've inspired me, and have more fun doing it than you do working for Blair. But it wouldn't be just yoga." She pointed to Grace. "We'd also sell your jewelry . . . and my paintings."

"Ooh, I like that." Grace rubbed her tiny hands together. "I like any plan that involves selling my jewelry."

"We'd position the studio as a place for people to relax, hang out with friends, and talk, maybe look at things from a new angle, or just a place to get motivated or inspired, in whatever way that makes sense to them."

Katrina gave Shana an anxious look. "What do you think?"

Shana bit her lip, then slowly shook her head. "Honestly, it sounds amazing. Really amazing. But I don't have the money for something like that, Kat. I'm sorry."

"I have some money, but other than doing taxes, I don't know squat about running that kind of business," Grace said.

Katrina leaned toward them and spread her hands on the table. "I know. That's why I spoke to Justin first."

Shana raised her eyebrows. "Justin?"

"Yes. He'd mentioned that he's always looking for new investment opportunities, so I ran my idea by him. He knows a lot about this sort of thing because he's been operating several small businesses for a while. Did you know that in addition to the coffeehouses, he owns three delis and two pubs?"

"Wow, who knew Justin was such a badass?" Grace said.

Katrina smiled. "He's so modest, isn't he? Anyhow, we talked about it, and then we sort of expanded on the idea a little bit. He had a lot of good ideas, actually."

"What do you mean, *expanded* on the idea?" Shana asked.

"Well, as I was trying to explain my thoughts to him—to convey that I wanted a quiet, friendly place where people could get together—I realized that his coffeehouse already has that vibe. So we got to talking, and we thought maybe we could add coffee and pastries to the mix. Nothing fancy, but make the place a combination yoga studio/coffeehouse with soft music playing in the background, and maybe a basket of newspapers and cool magazines for people to read if they're on their own. *Plus* Justin's amazing scones to nibble on. In blueberry *and* plain, of course."

"Sounds dreamy," Shana said. "And yummy. Totally up my alley."

"So Justin's on board with this?" Grace asked. "Like for real?"

Katrina nodded. "If we're in for the elbow grease, he's in to back us financially. He'd be the main investor, and he'd help the three of us work out the rest based on our availability, interest level, and skills. For example, Justin could teach me how to make lattes, but I could also do the books. And Grace could manage the tax side of things."

Shana's expression changed from excitement to one of confusion. "But what would all this mean for *you*? You're supposed to be going home soon to start that new job."

Katrina smiled. "I guess . . . my plans would have to change."

Shana clapped her hands together. "No way! You'd really stay here?"

Katrina nodded. "I really would. I can't believe I'm saying it out loud, but yes, I really would."

Grace turned her hand into a paw. "Meeeeooow. Way to *go*, Kitty Kat!"

Katrina removed a small notebook from her purse and opened it on the table. "I know it would be pretty life-altering—what am I saying, *totally* life-altering—to do this. But if there's one thing I've learned in my time here, it's that change is only scary if you let it be."

Shana clapped her hands again. "I love that! Can I use it in one of my classes?"

"Of course." Katrina removed a pen from her purse and tapped the paper. "Here's a detailed list of what we'd have to do to make it happen."

Grace rolled her eyes. "You and your lists. Some things will never change."

"This is terrifical," Shana said. "I'm so excited!"

"What are you thinking of calling this hippie-dippie yoga studio slash comfy coffeehouse slash place to show Kitty's paintings slash shop that sells my freaking amazing jewelry?" Grace asked, then put a hand on her jaw. "Damn, that was a mouthful, even for my big mouth."

Katrina pointed her pen at her. "Now *that* is a good question."

Chapter Twenty

"You all packed?" Justin asked as he took a seat across from Katrina.

She broke off a piece of scone and nodded. "All set."

He gestured to the tan suede jacket she had on, another gem she'd found at a consignment store. "Given how you never seem to wear the same outfit twice, I'm guessing you have quite a bit more stuff than when you arrived. Did you have to buy another suitcase?"

"Perhaps. You have a problem with that, sir?" She gave him a look of mock indignation, but she was secretly thrilled to be classified as any kind of fashionista—and that he'd noticed what she wore.

He laughed. "If you need to leave anything at my place while you're in California, you're more than welcome to."

"I'm fine, but thanks for the offer. I'm actually storing most of my stuff at Grace's apartment." She wondered what his house was like though. She'd learned he owned a single-family brownstone on East Twenty-Third and now lived there alone. Were he and his wife still speaking? Though she was curious, she didn't want to be intrusive.

"What time are you leaving for the airport?" Justin asked.

"Not until two. My flight's at four o'clock."

"I'm sorry I can't drive you there."

"Don't worry about it. You have a pretty good excuse. How are you feeling?"

"About my meeting?"

She nodded.

"Not great. I never imagined I'd be hiring a divorce lawyer to handle the separation of assets. To be honest, it sounds like something out of a soap opera."

Katrina frowned. "I'm so sorry. It's bound to get easier once you get through this part, right?"

He shrugged. "That's what I keep telling myself. That and *it's for the best.*"

"It *is* for the best. I'm sure of it. You deserve so much better. *No one* deserves to be treated like that, especially not you."

"I appreciate that. So what do you have there?" He pointed at a rectangular item propped against her chair. It was thin and wrapped in brown construction paper.

She felt her cheeks get a bit warm. "This? Um, well, this is for you." She reached down to pick it up, then handed it to him.

"For me?" He looked genuinely surprised. "What is it?"

"Open it and see."

He glanced over at the cash register. There was just one customer there, and Peter was taking care of him.

"Don't mind if I do." He carefully unwrapped the package to reveal a painting Katrina had done on the Brooklyn Promenade. It featured a lone empty bench, seen from the back. The Brooklyn Bridge rose up in the background on one side of it, the skyscrapers of Lower Manhattan on the other, but they were intentionally blurry, almost too blurry to make out at all. Only the bench was in focus—in addition to two items sitting on top.

A *New York Times* and a paper coffee cup.

Justin studied the painting. "Wow. It's beautiful, Kat."

She blushed. "That's kind of you to say."

"No, really, I'm not just saying it."

"I thought it might be nice for you to look at New York City from a different angle, especially now. For, um, you know, a couple of reasons."

"Thank you. I love it."

She pointed to the paper cup in the painting. "That's a skim latte, by the way."

He laughed. "No blueberry scone?"

"Maybe in the next one."

"I hope there is a next one." He held her gaze for a moment, and her pulse began to quicken. Could he tell how she felt?

Just before the silence turned awkward, he broke it. "I sincerely appreciate the thought, Kat. Thank you again." He stood up and tucked the painting under his arm.

She smiled. "You're welcome."

* * *

Katrina was just descending the front steps of her building when the town car pulled up to the curb. "Thanks for picking me up, Enrique. I'm so glad I didn't lose your card."

"That makes two of us, Miss Katrina. Did you have a nice time in New York?" He loaded her bags into the trunk, then opened the door for her and closed it behind her as she buckled her seat belt.

"I did, thanks. A wonderful time."

"Sad to be leaving us?"

"Not really."

He frowned as they pulled into the street. "Had enough?"

"The opposite, actually. I'm not headed home for long—just enough time to pack up and move back here."

"Is that so? For good?"

"I'd say for . . . indefinitely."

"I guess you'll have to hang on to my card then." He winked into the rearview mirror.

She smiled back. "I guess I will."

As the sedan rolled out of Manhattan toward JFK, Katrina mulled over how much had changed since she'd taken this trip in the opposite direction.

Professionally.

Personally.

Physically.

Her whole life was different now.

She wondered what else the future might hold for her, and the uncertainty was exhilarating.

* * *

"Did your parents freak out when you told them you're packing up and moving to New York in a few weeks?" Deb put her car in reverse and craned her neck to look behind her as she pulled out of the parking spot. It was eight hours later, and they were in the short-term lot at SFO. "I bet your mom lost it."

Katrina scrunched up her nose. "I sort of . . . haven't told them yet."

Deb snapped her head back around. "You're joking."

Katrina pressed her palms against her cheeks. "I couldn't do it, Deb. I really wanted to, but they were so excited about the job offer, especially my mother. When I told her about it, she sounded so, I don't know, *proud* of me. And you know she's never proud of me."

"Oh please, she's proud of you. She just has a hard time showing it."

"*Hard* is an understatement."

"So you choked and didn't say anything about anything?"

"You could say that."

"Why didn't you just e-mail them the news?"

Katrina sighed. "I couldn't. My father ingrained in me that important conversations *must* involve a human voice."

"How about voice mail? You could have left a message when you knew they weren't home. That's what I would have done."

"Not helping, Deb. I need to tell them in person, or they'll forever hold it over my head how rude I was."

Deb laughed. "Remind me to be far, far away when that conversation takes place. As in on the moon."

"Ugh. I'm so glad they're out of town right now. I'm not ready to face them."

"Where are they?"

"They had a wedding to attend in Santa Barbara over the weekend and are taking a few days to explore the coast on the way home. They get back the day after tomorrow."

"So that gives you time to give notice on your place? That way there's no turning back?"

Katrina nodded. "That's my plan."

"Not a bad one, actually. It'll force your hand a little bit, not that you need any forcing these days. You're like a new woman."

Katrina looked out the window as they merged onto the freeway. "Thanks. I kind of *feel* like a new woman." *Finally.*

"Are you going to ask your parents to start calling you *Kat*?"

Katrina coughed. "Can you imagine? Talk about pouring gasoline on the fire. My mother would throw a fit."

"Where are you meeting them?"

"Sundance in Palo Alto."

"Sweet. Nothing like a fat steak dinner at Sundance, regardless of who's on the other side of the table."

Katrina put a hand on her stomach. "Unfortunately, I have a feeling I'm not going to have much of an appetite."

"What about now? You hungry?"

"Starving."

"Want to stop by Stephens Green for a bite?"

"Can we pick up my car at my parents' house first?"

"Sure. I cleared my whole evening for you."

Katrina looked at her. "You did?"

"Yes, ma'am."

"I'm flattered."

"It's not every day my best friend comes back to town. And besides, I have nothing to eat in my fridge, so with or without you, I'm going out to dinner."

Katrina laughed. "Now I remember why I've missed you so much."

* * *

"Wow. This place is empty," Katrina said.

Deb glanced up from her menu and looked around the restaurant. "It is?"

"There are exactly four other people here." Katrina gestured to a couple sitting a few tables away from them, then at two men sitting separately at the bar, both of whom were watching a soccer game on the wall-mounted TV.

"So? It's a Tuesday at six o'clock."

"Was Stephens Green always like this?"

"Like this what?"

"This, I don't know . . . *dead*?"

Deb laughed. "We're in *Mountain View*, my friend. It's always like this."

"It is?"

"It is. Look who became a big-city girl."

Katrina thought of her first night in Manhattan, when she'd gone for a beer with Shana, Josh, and Grace. The memory replayed in her head like a movie—hearing the story of how Shana and Josh became a couple, seeing Grace's jewelry for the first time, being overwhelmed by her new surroundings. That had also been a Tuesday, and she'd been shocked at how crowded the bar had been. Stephens Green tonight seemed like a ghost town by comparison.

Has it really always been like this?

The place also looked different, but she couldn't put her finger on how.

What is it?

"Hello? You there?" Deb snapped her fingers.

"I'm sorry, what?"

Deb cocked her head to the right. A waitress was standing there, notepad in hand, waiting patiently for Katrina to order.

"I'm sorry. I'll have a garden salad with chicken and a Sprite, thank you."

"Got it." The waitress turned on her heel and left.

"Are you okay?" Deb gave her a look. "You're acting weird."

"I'm fine. Just a little disoriented, I guess."

"Culture shock?"

Katrina laughed weakly. "Maybe a little."

"I thought that might happen."

"You did?"

"Of course. New York and Mountain View might as well be on different planets."

Katrina nodded. "I expected it going out there, but I never really gave any thought to what it would be like when I came back."

The waitress set down their drinks and left again. Deb held up her glass of wine for a toast. "Here's to new beginnings."

"To new beginnings."

Deb clinked her glass against Katrina's, then frowned. "I'm so jealous. I can't believe I never got to visit you out there. Stupid promotion."

"Don't say that. You worked hard for that promotion, and you deserved it. Plus I suspect you love your fancy new title and everything that goes with it."

"Okay, maybe I do. But I still feel like I missed out."

Katrina took a sip of her Sprite. "Well, you'll have another chance to come visit me. I *love* my new neighborhood."

"What's it called again?"

"Brooklyn Heights. It's right across the Brooklyn Bridge, super quaint, lots of brownstones, very *Sesame Street.*"

"And your new apartment is just a few blocks from where the studio will be?"

"Yep, practically right around the corner. My street is a lot like the one I was on in Gramercy, only less busy. And cuter. And cleaner. And a bit cheaper."

"We all know how much you like clean, and what's not to like about cute and cheap? I can't wait to see your new place. It'll be months before I can get away though. My schedule keeps getting busier and busier. It's like the curse of the promotion, you know?"

Katrina smiled. "Actually, I *don't* know. And I don't *want* to know."

"Touché."

"If it's going to be a few months before you can get out for a visit, maybe you can come for the grand opening. That would be perfect timing. I'd love to have you there."

Deb sipped her wine. "Have you set a date yet?"

"If all goes according to schedule, it will be the fifteenth of May."

"That's not very far away. I mean it is, but it isn't, you know?"

Katrina nodded. "And we have a *lot* to do. We got a great deal on the lease, but part of that was because we agreed to take the space as is. It needs a lot of work to turn it into what it already looks like in my head."

"Sounds like this Justin knows his way around a tool shed. I'm sure he'll turn it into something spectacular."

Katrina hesitated for a moment before responding.

"What?" Deb asked.

Katrina waved a hand in front of her. "It's nothing."

Deb set down her wineglass. "You're lying."

"No, I'm not."

"Yes, you are."

"Okay, maybe I am."

Deb rolled her eyes. "Of course you are. You're like the worst liar in the whole world, did you know that? Literally on the entire planet."

"I'm well aware, thank you very much."

"Then what is it?"

Katrina sighed. "Well, the place needs a lot of fixing up before we can open for business, but lately, well, lately . . . I've been wondering if Justin will be fixed by then too."

"Fixed? You mean like neutered?"

Katrina laughed. "I just mean I wonder if he'll be healed from how much his wife hurt him."

Deb raised her eyebrows. "You mean . . ."

Katrina gave her a sheepish look. "Maybe."

"Crush?"

Katrina nodded slowly.

"Ooh, do tell."

"There's not that much to tell, really. It's just that I've been thinking about it lately, or *him*, I guess. I mean, thinking about him in a way I never did before. When we first met, I thought he was good-looking, but I saw his wedding ring like two seconds later, so I never thought of him that way, and we became friends."

True friends. Justin is a true friend.

The waitress appeared with their food, and they both dug in.

"Since *when* have you been thinking about him that way?" Deb pointed a curly fry at Katrina.

"Since the day I first talked to him about the studio. I was so excited to share my idea with him, not just as a potential investor but also because his opinion means a lot to me. But when I got to the coffeehouse, his wife was there. I think . . . I think seeing him with her made me look at him in a different way. It's like something suddenly kicked in."

Deb nodded knowingly. "The sudden kick-in. I've been a victim of that."

"And then later, as he and I were talking about the studio, I realized that I was as excited about the idea of working with *him* as I was about the idea itself, you know?"

Deb kept nodding. "Does *he* know?"

Katrina put a hand over her heart. "Oh gosh, I sure hope he doesn't. *I* don't even know. I mean, I *didn't* even really know. I mean . . . you know what I mean. Ugh. *I'm* not even sure I know what I mean." She slumped her shoulders.

"I *totally* know what you mean. And I think it's spectacular."

"You do?"

"I do. But tread carefully. That poor man's been through the ringer, and men take even longer to get over a broken heart than women do, at least according to *Cosmo*."

Katrina laughed. "Don't worry. It's taken me nearly thirty years to stand up to my parents, remember? And who am I kidding? I haven't even done *that* yet. I'm hardly an Olympic sprinter in the game of life. Plus he may not even like me back. To be honest, I'm afraid that if I slip up and let on how I'm feeling, he'll shoot me down, and then everything will be all awkward and terrible."

"I don't know the man, but he'd be a fool not to like you back. And as for timing, I'm sure we can figure out a plan. And speaking of your parents, did I tell you to remind me to get the hell out of Dodge before that conversation goes down?"

Katrina held up her Sprite in a mock toast. "Here's to getting out of Dodge. You have no idea how much I wish I could be in the car with you."

Chapter Twenty-One

Two evenings later, having officially given notice on her apartment, Katrina pulled into the parking lot of Sundance. It was 6:58 p.m. She spotted her mother's Lexus a few cars down and wondered what time her parents had arrived. She checked her face in the rearview mirror, adjusted the pink silk scarf around her neck, and applied some lip gloss before stepping out of the car.

You can do this.

You can tell them.

You're different now.

As she walked toward the entrance, she mentally went over her prepared remarks, which she'd been rehearsing all afternoon. She'd also practiced in the shower, while getting dressed and drying her hair, and during the entire drive to Palo Alto.

Opening observation about the restaurant and the evening in general.

Main statement and supporting points.

Closing expression of conviction and excitement for what lies ahead.

Just before she reached the entrance, she stopped, closed her eyes, and pressed her palms together, as if in one of Shana's yoga classes.

She inhaled deeply.

You can do this.

She opened her eyes and opened the door.

* * *

Katrina gave her father's name to the hostess. The young woman gestured toward her parents, who were having a glass of wine at the bar. Katrina glanced down at her coffee-colored sheath and walked toward them, forcing the corners of her mouth upward into an awkward smile.

"Hi, Mom. Hi, Dad."

They turned to face her at the same time. Though her mother stayed seated, her father stood up and gave her a hug. "Well, hello there, sunshine. Aren't you a sight for sore eyes?"

Katrina leaned toward her mother, who gave her a light kiss on the cheek. "I'm glad you made it home safely. It's good to see you back where you belong," she said.

Katrina nodded but didn't respond.

"What can I get you to drink?" her father asked.

"I think I'll just have some sparkling water."

"That's all? No wine?"

She shook her head. "Water is fine, thanks, Dad."

Her mother picked up her wineglass. "Is that a new dress?"

Katrina nodded. "I bought it in the East Village. What do you think? I got these boots there too."

"And those? I've never seen you wear jewelry like that." She pointed to Katrina's earrings.

Katrina's hand flew self-consciously to the hoops she was wearing. "My friend Grace designs jewelry. Do you like them? I thought they went well with the dress and boots."

"It's a nice outfit. I'm not convinced it's your style though. A little flashy for you, if you ask me."

Katrina's father handed her the sparkling water and sat back down on his stool. "I think you look beautiful. I especially like that scarf you've got on. Did you get that in New York too?"

"Sure did."

Her mother put a hand to Katrina's cheek. "Your face looks a little thinner. Have you lost weight?"

"Maybe a little. I've been walking a lot, and doing yoga."

Her mother raised an eyebrow. "Yoga? I've never heard you mention that before."

"I just started. One of my friends there is an instructor."

"Doesn't that take a lot of coordination?"

"I'm not very good at it, but I've grown to like it. I like it a *lot*, in fact."

Her father noticed the hostess, who was walking toward them. "Looks like our table is ready. Shall we?"

Katrina forced a smile. "Sounds great. I'm starving."

* * *

Katrina's father raised his wineglass. "To Katrina. You've got new clothes, new jewelry, even a new exercise routine. Sounds like you came into your own on the East Coast, sunshine. Good for you."

Katrina crossed her legs under the table, careful to keep her ankles touching even though her mother couldn't see them. "I did. Thanks, Dad." She was grateful for the recognition, but also dreading where the conversation was inevitably headed. "It was a really good two months for me."

"You spent most of your time sightseeing, I imagine? There's so much to take in there," he said.

She took a sip of water. "Yes, a lot of sightseeing. And I . . . I started painting again."

Her mother arched an eyebrow. "Painting?"

"I got into the habit of taking long walks to explore the city, and if I saw something along the way that inspired me, sometimes I'd go back later and paint it."

"That sounds nice," her father said. "You were always pretty good at that."

Her mother picked at her Caesar salad. "You and your brother are both talented—that goes without saying. Eric in particular has always had such a gift for drawing."

Katrina stiffened at the sudden memory of why she'd stopped showing her paintings to other people.

Her mother continued. "Anyhow, *regardless* of how you spent all that leisure time in New York, I'm just glad you kept your wits about you and stuck to your promise to look for a job while you were there."

Katrina nodded but didn't reply.

Her father dipped a piece of bread in olive oil. "When do you start this new job?"

Katrina swallowed. "Actually, I wanted to talk to you both about that."

"How so?" her mother asked.

Katrina's mind raced for her talking points.

Opening observation about the restaurant and evening in general.

It was a little too late for that now, but she decided to backtrack anyway.

"I love this restaurant. I'm so glad you suggested we come here."

Her mother gave her a strange look. "Katrina, dear, are you feeling well?"

"I'm fine, thanks. I . . . I just want to express my gratitude to you for choosing such a lovely place for dinner." She swallowed. "And . . . for supporting me in my decision to go to New York, even though I know that wasn't easy for you."

"Well, it's not like we had a choice," her mother said.

"And you *did* find a job while you were there," her father said.

Katrina took another sip of water and tried to keep going.

Main statement and supporting points.

She cleared her throat. "So, anyhow, about the job offer . . ."

Her mother quickly looked up from her salad. "Job *offer*? What do you mean? Was there a snag?"

Katrina hesitated.

Tell them!

"Katrina?" Her mother stared at her.

"I . . . turned it down."

"*What?*" Her mother glanced around the room, then lowered her voice and leaned forward. "You turned it *down*?"

Katrina inhaled deeply and stared at her lap for a moment.

Stay calm.

She tried to imagine she was sitting in one of Shana's yoga classes. A supportive environment. Relaxing and peaceful.

This is your life.

This is your *life.*

She looked up at her mother.

"Yes, I turned it down."

"Why?"

"Because I'm moving to New York."

"*What?*" Her mother's voice once again flared louder than she'd intended. She put a hand on her chest and looked at her husband. "Henry, did you hear that?"

"I believe I did." He blinked at Katrina. "Sunshine, did I just hear you correctly?"

Katrina nodded. "I've decided to move to Brooklyn and open a yoga studio with my new friends Shana, Grace, and Justin. We have a business plan, a financial backer, and a location."

Her mother's face turned ashen. "A *yoga* studio? In *Brooklyn*?" Katrina had never seen her look so aghast.

"A combination yoga studio, coffeehouse, jewelry display, and art gallery, actually. Or *my* art, at least. And Grace's jewelry. And Justin's pastries. And Shana's an incredible yoga instructor. But yes, in Brooklyn. Brooklyn Heights, to be exact." Once she'd uttered the words aloud, a weight had lifted and her confidence returned. She calmly took a sip of water.

Her mother looked at her father again. "Henry, say something! We can't let her throw her life away like this."

"I'm not throwing my life away," Katrina said firmly. Her voice was steady, but her pulse was still racing. She interlaced her hands under the table and squeezed them together.

Her father shook his head slowly, a look of pity in his eyes. "You're an *accountant*, sunshine. What do you know about running a business, much less a silly one like that?"

"It's not silly."

Her mother scoffed. "Yoga? Coffee and pastries? Please. That's about as silly as it gets."

"It's *not* silly. And my friends there know how to do it. They're doing it already."

Her mother pressed her palms against her temples, her thin fingers spread wide. "I can't believe this. All that education, wasted."

"It's not wasted. I'm starting a business, and I'm going to use that knowledge every single day."

Her mother didn't reply. Nor did her father.

"I'm going to do this," Katrina said. "You can't stop me."

Her mother groaned. "I think I'm getting a migraine."

Her father put a gentle hand on Katrina's arm. "You need to think about your *future*. Moving across the country, starting over, struggling financially. None of that is going to be easy."

"I know that, Dad. But this *is* my future."

"You're making a mistake," her mother said. "A terrible mistake."

Katrina took yet another drink of water and readied herself to deliver the final section of her prepared remarks.

Closing expression of conviction and excitement for what lies ahead.

She set down the glass.

"Mom, Dad, I *know* it's not going to be easy, that it's going to be quite hard, in fact. But this is something I *want* to do, something that will make me happy. I've spent too many years living a life that makes *other people* happy. All that did was make *me* miserable, and I just can't do it anymore."

"You're miserable?" her father asked, a look of surprise on his face.

"I *was*, but I'm not anymore. And I don't ever want to go back to feeling like that all the time, so this is what I'm going to do now. I'm starting over, *now*."

"But Katrina—" her mother began.

Katrina held up her hand. "I'm not finished. For the first time in a long time, maybe *ever*, I'm excited about the future. Maybe this will fail, or maybe it won't, but either way, it's something I feel I have to do. If you support me, then that's great. But even if you don't, my mind is made up."

Her mother stared at her.

"I've never seen you like this," her father said.

Katrina touched her scarf and felt her lips break into a tiny smile as she realized that during the entire conversation, her foot hadn't once begun to tap.

Chapter Twenty-Two

Six months later

Katrina had set her alarm for 6:00 a.m., but she was so wound up she woke up on her own fifteen minutes before that. There was just so much to do to prepare for the big opening, and she wanted every detail to be perfect—or at least nearly perfect, which had become good enough for her.

She opened her bedroom window and poked her head outside. The fresh morning air was cool, but to Katrina it seemed practically balmy compared to the harsh weather she'd experienced—and survived—during her first winter in New York. Even at this hour of the morning, the sun was already shining, with summer just around the corner.

After making her bed, she glanced at the calendar on her desk.

A small black circle was drawn around Thursday, May 15.

Today.

It was finally here.

She smiled at the calendar, then spontaneously grabbed a pen and drew a smiley face next to the circle.

That's more like it.

*   *   *

She spent most of the day at the studio getting everything ready for the launch party, crossing items off her list one by one.

Decorations, check.

Music, check.

Food, check.

Drinks, check.

Lighting, check.

Nerves . . . still working on it.

Grace and Shana arrived just after lunch, and Justin popped in and out throughout the day to make sure nothing needed hanging, hammering, or replacing. They'd hired Enrique the driver for a flat rate to lug anything that needed to be lugged, and they were getting their money's worth. Ferrying boxes of everything from paper plates to champagne and decorative lanterns, his car was continuously on the move, often with a harried Katrina in the backseat.

"I'm going to try to double-park, but this area can be tricky, so if I'm not here when you come out, I'm circling around the block," Enrique said as Katrina hopped out of the sedan. They were in Tribeca to pick up a batch of miniature cupcakes Brittany had insisted on buying for the party. Though Katrina knew she could easily find similar ones for half the price in Brooklyn, she also knew that arguing with a force like Brittany over anything—especially money—was not a winning strategy. But Brittany had gotten hauled into an all-day meeting at work and couldn't pick them up before the festivities started, so here Katrina was.

"Got it." She hustled into the bakery, checking her watch as she took her place in line. Deb's plane landed in an hour, so, assuming the cupcakes were ready, Enrique would have plenty of time to drop Katrina back at the studio before driving out to JFK to pick up Deb.

As she waited patiently for the teenager in front of her to purchase a cookie, she pulled her list out of her pocket and felt a sense of accomplishment when she saw how many items she'd already checked off. So far, things were right on track.

"May I help you?"

Katrina looked up at the woman behind the counter. "Oh, hi, yes, I have an order to pick up for Brittany Levin."

The woman smiled. "Oh, yes, of course. Let me get it from the back."

Katrina smiled back. *Pick up overpriced cupcakes, check.*

Moments later, she exited the bakery carrying the large box. She didn't see Enrique, so she turned and looked in the direction of oncoming traffic.

What she saw approaching made her jaw drop.

Or more to the point, *who* she saw.

It was Reid.

Reid Hanson, walking alongside an extremely pregnant woman.

It was too late for Katrina to move, and she didn't want to risk dropping the cupcakes, so she just stood there in the middle of the sidewalk, frozen. Reid looked equally surprised.

"Kat, hi."

"Reid." She was too tongue-tied to say anything more.

Reid cleared his throat. "This is my wife, Amelia. Amelia, this is Kat, a friend of a friend."

"Hi," Katrina said a bit awkwardly.

Amelia gave Katrina what appeared to be a warm smile, which surprised her. "It's nice to meet you. I'd shake, but it looks like you've got your hands full."

"Yes, um, cupcakes," Katrina said.

Amelia nodded toward the bakery entrance. "This place is amazing, isn't it? I had the worst cravings early on, for chocolate peanut-butter balls, of all things. Ten in the morning and I'd hustle down here for half a dozen of them." She put her hands on her bulging stomach.

"I'll have to try those sometime." Katrina was thrown by Amelia's friendliness.

"Why are you still in New York?" Reid gave her a curious look. "Weren't you here for just a few weeks?"

If he was afraid Katrina was going to rat him out, he didn't let on. He looked as unflappable as ever, and she wondered how many women in a position similar to hers were wandering around Manhattan.

Katrina held up the box. "Change of plans. Looks like I'm staying for a while."

"Oh, cool. Well, hey, we'd better get going." Reid put his hand on Amelia's lower back. "It was nice seeing you, Kat. Maybe I'll bump into you again sometime."

"That would be nice." Katrina smiled.

She knew she'd probably never see him again.

For a moment, as she watched Reid and Amelia walk away, she was curious to know what was really going on inside their marriage.

She was also delighted to realize that she didn't care.

*   *   *

"It's magical, Katrina." Deb tilted her head back to admire the light-blue ceiling of the yoga studio, which was sprinkled with a trail of bright silver stars leading to a half-moon on the far wall.

"Who's Katrina?" Grace appeared and handed them each a champagne flute.

Deb laughed. "I'm sorry. I mean, it's magical, *Kat*."

Katrina put her arm around Deb and gave her a squeeze. "*You* can always call me Katrina. I wouldn't want it any other way. To be honest, I still think of myself as Katrina, at least right now."

Deb held up her glass. "Well, Kat, Katrina, whoever you are, cheers to this beautiful place you've created."

"What are we toasting?" Shana walked up.

"Your engagement, of course," Grace said. "Just like we've been doing for the last three months."

"We are?" Shana giggled and held her left hand up to her cheek, a diamond ring glittering in the soft light.

"Barf," Grace said.

"What are *you* complaining about?" Katrina asked Grace, pointing to the other room. "Li's at the coffee bar right now, probably missing you even though you're only like twenty feet away."

"Who's Li?" Deb asked.

"He *was* Grace's pretend boyfriend, but he's not so pretend anymore," Katrina said.

Deb looked at Grace quizzically.

"He came crawling back," Grace said.

Apparently, Li *had* been telling the truth about his feelings for Grace, and they'd rekindled their romance a month earlier. Li had finally turned the corner and was ready to commit, but now, as Grace liked to say, she was the one "wearing the jock." This time around things would be on her terms—just the way she liked it.

"Come on, I'll introduce you." Grace grabbed Deb's arm and pulled her toward the front room.

The four of them left the yoga studio, passing down a short hallway into a large open space with a coffee bar on one side and clusters of plush lounge chairs sprinkled around the room. Justin and Josh stood like footmen in front of the bar, Justin dexterously holding a platter of Brittany's cupcakes, Josh carefully balancing a tray of champagne flutes and miniature cappuccinos. Beethoven's *Moonlight Sonata* played in the background. The coffee bar looked similar to Justin's shop in her old neighborhood, just as Katrina had envisioned.

Even more importantly, it *felt* similar.

Warm.

Inviting.

Friendly.

A Place for Yoga and Coffee was officially open for business.

Katrina's paintings, all for sale, hung on the walls. She'd recently completed a new series she'd done exclusively in Brooklyn Heights, after moving there. The subjects she'd chosen were simple, but she found them as inspiring and beautiful as the famous landmarks that surrounded them—if not more so. Cobblestone streets, mom-and-pop storefronts, tidy brownstones, meticulously tended flower beds. With each piece, she paid homage to something she adored about her new neighborhood, including what was possibly her favorite discovery of all: the stoop sale. Part garage sale, part flea market, 100 percent social hour, the stoop sale was an integral part of life in Brooklyn Heights, and no lazy Saturday was complete without stopping by at least one.

Or two.

When she'd arrived earlier in the day, Katrina had been surprised to see that Justin had framed one of her earlier paintings and positioned it prominently at the entrance. Fittingly, it was the one she'd given him of the bench on the Brooklyn Promenade, a few days after she'd come up with the idea behind A Place for Yoga and Coffee. A far corner of the main room featured a pretty tree-shaped display of Grace's jewelry—though given how many shops across Manhattan were now selling it, she hardly needed the exposure anymore. Grace was finally on her way, and Katrina hoped that one day she'd have similar success with her art.

As her friends chatted, Katrina twirled slowly in a circle, taking it all in, thinking about what it meant. All of them working together to create something special, something their future patrons didn't even know they wanted but that they would grow to love. Although not entirely certain how things would play out, she felt hopeful and optimistic.

For now, hope and optimism were enough.

The front door chimed, and Katrina turned around.

"Hey, there's Brittany."

"Who's Brittany?" Grace asked.

"She's the one person I knew before I moved here."

Deb elbowed Grace. "You mean back when she was still *Katrina*?"

Grace elbowed Deb back. "You mean back when she was rigid and uptight?"

"I prefer words like *organized* and *structured*," Katrina said with a tiny smile.

Katrina grabbed a champagne flute from Josh's tray and approached Brittany. In her black dress and heels—which put her well over six feet tall—she was as sensational as ever.

"Hi, Brittany, welcome!" Katrina said. "Thanks so much for coming."

Brittany took the flute. "It's my pleasure, hon. I can't believe how cute this neighborhood is, and so close to Manhattan! How have I lived in New York for nearly nine years and never been here? I need to stop ignoring Brooklyn."

"Given how popular Brooklyn is now, we're hoping to have a lot of business, even from fancy Manhattanites like you," Katrina said. "Oh, that reminds me: thanks so much for the fancy cupcakes. They're a huge hit."

"It's my pleasure. Your new apartment is near here?"

Katrina nodded. "In a brownstone around the corner. It's not big, but it's super charming. I'm madly in love with it."

"Look at you, all grown-up and making things happen. I'm impressed. Pretty soon you'll be teaching me a thing or two."

"I highly doubt that will *ever* happen, but thanks for the vote of confidence."

Brittany touched one of the spaghetti straps on Katrina's black cocktail dress, which she'd bought months ago at Chelsea Market. "I'm digging the frock. Did you buy that here?"

Katrina nodded. "To be honest, I don't wear many of my California clothes that much anymore. I've realized they're all a little, um, conservative, especially for New York."

Deb laughed. "Have I not been telling you that forever? Your wardrobe was conservative for *Mountain View*, for crying out loud."

Brittany gave Katrina's shoulder a squeeze. "Well, whatever it is you're doing, it's working. You look gorgeous."

She wandered off to mingle, and Deb turned to Katrina. "Do you think your parents will ever come to visit? I know your mom would love this place, no matter how much she pretended to hate it for a host of imaginary reasons."

Katrina shrugged. "Maybe, eventually. She's still upset with me for turning down that accounting job, but if she can't tell how much happier I am now, then it's really not my problem. My dad called to wish me luck today, though, for both of them."

Deb smiled. "It's so great to see this new attitude and confidence. I mean, I miss you to death, of course, but this really seems like the right place for you."

Katrina lowered her voice and leaned toward Deb. "Thanks, but just between you and me, *Katrina* has been tutoring rich kids in math on the side, just in case this all blows up in *Kat's* face."

Brittany reappeared from the crowd, a fresh champagne flute in one hand, a miniature cupcake in the other. She gestured with her eyes toward the coffee bar. "That guy serving the cupcakes is hot."

Katrina flinched. "Justin?" She doubted Brittany was referring to Josh.

Brittany nodded. "The tall one with the sexy stubble going on. I'm digging it. What's his story? I didn't see a ring."

"I thought you didn't care about marital status."

Brittany shrugged. "I don't. I just like to know what I'm getting into, that's all."

"He's divorced," Katrina said. "It's official—as of last week, actually." She'd noticed that he'd stopped wearing his ring several weeks ago, but she didn't feel the need to share that information. Plus she'd already learned her lesson about men and wedding rings.

Brittany raised her eyebrows and glanced in Justin's direction again. "Is that so? Interesting . . ."

"Don't go there," Deb said.

Brittany looked at her. "Why not? Is he dating someone already?"

"After tonight, he'd better be." Deb put her arm around Katrina.

Brittany smiled at Katrina. "You mean you and he . . . ?"

"Oh, no." Katrina felt her cheeks flush. "We're just friends."

Deb gave her a squeeze. "And as I said, if all goes according to plan, that will soon be changing. Little Miss Fraidy Cat here just needs to woman up and confess that she's got the hots for him."

Brittany laughed. "I like you."

"Right back at ya," Deb said.

Katrina scanned the crowd and noticed that Justin was looking in their direction. She wanted to wave a quick hello, but instead she found herself averting her eyes.

* * *

"You *suuuure* you don't want me to stay with you while you lock up?" Deb asked Katrina, fluttering her eyelashes, her voice loud enough for Justin to overhear. She was reciting from a script, which the two of them had written over the phone just yesterday.

Katrina shooed her away, trying to focus as she awkwardly delivered her own line. "I'll meet you there in ten minutes. I just want to give the floor a quick sweep."

Deb grinned at her, her voice still loud. "That sounds good. See you there."

Brittany draped her pale-green pashmina over her shoulders and looked at Katrina. "What's this place we're going to called?"

The script officially completed by Deb, Katrina answered freely. "Custom House. I guess you could call it a modern Irish pub, if there is such a thing."

Grace interlaced her arm with Shana's. "As long as they serve alcohol, I don't care *what* it looks like inside."

Brittany cocked her head toward Grace and said to Deb, "I like *her* too."

"Everyone likes me," Grace said.

"I'm glad I have such confident friends," Katrina said.

Josh walked up with Li and handed Shana her purse. "You ladies ready?"

Grace looked around the empty room. "Where's Justin?"

Josh pointed toward the hall leading into the yoga studio. "He said he'd catch up with us at the bar."

Deb winked at Katrina. "Right on cue."

Katrina led her friends to the front door and closed it gently behind them, the bells jingling as it locked into place. She closed her eyes and inhaled deeply.

You can do this.

She headed toward the closet to retrieve a broom, smoothing her hands down the sides of her dress as she walked. As she began sweeping the hardwood floors, she reviewed her prepared remarks in her head, trying to concentrate over the music still playing in the background.

Casual yet interesting observation about the evening.

Main statement and supporting points.

Closing expression of endearment.

Possible physical contact, if above goes well.

A moment later, the music stopped.

Katrina set the broom against a wall and turned around.

The time had come.

"Justin?" she called toward the yoga studio.

No reply.

"Justin? Are you there?" She began to make her way to the back room, the connecting hallway suddenly eerily silent. The door was open, but she didn't see him as she approached. She took a step inside and cautiously looked around the studio. It was dark save for a small lamp set against the far wall.

"Justin?"

Had he left?

"Right here." His voice came from behind her.

She jumped and swung around. Justin was standing right there, his face in shadow.

She put a hand on her heart. "Oh, you scared me."

He smiled. "I'm sorry."

"Where did you come from?"

He kept smiling. "I could ask you the same thing."

"What do you mean?"

He didn't answer the question. Instead, he walked to the middle of the room and looked up at the stars glowing on the ceiling. "Pretty good party, don't you think?"

"Yes, great party."

He turned to look right at her. "I think it's a good sign."

"You do?" She swallowed.

Do it now!

"Are you okay?" he asked. "You look a little pale."

She nodded slightly. "I'm fine, thanks."

Do it!

He began walking toward her. "Are you sure? Can I get you some water?"

She held out a hand against the wall. "I'm fine, I think. I mean . . . I wanted to talk to you about something."

"Shoot."

"I—" she began, but then completely forgot what she'd been planning to say. Her mind went blank, her entire speech gone.

She stood there in silence, her mouth agape.

After a few moments, Justin laughed. "Are you sure you're okay? You look a little strange just standing there with your mouth open."

She didn't reply.

"Okay then." He took a step toward her, then reached over and gently lifted her jaw back into place.

She searched the far corners of her brain, trying to remember any small part of her well-rehearsed declaration.

She came up empty.

Justin chuckled again and glanced around the room. "*Any*how . . . it's been a lot of work to get this place in shape, but I think it turned out pretty well, don't you agree?"

She nodded.

"Is it what you imagined when you first came up with the idea?"

She nodded again.

"Are you sure you're feeling okay, Kat?"

She nodded for a third time.

"Okay, if you say so." He took another look at the shimmering stars above, then settled his gaze on her. "It's a perfect night for new beginnings."

As he spoke the words, she couldn't help but notice his eyes.

Something about them, something about the way he was looking at her, was different.

The same, yet different.

"I'm proud of you for making this happen," he said. "For creating a brand-new life for yourself."

Words finally came to her, though they weren't the ones she'd practiced so many times in front of the mirror. Those were still MIA. "Well, I couldn't have done it without you, that's for sure." She winced at how stiff they sounded, how bland.

Why can't you just tell him how you really feel?

After all these months?

What's wrong with you?

Haven't you changed at all?

"When I said that, I wasn't just talking about the studio," he said.

She blinked. "When you said what?"

"That it's a perfect night for new beginnings." He lowered his voice. "I think *I'm* ready for a new beginning too."

She took a quick breath, flustered, her pulse quickening. She knew he wasn't talking about the shop. Or was he? Her goal tonight had been to nudge open the door. She hadn't let herself imagine a scenario in which he did it himself.

Her mind began to race.

"You are?" she whispered.

"Yes."

They stood there for a few moments, their eyes locked on each other.

Not speaking.

Just breathing.

"What did you want to say to me?" he finally asked.

She gave him a shaky smile. "I . . . I can't remember."

He smiled back at her. "Good, because I have something I want to say to you, something I've wanted to say for a long time." He took another step toward her, his face now just inches from hers. Slowly, very slowly, he touched her cheek. "I love your freckles."

She swallowed. "You do?"

He nodded as he slipped his arm around her lower back. "You have no idea."

Then he leaned down and kissed her.

Thank you!

For anyone who regularly reads this page in my books, the name Tami May McMillan is familiar by now, and once again I can't thank her enough for her help. Not only did she give me the confidence to keep writing *Katwalk* when I was mired in self-doubt early on, but she also provided some creative input at the tail end of the writing process, just when I needed it. I know in her mind she's only acting as any good friend would, but I hope she realizes just how much I appreciate both her thoughtful (i.e. no sugar on top) feedback and her unshakable belief in my ability to tell a good story. The same goes for Alberto Ferrer, Lori Rosenwasser, and Terri Sharkey, all regulars on this page who again came through for me in more ways than one.

As with all my books, I peppered *Katwalk* with nuggets from real life, and I would like to thank the following friends for providing such entertaining material: Steph Bernabe, Chris Conroy, Gloria Fong, Natalie Gonzalez, Joe Green, Joe Guggemos, Laura Curd Gunderson, Dave "Davio" Irving, DJ, Tanya Kalivas, Courtney Carroll Levinsohn, Brett Sharkey, Matt Strand, Jamie Tilotta-Green, Enrique Romero, Ithti Toy Ulit, and Garett Vassel. I feel lucky to know such smart, interesting, and funny people, because let's face it . . . without them I probably wouldn't have much to write about.

One friend who unwittingly played a major role in shaping *Katwalk* is Jenny Jongejan. Her adventurous approach to life is inspiring and infectious, and I thank her for not minding that I loosely modeled the premise of this tale after one of her bolder escapades. I'd also like to bow my head to all the wonderful yoga instructors I've had over the years. They've taught me to stay focused on what's really important in life—plus I can finally touch my toes!

I'm beginning to run out of ways to thank my longtime editor, Christina Henry de Tessan, whose talent continues to amaze me. I think she'd agree that she pushed me harder this time than in any of our previous collaborations, but I'm grateful that she did, because it helped me become a better writer. I also can't thank my dear sweet beautiful mother enough for her proofreading prowess. I keep wondering when I'm going to get an e-mail through my website asking if she's available for hire outside the family . . .

Last but not least, thanks to my amazing inner circle at Lake Union Publishing for their continued support of my writing career. Here's to you, Alex Carr, Terry Goodman, and Jessica Poore. I'm so lucky to have you in my corner!

About the Author

Maria Murnane left a successful career as a public-relations executive to pursue a more fulfilling life as a novelist and speaker. Her own "story behind the story" is an entertaining tale of the courage, passion, and perseverance required to get her first novel, *Perfect on Paper*, published. She is also the author of three sequels in the Waverly Bryson series: *It's a Waverly Life*, *Honey on Your Mind*, and *Chocolate for Two*, as well as *Cassidy Lane*. Maria graduated with high honors in English and Spanish from the University of California, Berkeley, where she was a Regents' and Chancellor's Scholar. She also holds a master's degree in integrated marketing communications from Northwestern University. She currently lives in New York City. For more information about her books, speaking engagements, and consulting services, visit www.mariamurnane.com.